D1244407

POWDERSMOKE JUSTICE

Center Point
Large Print

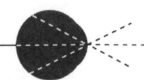

**This Large Print Book carries the
Seal of Approval of N.A.V.H.**

POWDERSMOKE JUSTICE

William Colt MacDonald

CENTER POINT PUBLISHING
THORNDIKE, MAINE

This Center Point Large Print edition
is published in the year 2010 by arrangement with
Golden West Literary Agency.

The text of this Large Print edition is unabridged.
In other aspects, this book may vary
from the original edition.
Printed in the United States of America
on permanent paper.
Set in 16-point Times New Roman type.

ISBN: 978-1-60285-892-3

Library of Congress Cataloging-in-Publication Data

MacDonald, William Colt, 1891–1968.
  Powdersmoke justice / William Colt MacDonald.
    p. cm.
  ISBN 978-1-60285-892-3 (lib. bdg. : alk. paper)
  1. Large type books. I. Title.
  PS3525.A2122P68 2010
  813′.52—dc22
                                                    2010020966

Contents

1. Buzzards Don't Lie

Early morning sunlight glinted along the damascened barrels of the double-barreled shotgun where it lay propped at an angle, twin muzzles elevated, on a small pile of stacked rocks. A chunk of sandstone rested across the barrels to weight the gun in place. From one trigger of the weapon a length of hempen cord stretched along the sandy earth to the rear of the walnut gunstock, circled the trunk of a mesquite bush, and reached forward several yards until the loose end came to rest on the ground near the right hand of the dead man.

The corpse lay on its back, legs straight, the motionless booted feet in the direction of the tilted gun muzzles. The right hand, fingers spread wide, as though they had just released the end of the death-bringing cord, lay close to the body. The left arm was bent at the elbow and rested across the dead man's chest. There was, apparently, nothing about the man's clothing to distinguish him from hundreds of other men in the Southwest cow country. His shoulders were broad; in height he had been above six feet. A gray sombrero with a beaded hatband of Indian design lay near by, and a Bull Durham tag on its yellow strings lay loosely adjacent to one pocket of an unbuttoned vest. A cartridge belt, with its accompanying holstered six-shooter, encircled the slim hips.

Generally, some indication of a man's age may be gained through an examination of his features. The dead man hadn't any features: in their place remained now only a gory, buckshot-chopped mask, the shotgun having accomplished its lethal task only too thoroughly.

The body lay near the edge of a dry wash which was littered with boulders of all shapes and sizes. Here and there grew a stunted mesquite tree, rising but slightly about the scattered clumps of brush. A few yuccas, still bearing the dried and withered stalks of last spring's blossoms, dotted the semi-desert landscape as it rose gradually to meet the foothills of the distant Torvo Range, the serrated peaks of which glittered brightly in the morning sunshine. Overhead stretched an inverted bowl of dense turquoise where a few fleecy clouds fled before the strong breeze blowing across the range country. In the distant sky to the south a black speck appeared and shortly resolved itself into a fast-winging buzzard. Time passed and three similar specks took form in the high dry atmosphere. It is said that a buzzard can scent death from afar, and that there also exist men who are unconsciously attracted to trouble as a piece of steel is drawn to a magnet.

Beyond a sage-dotted rise of land to the east three riders were loping easily in the direction of the spot where the faceless man lay still in death. These three riders of the mesquite country—the

Three Mesquiteers as they were known—carried the names of Tucson Smith, Lullaby Joslin, and Stony Brooke. Men had known them by other names as well—the Three Inseparables, the Cactus Cavaliers, and the Incomparable Trio. Probably the Three Mesquiteers fitted them best. Like the famous musketeers of the great Dumas, this trio was, indeed, "all for one and one for all." Their fame was known throughout the length and breadth of the Southwest. Those who defied the law grew to hate and fear their relentless upholding of justice. Law-abiding men swore by them and were grateful for their help in running to earth the crime makers of those early Western days. So great was the prestige of this trio that from time to time impostors came into being, claiming brazenly to be the Three Mesquiteers, but these were of brief existence under the keen scrutiny of all who could distinguish the genuine article from the spurious.

Leader of the Mesquiteers, if they could be said to have a leader, was Tucson Smith, his lean, weathered frame moving easily to the motions of the rangy buckskin horse beneath his saddle. Smith possessed slate-gray eyes and bright auburn hair; his face was long and bony, his nose arched. His mouth was wide with tiny quirks at the corners. There was something stern, sardonic, about Smith's face, though the small laugh wrinkles near his eyes attested his well-developed sense of humor.

On Tucson's left, astride a long-legged black pony, rode Lullaby Joslin, who was lanky, soft-spoken, with drowsy hazel eyes. His hair was as straight and black as an Indian's. There was something slouchy and indolent in the man's make-up. His clothing fitted loosely, the shirt sleeves exposing strong bony wrists. His Stetson was cuffed over one ear, and a brown paper cigarette dangled from one corner of his generous mouth.

Stony Brooke, the third man of the trio, was shorter than his companions, but what he lacked in height was compensated by breadth. He had a barrellike torso and carried in his shoulders the strength of a young bull. His nose was what is known as snub, and he possessed innocent blue eyes and a wide, gargoylish, good-natured grin. There was something deceptively cherubic about Stony Brooke, as more than one lawbreaker had learned to his lasting regret. Stony, in the final analysis, had always proved fully as tough, in a pinch, as the chunky chestnut gelding he was now riding with such easy grace.

The three men wore much the same type of range clothing—faded denims cuffed widely at the ankles of high-heeled, spurred riding boots, woolen shirts, neckerchiefs, more or less battered sombreros. All wore Colt's six-shooters and wide cartridge belts. Any casual observer would, doubtless, have put them down as just three ordinary saddle tramps looking for jobs, rather than the prosperous owners of the Three-Bar-O Ranch—or as some called it, the Three-Bar-Nothing—which was, by now, many weeks' riding to their rear. Generally, Tucson was the quietest of the three; Lullaby and Stony were forever wrangling, each trying to make some joke at the other's expense, when nothing more serious occupied their thoughts.

A long gradual slope lay ahead and the three riders pulled their ponies to a walk. Stony Brooke started to manufacture a cigarette. Just as it was completed, Tucson reached over and drew it from his hand, saying quietly, "Thanks. I was just craving a smoke." He scratched a match on his saddle horn and inhaled with keen appreciation.

Stony eyed him with speechless indignation, then resignedly commenced a second cigarette. "Damned if I know"—he spoke finally—"why I don't get wise to your taking ways, Tucson. You're always stealing my smokes—"

"I can explain that," Lullaby interposed in his slow drawl. "You don't get wise, because to get wise you'd first have to have brains."

"Is that so!" Stony retorted. He lighted the second cigarette he'd rolled. Smoke drifted from his open mouth while he spoke. "I've been told, more'n once, I had a mind like a razor."

"Humph!" Lullaby grunted. "You mean that razor you carry?"

"Sure. Any razor. Mine especially. I never saw such a sharp blade—"

"I noted already," Lullaby said insultingly, "that the handle is solid ivory, and if that ain't appropriate to your head, I'll eat my Stetson."

Stony groaned. "There he goes again, Tucson. Just can't get his thoughts off eating, and it's not more'n two hours since we ate breakfast back there in—what was that town? Torvo? Eat, eat, eat! Not only two breakfasts, but he finished your bacon and my pie."

"I like a mince pie," Lullaby commenced, "now and then—"

"You like anything immense, so long's it's food," Stony snapped.

Tucson chuckled. Lullaby's face reddened and, needing time to think over a proper reply, he reined his pony wide around a great clump of prickly pear whose pads were fringed with red fruit. Rejoining his companions, he went on, "I had a mince pie with brandy in it, once. Now there's something that would appeal to Stony. Fact is, he'd even eat cowhide, was it soaked in brandy."

"Most cowhides is brand-y," Stony grinned.

Lullaby, poker-faced, asked, "Is that meant to be funny? If so, your humor is wasted."

"It's always wasted on *you*. Besides, I'm not partial to brandy," Stony said. "Can't say I'm partial to any drink."

"I know," Lullaby sneered, "you don't care, you don't play any favorites—just so long as they got alcohol in 'em."

12

"Aw-w, I don't drink any more than you do."

"Not at once," Lullaby said. "Just oftener."

Tucson and Lullaby waited for Stony's reply and when it failed to come they glanced curiously at him. But the conversation of the moment had, apparently, been forgotten by the blond rider: his gaze was fixed toward the sky, beyond the crest of the next rise of land, where four buzzards dipped and soared on motionless wings, coming ever closer to the earth as they moved.

Tucson said, "What's on your mind, Stony?"

"Stinkbirds," Stony said. "Must be something dead over that way."

"Not necessarily," Lullaby said.

"Buzzards don't lie," Stony insisted. "They can smell death miles away. You see buzzards swoopin' low like old papers in the wind, and you can depend on it, they're fixin' to light on somethin' dead."

Lullaby snorted. "If that was the case, you'd have a whole flock of them birds hoverin' over your head all the time."

But Stony refused to rise to the bait. Gaze intent, straight ahead, he touched spurs to his pony and leaped in advance of his companions. Tucson said, "Probably a coyote-killed cow, or something similar. Come on, Lullaby, we might as well go see."

Ten minutes later the three had dismounted and, dropping their reins over their ponies' heads, were standing near the dead man. Flies buzzed angrily in the hot sunlight. Tucson removed a clean bandanna from his pocket and spread it over the faceless head. The strong breeze blowing across the range stirred the black hair at the side of the corpse's skull. Lullaby shook his head in perplexity. "I sure can't savvy why a man gets so low in spirits that he'll take his own life. You'd think there'd be something he could figure out, first, no matter what his troubles."

Stony nodded. "Poor cuss. I suppose he just walked out here"—his eyes shifted to the shotgun fixed on the pile of rocks—"arranged that scatter weapon in place, tied the string to the trigger, circled that mesquite until he was far enough away to pull the string—and then . . . well, all I can say, he had good aim. Wonder who he is?"

Tucson frowned. "He wears boots. I'm not so sure he walked out here. It's a long walk to Torvo or—what did that sheriff say was the name of the next town? Jackpot?"

"Jackpot is correct." Lullaby nodded. "The Torvo sheriff said it was just a ghost town, though, so this feller probably come from Torvo. I noted those boots, too, but where's his pony?"

"Probably strayed off," Stony put in. "I don't see any hoofprints, though."

Tucson's gaze ranged along the dry wash cluttered with granite boulders of various sizes. "A horse could have headed off that way, and not left any marks on those rocks, though I don't see why it should. It would more likely stay where there's brush to crop. Hereabouts, it's pretty sandy and there's considerable hardpan. With the wind blowing the way it is, any prints that were left might have been covered with loose sand."

Lullaby asked quickly, "Why do you say 'might have been'?"

Tucson shrugged. "I don't know. Guess I didn't want to jump to any conclusions. Anyway, it's not up to us to figure what happened. That's a job for the sheriff at Torvo. One of us will have to ride back and tell him about this. The body should be watched until it can be taken away."

"You stay here, Tucson," Lullaby proposed. "Stony and I can toss a coin to see who has to make that ride back." He drew a silver dollar from one pocket of his denims and addressed Stony, "Heads, I win; tails, you lose."

Stony nodded and the coin went spinning brightly into the air and returned again to Lullaby's calloused palm. "Tails!" Lullaby announced with a quick, straight-faced inspection of the dollar. "You lose!"

Stony craned his neck to glance suspiciously at the "tails" on Lullaby's outstretched hand, then nodded glumly. "You always do play in luck," he growled, and strode, disgruntled, to his horse. Gathering his reins from the ground, he climbed into the saddle and was just about to move off, when he abruptly checked the chestnut gelding.

His features had gone suddenly crimson. "You—you cheated!" he charged furiously.

"Huh?" Lullaby's voice, teeming with innocence, sounded hurt. "Why, what do you mean, pard?"

"I'm no pard of yours, you lowdown, unprincipled deadbeat! You slipped a fast one over on me. I never even had a chance to win that toss. The way you said it, even if it had come 'heads,' I would have lost. When a man can't trust a fellow he's—"

"Took you long enough to figure that out." A grin twitched the corners of Lullaby's lips. "And just a spell back you were telling how smart you are. What? No, I won't toss that coin again. You should be made to pay for your dumbness. But I will do this: I'll make the ride with you." Lullaby got into his saddle and the horses got under way. "Never let it be said," Lullaby added smugly, "that I'd let a pard make a long ride alone."

"Buffalo chips!" Stony scoffed. "I know why you're so willing to ride with me. You want to eat those sandwiches you're carryin', and then get some more when we reach Torvo."

"Maybe you ain't so dumb at that," Lullaby chuckled. "I'm beginning to have hopes for you. You'll learn, son, you'll learn—but only God knows when."

"Yaah! And you'll still be coming to me whenever you want to know something. . . ."

And so they wrangled, while, near the dead man,

Tucson Smith had seated himself on the earth to light a cigarette. After a time he rose, stepped on the cigarette butt, and then commenced a minute inspection of the ground in the vicinity of the corpse and double-barreled shotgun, the frown on his features deepening as he slowly circled the grisly scene.

2. A Matter of Elevation

It was mid-afternoon by the time Lullaby and Stony, accompanied by Sheriff Matt Yarrow, returned, and the westward-swinging sun was already painting the lower hollows of the Torvo Range with deep purple shadows and touching the highest peaks with glittering gold. Tucson had unsaddled his pony and lay stretched out on his blankets, his mind occupied with various abstractions, when the three riders arrived. Tucson rose to his feet as the sheriff and the others dismounted. Yarrow was a bulky-shouldered, middle-aged man with sweeping gray-blond mustaches, in tan corduroys, woolen shirt, and riding boots. His star of office was pinned to a stringy vest, and his sombrero in the vicinity of its hatband was stained with perspiration. There was a look of fatigue about the sheriff's blue eyes which Tucson had noticed earlier that day at breakfast, when they'd encountered Yarrow, shortly before daylight, in one of Torvo's all-night restaurants.

The sheriff nodded, solemn-faced, to Tucson, saying, "I sure didn't expect to be seeing you again so soon." His weary gaze shifted to the dead man. "I hope you haven't disturbed anything—"

"Not a thing," Tucson replied. Lullaby and Stony stood quietly by while Yarrow made a quick inspection of the scene, then asked, "Didn't see anything of this hombre's hoss, I suppose?" Tucson shook his head and mentioned that it might have strayed off. Next the sheriff lifted the bandanna from the faceless head and quickly dropped it back into place. "Nothing to be learned there to identify him," he grunted. He walked to the shotgun on the pile of rocks, broke it, and examined the empty shell, muttered something about "buckshot," and then left things as they were and returned to the corpse.

Reluctantly Yarrow now commenced going through the pockets of the dead man, turning him gingerly this way and that. Three letters were produced, all addressed to Mr. Jake Glendon and bearing the name of a Mexican town a few miles below the border; a clasp knife came into view; the vest pockets gave up two broken cigars and a sack of cigarette tobacco; there were two door keys and two handkerchiefs, one clean, one soiled; various cards advertising honkytonks and dance halls were exposed to view; a right-hand pocket of the pants gave up nearly two dollars in silver, a red poker chip, and a pair of well-worn dice; in a hip pocket was a roll of bills amounting to more than sixty dollars.

The sheriff sat back on his haunches, surveying the small pile of articles he had removed from the pockets. Tucson said, "I noted you looked rather surprised, Sheriff, when you read the addresses on those letters. Do you know the man?"

The sheriff pursed his lips and considered. Finally he grunted, "Not personally." He fell silent before continuing, then burst out, "This is a blessing if there ever was one. This here—this Jake Glendon has caused more trouble along the border than any ten men." Lullaby interposed a question and the sheriff went on, "Everybody hereabouts has heard of the Jake Glendon gang, though I never met anybody who'd admit he ever saw Glendon. He's been operating down below the border for the past three years—"

"Operating how?" Stony asked.

"Smuggling—diamonds and dope—mostly dope, I guess. All peace officers in this vicinity have been on the lookout for him. Tips have been received that were supposed to lead to his capture, but he always managed to slip through folks' hands. 'Bout all anybody knew about him was that he wore a hat with an Indian bead band"—nodding toward the sombrero that lay on the ground a few feet away—"and I never did read a description of him any place. A man hears word-of-mouth descriptions, now and then, but you know how they

19

go—nobody ever seems to agree on details. One month Jake Glendon would be short with dark eyes; the next he'd be tall with light eyes." Yarrow opened the letters he'd taken from the dead man's pockets and perused the contents, then replaced the papers with a grunt. "Cripes! A bill for gun repairs from somebody in Juarez, and two letters from lovesick women, in Phoenix and El Paso. The dates ain't recent enough to follow up."

"What you figuring to follow up on?" Tucson asked quietly.

"Nothing much, come to think of it," Yarrow said. "With Glendon dead, the case is closed." He tugged at his blond-gray mustache. "Now what in the name of the seven bald steers ever made Jake Glendon kill himself?"

"Probably had some trouble with his gang," Lullaby speculated. "Argument over leadership, perhaps. Maybe a fight occurred over the division of the spoils. It might be the gang had Glendon cornered and was set to wipe him out, and he preferred to kill himself rather than give his gang that satisfaction. Sound plausible?"

"Could be, could be," Yarrow conceded with a shrug. "The main thing is, Glendon is dead. This will be good news to the governor. The U. S. marshal's office has been asking him to do something, and the governor has been ridin' all hell out of us peace officers. I'll telegraph the capital when I get back. Maybe now I'll get some rest.

And there's a lot of other folks will rest easier in their minds with Glendon out of the way, too."

"Meaning who?" Tucson asked quietly.

"Relatives of peace officers," the sheriff replied. "I've lost two deputies—they were found dead, out here on the range. I always thought they must have run into Glendon when he was doing some smuggling. My present deputy has been threatening to quit. I figure him as having a streak of yellow. Two years ago my brother was found dead over in the foothills of the Torvos. He'd been prospecting over that way. Now I'm right sure he wasn't interfering with Glendon in any way, but he got a bullet through his heart all the same."

"The killers were never apprehended?" Stony asked.

"You can't apprehend a man unless you first know who he is and where to find him," Yarrow said heavily. "Frank—that was my brother's name—didn't have an enemy in the world." The sheriff sighed. "Well, that's the way it goes. Only thing I'm sorry for, this body wasn't over there, on the other side of this dry wash, when you found it."

"What difference does it make?" Lullaby asked.

"This dry wash is sort of the dividing line between Bandinera and Mesquital counties. If the body had been found in Bandinera I'd have been saved this trouble. Howsomever, I reckon it won't be too much trouble to report Glendon's death and see that he gets Christian burial—much as he don't

21

deserve same. I'll give the coroner a picture of just what's been found here and that will be the end of it, I figure." Tucson asked a question. The sheriff considered a moment, then shook his head. "No, I don't reckon it will be necessary for you to appear at the inquest. If you don't mind my askin', where you going from here?"

"Cattlemen's Convention, at Yubaville," Tucson replied. "We've got friends over that way and may visit for a spell. I don't know how long, but we'll drift back this way, in case you want to see us again. I'll give you the address of our home ranch, too, in case you want to get in touch later."

"I reckon that will be all right." Yarrow nodded. "Look here, if you're headed for Yubaville, there's no use you going through Jackpot, which is just a ghost town, anyway. You swing somewhat northerly when you leave here, and you'll hit a pass through the mountains that will save you some time. It's not a pass that a coach or wagon could make easy, but horses won't have no trouble. You'll have to make a dry camp tonight, of course—" He broke off to answer Stony's question. "No, there's no reason for you to wait any longer. I'll stay with the body until the undertaker arrives, which should be shortly after sundown. Get ridin' any time you feel like."

A short time later, having shaken hands with the sheriff, the Mesquiteers mounted and after picking a hoof-clattering way across the dry wash, headed their ponies in a swift lope toward the foothills of the Torvo Mountains, the clouds of dust kicked up by their ponies' hoofs being quickly whisked away by the strong breeze blowing across the brush and cactus-spotted terrain.

The sun was behind the mountain peaks by this time and the ponies were having harder going as they got into ascending ground. After a time the riders drew to a walk to rest their mounts. Cigarettes were rolled and lighted. Stony spoke first, "Why do you figure that Glendon hombre killed himself?"

"What interests me more," Lullaby said, "is why he came way out to the middle of nowhere to do it."

"It could be he was brought there," Tucson pointed out.

Stony glanced up sharply. "What you got on your mind, Tucson?"

"Mostly, a matter of elevation."

Lullaby said, "What are you driving at?"

"While you two were riding in to get the sheriff," Tucson explained, "I read sign a mite, and found out two or three things. I took a few measurements and made some calculations. Glendon was over six feet tall, but still not tall enough to receive a charge of buckshot from that scatter-gun—not with the gun muzzles placed at the elevation at which we found them. The shot would have gone well above his head when he pulled the trigger, if he was standing where we found the body."

"Maybe," Stony suggested, "he was standing closer when he pulled that cord, and then staggered back."

"I thought of that." Tucson nodded. "In that case, I don't think the buckshot would have spread enough to wipe out his whole face the way it did. Without knowing more of the gun, I couldn't say for certain, of course. I'm just telling how it looked to me."

"A shotgun has a terrific kick," Lullaby pointed out. "Maybe when it went off the kick threw it to a higher angle."

"I gave that some consideration too," Tucson replied. "You'll remember there was a chunk of sandstone laying across the barrels to weight the gun in place—supposedly." Lullaby demanded to know what he meant by "supposedly." Tucson explained, "Whoever placed that sandstone on the shotgun didn't give enough thought to what he was doing, or he'd have realized a rock that size wasn't heavy enough to hold the gun solid when it was fired. The kick of the gun would have flung it to one side."

"What in the devil are you driving at, Tucson?" Stony frowned.

"Simply that Jake Glendon didn't commit suicide. He may have originally been murdered by that shotgun, but not at the place where we found him. Somebody killed him and then brought the body out there, and set the stage to make it look like suicide. Whoever did it likely figured that the death of a man with Glendon's reputation wouldn't arouse enough interest among peace officers to entail a thorough investigation. Oh, there were other things to make me suspicious too. For instance a man with his head half blown off would stagger back and fall with his arms and legs sprawled in all directions. Glendon lay very straight, legs close together, just as he had been laid down by whoever carried him there. One arm had even been dropped across his chest. There were no heel marks in the sand such as a staggering man might make—"

"You sure make it look like murder." Lullaby nodded.

"I don't see how it could be anything else," Tucson said. "I'm no medical examiner, but I felt Glendon's flesh and I judge that he was killed sometime last night. Now will you tell me why a suicide should go out there in that open country and fumble around in the dark to set the stage that way before killing himself—especially when he had a six-shooter in his holster that would have done the job just as well? And why should he go so far from town to do the job?"

Lullaby grunted disgustedly, "Damn it, I'm getting careless in my old age. Somehow I never gave a thought to that six-shooter."

"The murderer planned on folks being careless," Tucson said, his body shifting easily to the movements of his horse. "The very fact that nearly sixty-five dollars was left on the body tends to make it look more like suicide. So often a murdered man is found to have been robbed, whereas a suicide—" He broke off, then continued, "Like I said before, folks won't be likely to consider details much with Glendon dead. They'll just be thankful, and then forget the whole business."

"Look here," Stony put in, "if somebody killed Glendon and then carried him out there, why didn't we notice sign of some sort?"

"I did," Tucson replied. "I found a freshly broken limb of brush that had been used to sweep over tracks. I even found a few blood spatters, here and there, that the murderers overlooked. I followed down that dry wash for a spell, and while hoofs don't leave much mark on those granite boulders, I did locate a few scratches. I figure there were three horses—two riders and an extra bronc to tote Glendon's corpse. I followed the sign until the riders left the wash and headed west, then didn't look any farther."

Lullaby asked, "Why didn't you mention all this to Yarrow?"

"From what Yarrow told us about Glendon," Tucson replied, "I figure it's a case of good riddance. But if the sheriff had the least inkling that Glendon had been murdered, he'd feel it his duty to get on the murderer's trail. He might even catch him, and then the county would be put to the expense of a trial to convict a man who is, more than likely, a public benefactor, if Glendon was engaged in smuggling narcotics, as the sheriff said. Lord! How I do hate a dope peddler. They cause more misery than all the gunmen and bandits in the country."

Stony and Lullaby nodded agreement. For a few minutes only the sounds of the horses' hoofs broke the silence. A huge jack rabbit scurried from beneath a clump of spiny cholla, darted frantically past the hoofs of the ponies, and went bounding off through the brush until it had been lost to sight. The riders looked after it a moment, then their thoughts returned to the matter of the Glendon "suicide." Tucson concluded, "Anyway, that's why I didn't mention my suspicions to Yarrow. He already looks sort of worn down. l didn't see any reason to add to his burdens."

Stony nodded. "You probably did right. Let sleeping dogs lie, as the saying goes."

"Goes where?" Lullaby wanted to know.

"Where sayings always go," Stony replied testily. "You know—just round and round—"

"I don't know," Lullaby insisted. "That's why I asked you. And now I don't think you know either. 'Let sleeping dogs lie.' I ain't stopping them, but how can they tell lies if they're asleep? Even if they could talk in the first place."

"I didn't mention any particular place they talked," Stony defended himself. "There just ain't no satisfying some folks. I try to tell you about a dog that can talk, and you insist he has to talk in some particular place."

"*You* try to tell me," Lullaby snorted. "It was me that brought it up."

"You think that's something to brag about?" Stony sneered. "Anybody can bring up a dog. I've brought up many a dog."

"What kinds?"

"I had a sheepdog once—"

"Sheep!" Lullaby's nose wrinkled contemptuously. "And you call yourself a cowman."

"—but the best dog I ever had was a cross between a hunter and a setter—"

"Hunted for bones and then set down to gnaw 'em, I'll bet," Lullaby guffawed.

"If that ain't like you," Stony said disgustedly. "Always trying to bring the conversation around to the subject of eating."

"Knowing your predilections for drink," Lullaby snapped, "I'm amazed that you never had one of them dogs that comes with a little keg of brandy slung to his neck, that saves travelers lost in the snow."

"I never lived where there was enough snow for a Saint Bernard dog—"

"And besides, you'd never let a keg of brandy get that far away from you. I'm surprised you never moved to one of them snow countries, though, and made a life career out of being saved."

"I already been saved," Stony said piously. "That time I took up religion and became a missionary among the Yaquente Indians."

Lullaby gasped. "If you can't make up the damnedest lies! You hear that, Tucson, Stony claiming he was once a gospel spreader among the heathen?"

"I never said anything about spreading the gospel," Stony said modestly. "The padres did that. I just helped out, and taught the savages to till the soil and plant and such."

"What did you plant?" Lullaby asked suspiciously.

"Oh—corn and punkins and joshin' seeds—stuff like that," Stony said casually. "Those Yaquentes became real civilized—"

"Now wait a minute," Lullaby interposed. "Corn and pumpkins I can savvy, but what's this about joshin' seeds? I never heard of 'em."

"Never heard of joshin' seeds?" Stony snickered. "Let me enlighten you, my friend. You plant 'em in the spring and in the fall they sprout the answers to damn fool questions." He gave a sudden whoop of delight.

Tucson chuckled and Lullaby looked disgusted. "Serves me right," Lullaby said darkly, "for associating with somebody whose mind ain't never developed beyond the childhood stage."

"Hear that, Tucson?" Stony grinned. "He don't appreciate us. I wouldn't let him say that about my mind, was I you."

"I'll let it ride for the present," Tucson said dryly. "Meanwhile, if we're going to reach that pass before sundown, I figure we'd better hightail it some."

The men touched spurs to their ponies and the animals once again broke into a long, ground-devouring gait that carried them through the foothills of the Torvo Mountains, now towering high above their heads.

3. Sheriff's Luck

Torvo lay sweltering under the midmorning heat. Pitch oozed stickily from the plank sidewalks along Main Street, which was bordered on either side by various false-fronted frame structures, or buildings constructed of rock and adobe. There were several saloons, three general stores, barbershops, restaurants, and numerous other places of commercial enterprise. The Torvo House, a two-story hotel, stood on the northeast corner of Main and Deming streets, and the livery and corral at its rear ran clear through to First Street, which was mostly filled with residences. At the corner of Main and Waco streets the Torvo Savings Bank raised a faded brick façade, while diagonally across from it, on the southeast corner, stood the sheriff's office, with, stretching to its rear, a long, barred-windowed jail. The streets of Torvo were dusty and unpaved. There weren't many people abroad at this hour of the day. Mostly Torvo's residents were remaining within doors, or at least in the shadows cast by the wooden awnings that reached above the sidewalks. An almost unbroken line of hitching racks flanked both sides of Main, at which stood a few cow ponies, lazily switching tails at the flies. In the vicinity of the general stores there were a few wagons and buggies to be seen.

Sheriff Yarrow moved out of his office and stood a moment on the small porch fronting the building, while he gazed in both directions along the thoroughfare. A man in cowman's dress sauntered past and received a pleasant "Good mornin' " in reply to his salutation. A hen scratched futilely in the dusty street. It was, probably, the sheriff considered, from Ma Henderson's coop, over on Second Street. It passed through Yarrow's mind that he'd have to tell Ma Henderson to keep a better check on her chickens; they were forever getting loose and wandering over to Main, where they generally got killed, one way or another, and that always made one more complaint for the sheriff's office. As though there weren't more serious complaints to worry a man. Yarrow glanced again at the sheet of paper he carried in his hand and, frowning, folded it and thrust the message into one pocket.

His attention came back to the chicken, stirring up small puffs of dust, and he strode out to the middle of the road making "shooing" sounds and waving his hands until the hen beat a reluctant retreat in the direction of Waco Street. The sheriff stood looking at it a moment, then crossed the remainder of the way to enter the Sundown Saloon, whose cool dim interior furnished a welcome relief after the heat of outdoors. Hank Rittenhouse, proprietor of the Sundown, was polishing glasses behind the bar when the sheriff entered. There were no customers at the long mahogany bar, and Rittenhouse turned with a smile of welcome on his round, smooth-shaven features, at sound of the sheriff's step. His hair was sandy-hued, streaked with silver, and slicked down on his forehead; a bar apron was knotted about his bulging middle. "How's it this morning, Matt?" he queried, setting out a glass and bottle of beer.

The sheriff replied shortly that it was "Hot," and didn't speak again until a glass of the foamy amber liquid had disappeared down his throat. Then he gave a long sigh of satisfaction. "Hank, you're the only barkeep in town that keeps beer at the correct temperature. Most fellers serve it warm, or if they've got ice they dang nigh freeze it solid, seems like. Chilled beer can be bad for a man's stomach."

"If I don't get a shipment of ice on this noon's train I won't have any cold beer either. I did manage to keep that bottle cold for you, but my ice is near gone. Lost quite a bit of business this mornin', because I had to turn customers away. But that's a barkeep's luck for you."

"I'll take it in preference to a sheriff's luck any day," Yarrow said moodily. "If I'd had any sense I'd gone pardners with you twenty years ago, as you wanted. But no, I had to get into politics."

"Something got you upset, Matt?" Rittenhouse asked quietly.

"Another telegram from the governor this mornin'. He's threatenin' to replace me unless something is done about the Jake Glendon gang. Yeah, some more stuff got through—morphine and opium. They always get wind of those things after they've happened, of course."

Rittenhouse shook his head sadly. "That's bad. Seven weeks ago, when Jake Glendon's body was brought in, I thought that would be the end of the business, but the gang seems to go on just the same."

"I felt the same way," Yarrow said bitterly. "Foolishly, I let down and gave up riding nights, the way I'd been doin'. Not that my ridin' done any good, but I kept tryin'. If I could only get another deputy to share the work, but nobody wants the job, 'pears like. With the Glendon gang still operatin', it looks too dangerous— particularly in view of my losin' two deputies, shot to death."

"By the way," Rittenhouse said, "Owney Powell is in town." Yarrow asked for details. Rittenhouse continued, "I was down to the Boston Clothing Store to buy a shirt, and when I came out Owney and three of the Box-V outfit were just going in the Silver Spur Bar."

Yarrow frowned. "I wondered what became of him. He's probably been living at the Box-V since I took his badge away. Maybe he's taken a job with Luke Vaughn. I don't figure Vaughn's the type that would feed a man for nothin'. Well, he's welcome to Powell. I don't want any more of him. Only made him a deputy in the first place because I couldn't get anybody else. I should've knowed better."

"You never did say why you sacked Powell."

"Huh? I thought I told you, Hank. Well, to make a long story short, the U. S. marshal's office sent me a tip they'd got someplace, that the Glendon gang was bringin' a load of dope through Lamedero—you know, that little Mex settlement on the salt flats down near the border. This was about two weeks after Jake Glendon's dead body had been brought in. Well, you know how tips are—mostly unreliable, but they have to be checked into anyway, and the U. S. marshal can't handle everything himself. So I should have been on the job. But what happened? I was out of the office when the marshal's telegram arrived and Owney Powell took it. Then he neglects to tell me and disappears on a week's drunk. By the time he sobers up and gives me the telegram it's too late for me to do anything about it." The sheriff swore long and fervently. "And so I kicked him out of the job; tore the badge right off'n his vest."

"You done right, Matt," Rittenhouse nodded. "As a deputy, Owney Powell was a no-good."

"Just call him a no-good at anythin'," the sheriff growled. He poured the remainder of the beer into his glass and sipped reminiscently. "Funny thing, though, Powell sure acted like he hated to lose the job. That surprised me plenty, as he'd always been talkin' about quittin', before that, and I'd put him down as bein' yellow for fear of gettin' into some sort of trouble with the Glendon gang. For that matter, I still think he's yellow. As for runnin' counter to the Glendon gang"—bitterly—"it don't look like there's much chance of that, unless somebody can get a line on 'em and find out who they are."

"You don't even know where they hang out?" Rittenhouse asked.

Yarrow scowled. "Either this side of the border or on the Mexican side. That's about all anybody knows. The Mexican Government is working with the United States authorities, wherever possible, but neither side seems able to learn anything definite—"

The sheriff broke off as the swinging doors of the Sundown Saloon banged open and four men approached the bar, their spurs jangling across the pine floor boards. The three men in the lead nodded to the sheriff and took up a position farther along the bar. The fourth, a fellow of around twenty-five with sideburns and a thin mustache, lingered a moment to say, "H'are you, Matt! How's crime?"

"It might be on the increase," Yarrow said coldly, "now that you're back in Torvo again."

Owney Powell, Yarrow's ex-deputy, stiffened. "Just what do you mean by that remark?" he demanded uneasily.

"Owney," Yarrow explained, "when a man has shown definite that he ain't any good puttin' down crime, and don't even try, I'm inclined to figure him as bein' on the other side of the fence, until such time as I'm proved wrong. That clear?"

Powell's long lantern jaw jutted belligerently for a moment, then he forced a laugh. "Damn if you ain't a card, Matt. Always joshin' folks." He left the sheriff and joined his companions at the far end of the bar.

The sheriff's lips tightened as he looked at the four men: Luke Vaughn, owner of the Box-V Ranch, a big man with thick shoulders and black eyebrows forming a straight line across the bridge of his hooked nose; Bart Fielding, puncher for the Box-V, hard-bitten and narrow-eyed; the tow-headed Tulsa Nash, thin and wiry, with washy blue eyes and crooked teeth. Nash carried a reputation as a gun fighter, though so far as Yarrow knew he'd never been involved in any killings in the vicinity of Torvo. Everyone knew, however, that the man was of a quarrelsome disposition and he was generally given a wide berth. All four men were in cow-country togs and carried six-shooters in holsters. Only Powell's clothing looked new, and the sheriff noted that Powell's six-shooter sported an ivory butt.

Luke Vaughn had asked for cold beer, when Rittenhouse went to take the orders, but upon being told there was no more cold beer, had accepted whisky as had the others. With the drinks consumed, Powell and Vaughn carried on a low-voiced conversation. Eventually Powell drifted along the bar until he was standing beside Yarrow.

"Y'know, Matt," he said good-naturedly, "there ain't no use of you and me bein' enemies."

"I've seen nothing to warrant us bein' friends either," the sheriff replied in brittle tones.

"Now, now," Powell laughed, "you shouldn't take that attitude. You and me had our differences, and I ain't saying you were in the wrong. I guess, as a deputy, I was just a round peg in a square hole. Maybe I didn't take the job as seriously as I should. I realize that now, however, and—"

"Cut out the palaver, Owney," Yarrow broke in. "What you getting at?"

"I hear you haven't been able to get a deputy yet, Matt."

"You hear correct. What's it to you?"

"I hate like hell seeing you carry the burden of office all by your lonesome. You'll work yourself to death."

"Gawd, you're sure getting tenderhearted," Yarrow stated sarcastically. "Since when have you commenced worryin' about me?"

"Ever since I left your office," Powell said earnestly. "I let you down, Matt, let you down bad. I'd like another chance."

"At being my deputy?" Yarrow's eyes widened, then a harsh laugh parted his lips. "You fool, you should know better—"

"You'd better think twice, Matt." Powell's cheeks had grown red. "You've tried and tried to get somebody to take my place, and you ain't had any luck. Now you could swear me in and make things a heap easier—"

"Owney," the sheriff said steadily, "I wouldn't put you back on that job if you were the last man on earth—"

"Don't say anything you'll regret, Matt," Powell snapped.

"I'm not!" Yarrow's anger burst into sudden flame. "Powell, you're no good and you never will be any good. Before I'd make you my deputy I'd give the badge to the first lousy, stinkin' bum that hit Torvo. I'd know what to expect from a bum, at least."

"By God, Matt, that sounds like war talk to me," Powell flared.

"War talk it is then," Yarrow said hotly. "What you aimin' to do about it?"

Powell fell silent before the sheriff's wrath. The

other men had been listening to the conversation, and now Tulsa Nash's sneering voice broke in. "Yarrow, you'd best take Owney up on his offer. You won't find anybody else willin' to take that deputy job—"

"You, Tulsa," Luke Vaughn growled, "keep your mouth out of other men's business. Come on, we're heading out of here." Nash fell silent and Vaughn moved toward the doorway, pausing a moment before the sheriff. "Matt, my outfit don't want any trouble with you. If any of my boys get proddy, you say the word and I'll put the quietus on 'em." He glared balefully at Powell. "That goes for you too, Owney. If you ain't satisfied with the job I gave you, quit right now. I'll be damned if I intend to feed you any longer, if you keep lookin' for another job."

"The Box-V suits me," Powell said tonelessly.

Vaughn nodded shortly and started for the street again, Nash and Bart Fielding at his heels. Powell lingered but a moment longer, saying, "Sorry we couldn't get together, Matt, but if you change your mind, just say the word."

"I'll not be changing my mind," Yarrow snapped. "What I said still goes—any bum that happened to hit Torvo would make a better deputy than you."

"Someday you'll regret saying that," Powell half snarled.

"That sounds like a threat to me," Yarrow said, level-voiced. "Now you'd best watch your lip, and your actions, Owney, or I'll put you in a cell. Now go on, get out of here, and see that you keep the peace so long's you're in town."

Powell hesitated but a moment longer, then without speaking further pushed open the swinging doors and joined Vaughn and the others on the sidewalk.

Yarrow turned back to the bar. "Damn insolent pup. I nigh lose my temper when I talk to a man like that."

Hank Rittenhouse placed another bottle of beer in front of the sheriff. "Talking is dry business," he observed.

"Thought I heard you tell Vaughn you didn't have any more cold beer."

"I didn't—except this I saved for you. I knew you'd be wanting it."

"You're a friend, Hank." The sheriff drank beer in a moody silence for a few minutes, then, "Just what did you make of all that?"

Rittenhouse frowned. "I was watching Vaughn and them others. I could have sworn Vaughn put Owney up to asking for his job back, but seems like he got mad at Owney for asking."

"That's the way it looked to me too," Yarrow said. "Maybe when he saw the idea didn't go across, he decided he'd better pretend like he'd had nothing to do with it."

"Maybe so," the barkeep agreed. "I never could figure out Vaughn. He and his outfit always seem to have plenty of loose cash. At the same time, they don't appear to work too hard. I heard a couple of Rafter-H hands talking last fall about the small shipment of beef animals Vaughn sent off—small, that is, considering the size of his herd. And it's a pretty good-sized crew he keeps on his pay roll too. Now if there'd been any rustling complaints hereabouts, and Vaughn was in the habit of making large shipments, I might have my suspicions."

"Thank God there've been no rustling complaints," Yarrow said fervently. "If I had rustling as well as smuggling to contend with—" He paused. "Hell! What's the use of talking? I'd best be getting along. The noon train is nigh due."

"Should you see Bud Yeager down to the station," Rittenhouse said, "tell him not to lose no time gettin' my ice here. That is, if you'll be expecting cold beer tomorrow."

"Which same I will be, Hank. I'll mention it to Bud."

4. A Fighting Hobo

The sheriff left the Sundown Saloon and recrossed the street, his moving shadow making a black silhouette against the sun-baked dusty roadway. Stepping into his office, he remained there for a time, then emerged to saunter leisurely in a westerly direction along Main. At the corner of Deming Street he turned south, proceeding along

41

the side wall of Petten's General Store, grateful for the shade in which he now walked. Ahead, he could see the twin gleaming rails of the T. N. & A. S. Railroad, and beyond them, except for a few scattered adobe shacks, all open country dotted with cactus, mesquite, and creosote bush, all the way to a rugged-peaked mountain range in Mexico, now somewhat hazy in the distance, due to the shimmering heat waves rising from the sandy, parched earth.

Yarrow rounded the rear of the general store building, glanced along the numerous piles of ashes, tin cans, and other refuse standing near the back doors of buildings fronting on Main Street, then walked another seventy-five feet to the platform of the T. N. & A. S. depot, which was constructed of heavy pine planks raised but slightly above the level of the ground. Standing in the center of the platform was a frame building, painted a sun-faded brownish red, which constituted the railroad ticket office and waiting room. Partitioned off, at the far end was the freight shed. The usual town loafers, some of whom had already made too many visits to Torvo's drinking emporiums, lounged about the building. In addition a number of the town's more staid citizens were on hand; as no newspaper as yet existed in Torvo, many men made it their business to be on hand when the daily trains arrived in the hope of gleaning some news from other parts of the country, and to see what passengers, if any, descended from the coaches. There were only two or three women to be seen.

Various individuals spoke to the sheriff as he stepped to the platform. Nodding, he passed on and entered the depot proper. Approaching the ticket window, he spoke through the grill to a girl with taffy-colored hair and eyes the hue of dusty violets, who was making *clickety-click* sounds over a telegraph instrument. The girl shifted a slim boyish form in brown gingham and started to rise from her chair.

"Don't get up, Jane," Yarrow said. "I just wanted to know if anything more came in for me."

"Nothing since that wire this morning, Uncle Matt."

An expression of relief passed across Yarrow's face. "The governor must have forgotten me for a spell," he observed.

"Uncle Matt, stop worrying," the girl exclaimed with some exasperation. "Everybody knows you're doing your job as well as possible. If the governor knew you were running your office shorthanded—by golly! I'd tell him you haven't been able to get a deputy—"

"What sort of a sheriff is unable to get a deputy?" Yarrow asked gloomily. "That makes it look like I can't run my job proper—"

"Fiddlesticks!" The girl had started to say more when the long-drawn whistle of a locomotive reached their ears, and the sheriff departed in the direction of the outer platform. He noted as he emerged from the depot that Bud Yeager's wagon was drawn up near the tracks, awaiting the arrival of ice. Grouped near the wagon seat upon which Yeager sat were the four Box-V men—Vaughn, Nash, Fielding, and Owney Powell. The sheriff approached the wagon, ignoring the Box-V men. "Bud," he said, "Hank Rittenhouse wants you should get the ice over to the Sundown first off."

"Surely will, Sher'f," Yeager responded, "just as soon's I've made a delivery to the Silver Spur. Luke, here, tells me the Silver Spur is plumb melted out—"

"The Sundown, first off," Yarrow repeated. "As a personal favor to me."

"We-ell, if you putten it that-a-way." Yeager nodded.

The sheriff said, "Thanks," and turned away.

Owney Powell uttered a sneering laugh. "Using your office to get favors now, Matt?"

Yarrow's features crimsoned. "And what's it to you if I do?" he growled, swinging back.

"No offense, Matt," Owney said, backing a step. "I was only joshin'. Just the same, it don't seem right for a sheriff to run errands for a barkeep. You should have a deputy for such jobs."

Yarrow laughed without humor. "Yeah, I should have," he admitted, "but no bums for the job have hit town yet, and I got to get somebody that rates higher than my last deputy."

Without giving Powell time to answer he again turned back toward the center of the platform. The locomotive whistle sounded again, a quarter mile distant, and the tracks commenced a vibrating hum. Loungers in the shadows straightened and moved to the edge of the platform. Within the next minute the train ground to a braking stop among a shower of cinders and hissing steam. Black smoke billowed about the depot. This noon train was a combination affair: three freight cars and two passenger coaches, though today no passengers had bought tickets to Torvo. Two of the three freight cars had been opened and while ice, crates, and boxes were being unloaded, a small knot of men had collected near the locomotive in hope of hearing news of the capital from the engineer. Finally the doors of the boxcars were closed, and the conductor yelled his "All ab-boar-rd-d-d!"

The locomotive started to make chuffing noises. Again black smoke clouded down about the depot in a rain of cinders. Steam hissed. The wheels of the engine hadn't yet started to turn when there came a loud bawling from the conductor, "Hold 'er, Jim, hold that kettle! Wait a minute! Don't start 'er!"

Swift words passed between conductor and engineer. A brakeman came running to learn what was holding up the train. A crowd gathered about the two. "—and just as we was ready to roll," the conductor was explaining, "somebody inside that first boxcar started to open the door. There's somebody in there. Some damn dead-beat—"

"You sure, Charley?" the brakeman demanded. "We finished emptyin' that car at Turnerburg—"

"Then some hobo must've sneaked in at Turnerburg," the conductor insisted angrily.

The brakeman swung around. "Ain't no 'boes going to ride on my train," he announced. "We'll see about this." He ran to the freight car in question, slid back the door, and climbed into the car. Immediately an oath left his lips as he darted toward one end of the car. Sounds of a commotion instantly filled the air. The crowd pressed closer. There came a loud smacking sound and the brakeman again appeared in view, this time staggering backward to go tumbling to the earth.

A delighted yell rose from the crowd. "Looks like Hugo needed help," the conductor snapped, and hurried to the rescue of his brakie. By this time the brakeman had regained his feet and was again within the boxcar. The tussling sounds were renewed and within a minute the struggling forms of the brakeman and another man appeared in the open doorway of the car, though now the brakeman was bawling lustily for assistance. The conductor started to climb up, but one foot of the hobo caught him in the chest, sending him staggering back. Now the fireman of the locomotive came running

46

to the rescue. Pausing only long enough to help the conductor to his feet, he too climbed into the car.

The sounds of violence were renewed. The crowd cheered wildly. Standing in the shadow of one depot wall, Sheriff Yarrow watched with interest while struggling figures swayed back and forth in the open doorway. By this time the engineer had clambered down from his cab and stood watching above the heads of the crowd. Seeing the sheriff, the engineer said, "How about doing your duty and arresting that 'bo, Yarrow?"

The sheriff smiled. "Want I should spoil Torvo's enjoyment? 'Sides, that hobo is on railroad property. Toss him off and I'll make an arrest. Meanwhile, it looks like you got enough men to handle him—or maybe you haven't." The brakeman had again come hurtling through the open doorway of the car, leaving the fireman and conductor to carry on alone. This time the brakie was slower in gaining his feet.

Owney Powell sidled up to Yarrow. "Remember what you said about making a deputy out of the first bum to hit town?" Powell sneered. "Here's your chance, Matt."

The sheriff flushed. "Right now that bum, whoever he is, is provin' himself a better fighter than you, Owney. You've allowed you're somethin' of a fighter, yourself, in the past. Why don't you give that train crew a hand, seein' you're so tough?"

"By God, I'll do just that!" Powell exclaimed and

47

started for the train, arriving just in time to give the brakeman a shove up into the car and climbing up after him. Momentarily the battling men were lost to view beyond the wide door opening, but the sounds of violence were increased. The crowd rent the atmosphere with its yelling. From within the car a yell of triumph lifted from Owney Powell's throat, only to be cut short in a gasping grunt. Feet thudded loudly within the car. There were grunts, groans, curses.

"By Gawd," Yarrow told himself, "that 'bo's a scrapper—"

He broke off as a knot of struggling figures again appeared in the doorway of the boxcar. Owney Powell and the fireman were clinging doggedly to the legs of the hobo. The brakeman and conductor had their arms about the tramp's upper body. All five teetered on the edge of the car doorway a brief moment before going over and landing on the earth beside the tracks, the shock of the impact loosening the holds of the attackers.

The hobo was first to regain his feet. His overalls and shirt were in tatters. Somehow, through all the melee, he had managed to retain his hat, a shape-less soft object which might have, at one time, been a gray sombrero. He was unshaven, smoke-grimed, and toes showed through one boot; the other boot was heelless. He was, in short, as disreputable a figure as Sheriff Yarrow ever remembered seeing.

"My grief!" It was the voice of the lady telegraph

operator standing in the depot doorway, near the sheriff. "Do you mean to tell me that—that scarecrow—put up all that fight?"

She stopped. Powell and the brakeman had also regained their feet now, and Powell's fist was swinging in a wide arc intended to land in the hobo's face. He sidestepped suddenly and the fist landed on the brakeman's jaw. A roar of laughter rose from the spectators as the brakeman went staggering into the crowd.

"Who in hell you pushin'?" a spectator demanded angrily. He had been drinking and wasn't quite responsible. "Just 'cause four of you can beat up on one bum is no sign you can ride roughshod—" Rage overcoming him, he swung wildly at the brakie and connected, his victim striking the ground heavily from the force of the blow.

With an angry curse, the fireman sprang to the aid of the brakeman, the hobo forgotten in this new altercation. An instant later the drunk had joined the brakeman on the ground. That started things; many in the crowd decided to take sides. Powell had started another blow at the hobo, but one of Torvo's citizens knocked Powell from his feet. Thereupon the fireman and conductor, rushing to Powell's assistance, found themselves in turn borne to the ground by the weight of numbers as some twenty men got warmed up to the fight. In an instant the vicinity of the depot was a scene of milling, cursing men whose fists were flying in all directions. Cooler heads formed a circle about the combatants and filled the air with impartial yells of encouragement. Dust rose in clouds about the cluster of straining, cursing fighters.

Yarrow was dancing around the edge of the brawl. "Stop it, you damn fools, or I'll put every mother's son of you in the hoosegow. Stop it, I say!" He plowed into the melee, trying to separate two of the fighters, but neither words nor actions were of any avail. Finally, with a growl of disgust, he retired to the shadow of the depot, where a slow grin broke over his face. An instant later he was doubled over with laughter. "Of all the fool nitwits I ever saw," he gasped. "There ain't but two or three of 'em knows what they're fightin' about, and even they ain't certain. Serves 'em all right!"

"Right smart little fracas, eh, Sheriff?" queried a cool voice at Yarrow's elbow.

Yarrow turned his head, his jaw dropping. Standing by his side, a broad grin on his smudged, unshaven features, was the cause of the trouble—the fighting hobo—looking even more disreputable than Yarrow had first thought him.

"Where in hell did you come from?" the sheriff blurted.

"Yonderly from that mass of stamped critters," the hobo replied cheerfully. "It was getting too hot for me. A feller could get hurt fooling around that way."

"Why, damn your lousy hide," Yarrow burst out, "it's you them hombres is scrappin' over."

"No fault of mine," the 'bo defended himself. "I was riding plumb peaceful until that brakie decided to throw me off here. Just plain minding my own business and now look—" gesturing toward the milling men. He drew a long pious sigh. "It's disgraceful the way a fellow creature will turn into an animal like that. And no fit sight for a lady's eyes. And the language. Tut-tut!" He had just seen Jane Yarrow standing in the doorway of the depot, her face suffused with mirth.

"Never mind the lady," Yarrow said sternly. "She happens to be my niece, and is no concern of yours. Whether you wanted this fight or not, it's your fault the whole thing's started." He couldn't feel really angry at the tramp. "Mebbe you have some idea how to stop it."

"Maybe I have," the hobo admitted. "That locomotive engineer is trying to get his fireman out of there now, but he's not having any success. I'll pull the engineer loose, and when I do, you grab him and tell him to blow hell out of his whistle. C'mon."

Without waiting for the sheriff to agree, the hobo plunged into the brawl. A moment later he emerged, hauling after him the engineer of the train, who was already sporting a black eye. "Damn you," the engineer swore, recognizing the tramp, "it's you that caused this—"

That was as far as he got when he felt himself seized by the sheriff and hustled in the direction of his locomotive. "You get up on your engine and blow the tootin' entrails outten your whistle," the sheriff said sternly. "Get your train out of here pronto, before I lay suit against the T. N. & A. S. for creatin' a disturbance in Torvo. Go on, now, get started!"

Without a protest the engineer climbed into his cab. The sheriff turned back to see the hobo emerging once more from the cluster of brawling men, dragging behind him the fireman, who was too groggy to put up any resistance. "Your engineer's on his engine," Yarrow snapped. "You get up there with him and fire like hell." Meekly the fireman started in the direction of the locomotive.

"Who else do you want?" the hobo chuckled.

"You," Yarrow grunted, seizing the tramp's arm, which proved to be decidedly muscular beneath the tattered shirt. "You needn't think you're goin' to get off so easy."

"But look here," the 'bo protested, "I haven't done a thing."

"Don't cry about it. You're goin' to have plenty of opportunity, before you leave Torvo—"

It was at that moment the engineer sounded his whistle, giving out a blast that drowned all sounds of the fight. White steam filled the air in a screeching crescendo. Men picked themselves from the earth or lowered their fists and gazed in astonishment in the direction of the engine. The brakeman and the conductor wrestled themselves loose from their opponents of an instant before and started a mad dash in the direction of the train, the conductor yelling wildly as he ran, "All aboard, you bustards, all aboard!"

By the time the contestants had stopped and looked about, the locomotive's wheels were starting to revolve. A few passengers who had descended from the coaches clambered frantically back up the steps. The train commenced to move. A moment later, with an angry, half-defiant tooting of the whistle, it was rolling down the tracks, gathering speed with every turn of the ponderous steel wheels.

With this abrupt termination of the fight, tempers started to cool. The contestants gazed foolishly about, for the first time commencing to wonder just how they'd become embroiled in such an affair. It was a sorry-looking group that faced the sheriff and the hobo, now standing in the shade of one depot wall. Torn shirts, black eyes, swollen and cut lips, bloody noses appeared to be the general reward of those who had engaged in the battle. The tramp chuckled and then broke into loud laughter. At the sound, angry tempers started to rise again. Led by Owney Powell, a number of men converged on the sheriff and his prisoner.

"There's the stinkin' buzzard we want," Powell snarled.

"Let's string him up," Bart Fielding shouted.

The group closed in on Yarrow and the tramp, raising menacing fists. The sheriff slapped his holstered gun. "If you hombres think you're takin' my prisoner," he announced grimly, "you got another think comin'. Now go on about your business, the hull kit an' kaboodle of you, before I start shakin' lead outten my gun barrel."

The crowd fell back, leaving only Powell and Fielding facing the sheriff and his prisoner. Powell swore. "By God, I'm going to settle with this vag or—"

"You'll settle nothing," the hobo said calmly, "not unless you're craving another black eye to go with the shiner you already gathered."

"Don't take nothin' from him, Owney," Fielding encouraged. "I'll help you—"

"You're flirting with a mean bruise if you try to help anybody," the hobo told Fielding. "If the sheriff will just—"

"Tramp's advice ain't necessary," Yarrow cut in. "You keep your lip out of this, feller." His gaze ranged over the crowd and spied Tulsa Nash and Luke Vaughn, who had been smart enough to keep out of the fight. "Luke, you'd best call off these would-be fire-eaters of yours, or the Box-V will be short two hands. I'm making it clear, I don't want no more trouble."

"That suits me, Matt," Vaughn growled. "I was just waiting in hope you'd turn loose that vag on

Fielding and Powell. A mite of comeuppance would do 'em both a lot of good. Come on, you hombres, we're getting out of here."

Fielding and Powell started reluctantly away. Powell said, "You take my advice, Matt, and you'll keep this hobo in a cell. If I meet him on the street I'll—"

"Get on about your business, Owney," Yarrow snapped.

"I'm gettin', but you won't get any place protectin' that bum—"

"It's a habit I acquired when I made you a deputy, some time back," Yarrow said, tight-lipped. "Protectin' one more bum won't make much difference."

Laughter rose from the spectators. Powell's face reddened. "Probably aiming to make a deputy of him, too, I reckon," he said insolently.

"By Gawd," the sheriff flamed, "I might do just that to prove my point. Now go on, make yourself scarce."

The Box-V men retreated in the direction of Main Street, and the crowd gradually dispersed. Yarrow said to the hobo, "Well, you and me had better be getting over to the jail."

"Just's you say," the tramp said agreeably, glancing around, "but I'd like to apologize first to that young lady for any part I had in the disgraceful scene of a few minutes ago."

"The young lady," Yarrow said coldly, "has

returned to her job, and wouldn't be interested in your apologies, nohow, anyway."

"What's her job?" the tramp asked casually.

"She's the telegraph operator, days, and helps out the stationmaster, now and then—" Yarrow broke off, angrily. "What in hell's business is it of yours, I'd like to know? Now come on; you step along smart." They started toward Main Street, turning on Deming. At the corner of Deming and Main, Yarrow drew his prisoner's attention to the old frame two-story building across the way. "That's our courthouse," he commented carelessly. "What do you think of it?"

"Looks right ramshackle to me," the hobo said airily, "and no fitting place to bring *me* before the justice of the peace on a charge of vagrancy. I'll swear that building is as disreputable as any prisoner you might bring in. Looks about ready to collapse, too."

"Exactly what Torvo thinks of it," Yarrow said blandly. "We're erecting a new one, of cement, down the street a spell. Just started it last week."

The tramp looked at him in some alarm. "You mean I won't get a hearing until it's finished?"

"I didn't say that either," Yarrow replied. "That's something we'll discuss when we reach my office."

5. Smoky Jefferson

Yarrow and his prisoner entered the sheriff's office, which contained at one side a roll-top desk from which most of the finish had long since vanished. Across the room was a cot with neatly folded blankets. Four straight-backed chairs stood about. On the walls were various calendars from meat-packing companies, a topographical map of Mesquital County, and a few yellowed, flyspecked "wanted" bills, giving the descriptions of outlaws with prices on their heads. Light from a front window shone on a rack of shotguns and rifles placed against the back wall, and next to the rack a closed door showed the way to the jail cells. Yarrow kicked a chair in the direction of the hobo and seated himself sidewise at his desk. For a few moments he sat in silence, then asked abruptly, "Ever mix cement?"

The 'bo chuckled. "Not me. That sounds like work."

"It is work. Hard dusty work. The cement dust gets into a man's lungs somethin' fierce. But somebody's got to build that courthouse. We've sort of figured the labor could be done by the vags I arrested. Trouble is, there ain't many vags hit Torvo any more. I reckon news of our courthouse has spread, and the tramps are sheerin' wide of the town." He sighed deeply. "It's goin' to be mighty tough on you, wheelin' cement every day, not to mention the mixin'. Just tuggin' the bags around is backbreakin' labor—"

"Hey"—the hobo sounded alarmed—"you talk like I was elected to furnish all the labor."

"I know, son, it's tough," Yarrow sympathized, "but you can realize my position. I'm supposed to furnish the labor, and if I only manage to take in one vag, then one vag has to do the work—"

"Regardless how long it takes?"

Yarrow shrugged his bulky shoulders. "What's time to a hobo? Two or three years should see your sentence finished. Might take less if I can get some more vags—"

"Now look here, Sheriff, that sounds like a right stiff sentence. It's not fair."

"I already admitted that," Yarrow said blandly, "but I don't see no way out. A little work won't hurt you."

"Work!" The tramp shuddered. "Somebody's always tryin' to make me work. For all they know I might have a delicate constitution. Suppose I got some of that cement dust in my lungs? I might get consumption."

"In that case," Yarrow pointed out brutally, "your sentence would be concluded that much quicker. It ain't like we wouldn't feed you regular. And on Sundays you could have a cell all to yourself to get rested up." He added in a sudden burst of generosity, "I'll even furnish the liniment for your back, and if your lungs get real bad I'll get the doctor in. What do you say?"

"Do I get a say in the matter?" the 'bo asked hopefully. "Then I say no. I never could get used to labor of any sort. Cement mixing would be the death of me. Haven't you got anything easier?"

Yarrow considered. "We-ell, I don't like to be hard on you, son. I do have one other little job you might do—"

"So long as I don't have to work with cement—"

"You see, I've been needin' a deputy. I might give you a whirl at that. I don't know though—you've never had experience—"

"I'm a smart learner," the tramp said quickly. "I think that deputy job would be fine. No work concerned that amounts to anything."

"Course," Yarrow said carelessly, "I've had a couple of deputies die on the job. Little case of lead poisonin'."

"I could keep out of that kind of trouble," the tramp said. "Far be it from me to get into a ruckus of any sort."

"I noticed that, today, down to the depot," Yarrow said dryly. "But you do 'pear capable to take care of yourself." He sighed. "I'm a damn fool, but that Owney Powell makes me so blame mad. I'd just like to show him—"

"I don't get what you're talking about."

"It don't matter, son. Likely I should be sent to some sort of institution for the feeble-minded, but

I'm going to take a gamble on you. Ever ride a hawss?"

"Once or twice," the hobo admitted. "They jostle a feller around something terrible, though."

The sheriff groaned. "Oh, Gawd . . ." With an effort he continued, "Can you shoot a gun, if somebody shows you where the trigger's located?"

"You mean one with cartridges in it?"

Yarrow's face crimsoned. "What in the name of the seven bald steers would I mean? Moses on the mountain! One with cartridges in it! Oh, my Gawd! No, never mind. Don't answer me. I'm a fool, all right, but a desperate situation requires desperate measures. You're going to be a deputy if it kills you. How long you'll last is up to you—but I can't hold out much hope."

He rose and from a wooden peg driven into the wall took a woolen shirt, a pair of tan corduroy trousers, and a well-worn gray sombrero. A dusty pair of high-heeled boots standing against the wall received a kick from the sheriff that sent them flying toward the hobo. "These togs belonged to one of my deputies, and should about fit you." Yarrow moved back to his desk and flipped a cake of brown soap into the tramp's lap and followed it with a razor. "At the rear of the cell block you'll find a tub. Out back, there's water. Go see if you can get that dirt off, then come back here. If my nerve holds up we'll go through with this insane business." The sheriff came suddenly to his feet, roaring angrily. "Get along! Move, will you! And for Gawd's sake, let's see somethin' different next time I look at you." Swearing hotly, Yarrow turned his back on the hobo and busied himself with some papers on his desk.

Half an hour later, while the sheriff was working over his monthly expense account, a step sounded at the door giving on the cell block. Swiveling around in his chair, Yarrow saw a dark-haired individual of twenty-five or -six, with smoky gray eyes and good mouth and chin, leaning nonchalantly against the doorjamb. Yarrow swore. "That damn bum must have left that rear door open. What can I do for you, mister?"

The reply came in an indolent tone: "I've been sort of wondering that myself, Sheriff."

Yarrow frowned, thinking the voice sounded vaguely familiar, and at the same time noting the slim hips and broad shoulders of his visitor. "Do I know you?" the sheriff commenced, then, "My sufferin' Aunt Tabitha!" he exploded suddenly. "It's the hobo!"

"The nomad of the wastelands, let us say," came a polite reproval. "It sounds more dignified."

"Nomad!" Yarrow sputtered. "Dignified my eye!" Gradually a more contented expression came over his features as he added softly, "You don't look nearly so bad as I expected. Mebbe you ain't the fool I been thinkin'. Come on in here, and we'll go through with it." Fumbling in his desk, he produced a deputy's badge which he proceeded to pin to the tramp's shirt. "S'help me, I aim to swear you in. What's your name?"

There was a momentary hesitation. "We-ell, some folks call me Smoky."

"Smoky what? I asked for your name."

Again that hesitation. "Er—ah—just Smoky Jefferson, let us say. Will that do?"

"I reckon it will have to. Where you from? No, nev' mind that. You'd just give me some fool answer. Raise your right hand. Do you solemnly swear and promise to the best of your ability to carry out and enforce the laws of Mesquital County and obey any and all orders . . ." Quickly, pausing only now and then to refresh his memory, Yarrow gave the oath of office, fairly rushing through the final "s'help me Gawd," as though fearing some small measure of intelligence would bring him to his senses before he'd finished swearing in his new officer. "There you are," he concluded with considerable relief. "You are now a legally appointed deputy of Mesquital County. I hope you'll be a credit to the job—"

"You've not said anything about the salary," Smoky Jefferson commenced.

"And I don't intend to," Yarrow snapped. "You're working out a sentence for vagrancy, remember."

"But I have to eat."

"I don't know why," Yarrow said tartly, then relented and drew from his pocket a silver dollar which he handed to Jefferson. "Let me know when that's gone. But don't make it too soon. And now we'll go out back and I'll try to instruct you in the use of firearms." He got a cartridge belt and pair of short-barreled .45 six-shooters from the gun rack on the wall, then replaced one of the guns. "Should I turn you loose on this town wearin' two guns, you'd be bound to get in trouble. Anyway, it'll be enough of a task to teach you to handle one weapon. Now, see, you load your cylinder this way. See? Just five ca'tridges, and we'll let the hammer rest on his empty shell . . ." The sheriff continued instructions for a few minutes, while Jefferson nodded understandingly, his lips twitching at the corners now and then. Finally Yarrow jammed the gun into the holster of Jefferson's belt and strapped the cartridge-lined leather about his deputy's hips. "Come on out back; I'll teach you the first fundamentals of shooting."

Yarrow led the way back through the cell block, past the empty, barred cells. Jefferson said, "I note you haven't any prisoners in here."

"No crime in Torvo," the sheriff grunted. "It's the crime outside town that bothers me." He unlocked the rear door and the two men stepped into the open.

Beyond stretched the tracks of the T. N. & A. S. Railroad and up the tracks a short distance stood the red-painted depot. Nearer at hand were various piles of rubbish, and some fifty or sixty feet back of the jail was a stack of old crates and packing cases. The sheriff stooped and picked up a rusty tin can, then tossed it aside. "Nope, that would be too small for you to start shootin' at. Lemme see . . ." He gazed about, seeking a sizable mark at which to shoot, until his eyes fell on the stack of wooden crates. "Jefferson, you see that packin' box, yonderly, the one that says 'Cooper Furniture Company' on it? Well, a box that size is about right for you—"

A burst of gunfire interrupted the words, as five explosions blended almost into one. Miraculously five holes had appeared in the first five letters of "Cooper." Yarrow swung around, mouth agape, just in time to see Smoky Jefferson replacing a smoking six-shooter in his holster.

"D-di-did you do that?" Yarrow stuttered.

Jefferson nodded, a sheepish expression crossing his face. "Darn gun started going off and I didn't know how to stop it—" he commenced, then halted suddenly.

Wild yells had been heard from the vicinity of the packing cases and Owney Powell and Bart Fielding burst into view, arms high above heads. "Don't shoot again," Owney cried frantically. "We're not doin' anythin', Matt." Both men began to move quickly away from the stacked crates.

"Put your arms down, you damn fools," Yarrow

said angrily. "We're not shootin' at you. What you two hidin' out there for?"

"Weren't hidin' out," Fielding protested. "Me'n Owney were just takin' a snooze in the shade, when all hell busted loose—"

"It couldn't be, could it," Yarrow asked blandly, "that you two was hangin' around to devil my new deputy a mite?"

"Swear t'Gawd we wasn't, Matt—" Powell commenced, but had no time to say more, as a number of men came running to investigate the sound of the shooting. The sheriff explained that he and his new deputy—"Smoky Jefferson, gentlemen"—had been indulging in a little target practice, there was nothing to cause any alarm, and everybody could now return to whatever business had been occupying his attention before the shooting had occurred. The crowd took the hint and dispersed, but not before two or three men had asked whether the sheriff or his deputy had punctured the letters on the packing case. "That," Yarrow evaded, "was just a matter of luck, I imagine." The crowd drifted off, Powell and Fielding disappearing at the same time. Yarrow and his deputy were once more left alone.

The sheriff drew a long breath. "Reckon nobody recognized you as that bum that hit town a spell back. Probably just as well."

"I don't think you'll be able to keep it quiet, Sheriff," Jefferson replied. "When I came out for that tub of water to wash up, I noticed Powell and Fielding dodging behind those packing crates. I figure they've been spying to see what you did with me."

"They found out, damn 'em," Yarrow said grimly. His gaze strayed back to the plugged letters on the wooden case. "So the gun just kept going off and you didn't know how to stop it, eh? Bosh! You done right well for a greenhorn. I wa'n't whelped yesterday, y'know. And I suppose it was just accident you hit them five letters in 'Cooper,' too."

"Like you said," Jefferson said modestly, "it was a matter of luck."

"Luck in a pig's eye," Yarrow growled. "And *I* was goin' to teach you to use a six-gun." He swore again. "Mebbe I *was* whelped yesterday. I'm commencin' to wonder. All right. It could be I've got more than I bargained for. But I'm warnin' you, the first reward bill that comes in, bearin' your description, I'm aimin' to slam you into a cell so fast it'll make your head swim."

"Yes, sir, Sheriff," Jefferson said meekly.

"And don't call me sheriff," Yarrow snapped. "My friends call me Matt. Come on, I got to buy a cold beer for the hombre that can knock out five letters of a six-letter word—by accident."

"There was only five cartridges in the gun, Matt," Jefferson ventured, lips twitching.

"What?" Yarrow glared at his deputy. "And if you'd had six, I suppose—oh hell, the drinks are on me. Let's go get 'em."

66

6. Concealed Identity

Afternoon sunlight sifted through the windows of the sheriff's office where Yarrow and his new deputy sat talking. The two had imbibed their cold beer and then taken a walk about the town that Torvo might become acquainted with Smoky Jefferson. By this time it was no secret that Jefferson was the hobo who had been thrown off the train a few hours previously. Men had viewed the newly appointed officer with quizzical looks in their eyes, admitting that Smoky Jefferson didn't look too bad, but his mettle was yet to be proved. After all, Owney Powell and Bart Fielding had been making certain threats in various saloons. Once Jefferson was out from under the protecting wing of Sheriff Yarrow, the deputy might prove to be entirely without nerve, and Yarrow would become a laughingstock in Torvo. It was something to look forward to, men said, and winked slyly in the direction of Yarrow and his deputy as they passed.

Meanwhile the sheriff had been giving Jefferson a quick fill-in on the crime situation in Mesquital County, as they sat in the sheriff's office smoking brown paper cigarettes. ". . . and that's the story," Yarrow concluded. "The Jake Glendon gang is still runnin' dope through my county, and—"

"I thought you said Glendon was dead," Jefferson put in.

"He is, but for want of a better name, we still speak of the crew as the Glendon gang. Somebody—we don't know who—has taken over the gang and continued operations—"

"Who do you mean by 'we'?"

"Law officers—the U. S. marshal's office—hell, Smoky, there's a lot of us on the job, and the U. S. Customs Bureau is pushing us hard. I've been catching merry hell from the governor."

"But why you?"

"The stuff is being smuggled into my county. No, we don't know where it goes from this neck of the range, or how the dope is gotten out of Mesquital. We get tips, now and then—but we can never seem to catch anybody, or tips come through too late to do any good. No, I'm not telling you anything everybody else in Torvo doesn't know. The whole business is a disgrace to the county."

"You said something about two deputies being killed."

Yarrow nodded. "Found dead, over near Jackpot. They'd been shot. I've always felt they'd run onto the Glendon gang and had been shot to keep their mouths shut."

"Where's Jackpot?"

"That's an old ghost town. Not in my territory. It's in Bandinera County. What? Of course the Bandinera sheriff is working on the case too, only I reckon Jackpot is sort of far from his county seat.

The Torvo Mountains lay between Bandinera's county seat and Jackpot."

"Looks to me like Jackpot might stand some investigation."

"Now you just get that idea outten your head, son. Both my deputies that was killed had that same idea. They'd no business over there. It's out of my territory. I've no jurisdiction in Bandinera County."

"Tell me some more about Jackpot."

"There's little to tell. Jackpot's deserted. You know what a ghost town is, don't you?" The tramp deputy nodded and Yarrow continued, "Jackpot boomed when the old Jackpot Mine was producing big. Then an epidemic of smallpox hit the town; that wiped out a lot of people. Next thing, a bad fire did for a bunch of the buildings. About the time folks started to rebuild, the mine petered out. So the people of Jackpot just up and left, thoroughly discouraged."

"And nobody lives there now?" Smoky Jefferson asked.

"Nope, except one old coot that folks call the Cactus Man, who uses one of the buildings as a headquarters."

"What's he do?"

"Moseys around the country over there, diggin' up cactus plants of different sorts to ship back East and out to California. Seems there's a lot of horty—horty—"

"Horticultural gardens?"

"That's it. Thanks. There's a heap of them gardens and scientists interested in cactus, Gawd only knows why. And this old coot, name of Joel Wyatt, digs up specimens and ships 'em off. Imagine folks plantin' cactus in their garden! Though I got to admit some of them spiny plants has got real pretty flowers when they bloom in the spring."

"And this Cactus Man is the only person around Jackpot?"

Yarrow nodded. "No, he ain't never seen anythin' of the Glendon gang; leastwise, that's what he told a U. S. marshal who questioned him." Yarrow tugged at his blond mustache. "My brother Frank used to prospect round Jackpot, but he was found killed, two years ago. I always figured he must've run afoul of the Glendon gang in some manner. There was no need for anyone to kill him. Far's I know, he hadn't an enemy in the country."

"That girl at the depot—she was your brother Frank's daughter?"

"That's right. Jane and her pa and ma lived in Jackpot for years. Then about the time the Jackpot Mine petered out, her ma died, so Jane came on to Torvo to keep house for me, bein' I was alone. She studied at that telegraph contraption and works at the depot as an extra man—extra girl, that is—anyway, she fills in when one of the regular operators is sick, or off huntin', or something. But we never could get Frank to leave the Jackpot

70

country. Last time I saw him, before he was murdered, he was still hopin' to make another strike like the one that set off the big boom, thirty years ago. But, shucks, the ore's played out—"

"Uh-huh, I expect so," Smoky Jefferson said absentmindedly. He seemed, momentarily, to have lost interest in the subject. "You don't sleep here, then?" he asked finally, gesturing toward the cot with its folded woolen blankets.

"I already told you that Jane keeps house for me. I eat and sleep at my home, over on First Street. That cot's for you."

"And I eat with you?"—hopefully.

"You do not," Yarrow snapped. "You'll eat—at county expense—at any one of several restaurants you'll find in town."

"Anyway"—Smoky spoke resignedly—"eating on the county will be something." He hesitated. "I suppose your niece is a good cook."

"She is," Yarrow said smugly. "Too bad you won't never have a chance to find out how good." He scowled suddenly. "I'll thank you to keep your mind on crime—not on cookin' and eatin'."

"I'll try my best," Jefferson promised.

"You'll do more than try," Yarrow threatened, "or you'll be transferred to that cement job, plumb pronto."

There was silence for a few moments, while the deputy twisted a new cigarette, scratched a match, and then fanned his lungs deeply with the smoke.

71

"You know," he said at last, "I've been wondering what that Glendon fellow looked like. Can't you give me a description?"

"How in hell can you describe a man with no face?" Yarrow snorted. "I already told you the buckshot tore his features plumb off'n his head."

Jefferson nodded. "I remember now you did say something like that," he responded lazily. "It would certainly be a good way."

"To commit suicide?" the sheriff asked.

"No, to conceal a man's identity."

"What in hell you talkin' about?"

"Suppose," Jefferson speculated dreamily, "that that corpse wasn't Glendon, but somebody else—"

"Huh?" Yarrow's eyes widened, his jaw dropped. Then he shook his head. "Nope, you're wrong, Smoky. There was letters on the body addressed to Glendon."

"The letters could have been planted on the corpse."

The sheriff looked troubled. "No, I can't believe it."

"But it's possible."

"Goddammit!" Yarrow swore. "Anythin' is possible, but—"

"And you can't give me any information as to description. Didn't nothin' stand out that you'd remember?"

"Like I told you, the corpse had been a good-sized feller, but he just had on ordinary cow-range togs. Without a face, I couldn't—"

"Not even any hair left?"

"Oh, sure," the sheriff said readily, "above the ears and at the back of the head—"

"What color?"

"Black," Yarrow said readily, then his eyes narrowed. "As black as yours."

Jefferson chuckled lazily. "Now don't you go to suspecting me. Black, eh? Any gray in it?"

"Now you speak of it, yes," Yarrow replied. "But not the usual gray, not sprinkled all through, or just at the sides of the head. This was an almost white streak running diagonally across the back of the head; probably a half inch wide. The coroner investigated some and said the dead man had a scar under that white hair, like he'd been bad hurt at some time or other—Hey! What you lookin' that way for?"

The hard, narrow-eyed look that had crossed Jefferson's face passed as quickly as it had come. "Didn't realize I was looking any particular way, Matt. I swallowed a couple of flakes of tobacco from this cigarette; they got stuck in my throat."

Yarrow tugged at his mustache and looked relieved. "For a minute there, you looked right mean."

"Blame it on the Bull. I never could go for eating tobacco." Smoky considered. "These fellows that found the body—claimed they found the body, leastwise—what about them?"

"Y'know"—Yarrow frowned—"I've been sort of wonderin'—"

He broke off as a shadow darkened the open doorway. A tall lean man in dark blue corduroys, riding boots, black sateen shirt, and stiff-brimmed, flat-topped sombrero stepped into the sheriff's office. A dark blue bandanna was knotted about his throat.

"Come in, Captain, come in," Yarrow said heartily. "Find a chair and rest your boots a mite. Smoky, shake hands with Captain Rafe Chandler, of the Border Rangers."

The two men shook hands. Chandler was a blond-complexioned individual with blue eyes, and a smooth-shaven sinewy jaw. His eyes twinkled as he dropped into a straight-backed chair. "I've been hearing around town about your new deputy, Matt." Then to Smoky, "You just alighted from the train this morning, didn't you?"

Smoky Jefferson laughed. "I'm not certain 'alighted' is the right word for it. Maybe 'descended,' or better still, just say I was precipitated from the train."

Chandler chuckled. "At any rate, you've given this town something to think about. I'm glad to see Matt has some assistance at last."

Yarrow put in a question. "You got anything new, Captain?"

"Not one single thing." Chandler's face darkened. "I just dropped in to Torvo to get a fresh mount. You don't know anything, I suppose."

"Not a solitary tip," Yarrow grumbled. "And the governor's been raisin' hell, too."

"These politicians!" Chandler said somewhat bitterly. "If they had to ride out to do a job they'd know what we're up against. This morning I rode—" He hesitated and glanced inquiringly in Smoky Jefferson's direction.

"You can speak up," Yarrow said. "I've already given Smoky an outline of the Glendon gang."

"Just wanted to be sure," Chandler said to Jefferson.

"Anything you say before me won't travel any farther," the deputy replied.

"Trouble is, there's nothing much to say," Chandler said. "This morning I rode over to Jackpot, just in the hope of running across something, but didn't have any luck. The Cactus Man had just returned from a trip and was packing some plants. Aside from him and some buzzards, I didn't see a living thing." He got to his feet. "Well, there's no rest for the weary. I've got to be pushing along. I'll see you again, Smoky. So long, Matt." Chandler left the office and a moment later the squeaking of saddle leather and sound of moving hoofs were heard as the Border Ranger moved off down the street.

"So the Border Rangers are working on this smuggling business too," Smoky Jefferson observed.

Yarrow nodded. "The government at Washington asked 'em to take a hand a spell back. They're a right efficient body of men. This is the third time Rafe Chanldler has been in Torvo in the past three weeks. He sure covers a lot of country, riding, in the hope of uncovering something. His horses are just about beat down when he rides in for a change—Hell! I should have mentioned your theory that the face was shot off Glendon to conceal somebody else's identity—"

"If it was Glendon's face that was shot off."

"You think Glendon might still be alive?"

"I didn't say that either. You were telling me about the three fellows that found the body, when Chandler's arrival interrupted."

Yarrow's face darkened. "Yeah. The more I think about them, the more I wonder. Y'see, they claimed to be on the way to a cowmen's convention at Yubaville, but that's a hell of a long distance from the home address at their ranch they give me."

"Meaning what?"

"Why travel all that distance on hawssback? A train would be more logical."

"Seems like it. What did you say their names were?"

"Smith and"—Yarrow searched his recollections—"Joslin and Brooke."

Jefferson sat straighter in his chair, brow furrowed with thought, eyes narrowing. "Do you remember, Matt, if Smith was called Tucson?"

"That's the name! And the other two . . . lemme see . . . Melody? No. Lullaby! That's it. Lullaby Joslin and Stony—Brooke."

The deputy laughed suddenly. "Sure as hell it's them."

"Who you talkin' about?"

"The Three Mesquiteers—the greatest trio of law busters ever to hit this Southwest country. If they went by horse, all that long distance, it's because they wanted to and had the time—and the money— for such traveling. You've heard of the Three Mesquiteers, Matt."

"By Gawd, I have, now you mention 'em. I'll be damned! Just never give it a thought when they were here, my mind bein' occupied with Glendon's suicide, like it was."

"Too bad they couldn't have remained in Torvo. From all I've heard, Tucson Smith and his pards could run down that Glendon gang in quick order. They've got a rep that's really fabulous—" Smoky broke off, musing. "I wonder . . ." he muttered, half to himself.

"You wonder what?"

The deputy chuckled. "If I've guessed a mite smarter than Tucson Smith. That would be a feather in my cap, outthinking the best law buster in the country."

"Seems to me," Yarrow growled suspiciously, "you know an almighty lot concernin' law busters—"

"Now don't get proddy, Matt." Smoky smiled. "I

was just thinking it was odd Tucson Smith didn't think of that face-shot-off business as a nice method of concealing a man's identity."

"If this Smith is as smart as you say," Yarrow snapped, "he probably did think of it and disregarded the notion as bein' a lot of poppycock. After all, there was letters addressed to Glendon and that beaded Indian hatband Glendon was known to have wore. What more evidence do you need?"

"Not too much more, not too much more, Matt," Jefferson replied cryptically. "All the same, I'd like a chance to talk to Tucson Smith."

"I'll give you his address," Yarrow said sourly, "and you can go visit him—after you've finished that cement job. It don't look like I got any prize, gettin' a deputy that tries to use his head, so I'd best take your badge away. If you'd only learn to let me do the thinkin', and just obey orders. By the seven bald-headed, short-horned steers, I swear I'll—"

"Don't swear, Uncle Matt, it's bad for your blood pressure," said a voice at the doorway.

Both men glanced up. Jefferson got to his feet. "What? Huh!" the sheriff said, then relaxed. "Oh, it's you, Jane. By cripes! Some things is enough to make a man swear."

Neat in blue checked gingham, hatless, the girl stood smiling in the doorway, while Smoky Jefferson stood admiring the contrast of taffy-colored hair against the dark healthy tan of smooth skin. Jane Yarrow said with mock severity, "It's bad manners to swear. You should always remember your manners, Uncle Matt."

"Huh? What you talkin' about? Oh"—reluctantly—"Jane, let me make you acquainted with my new deputy, Smoky Jefferson." The girl smiled and acknowledged the introduction. Smoky said he was tickled to death—and he looked it. The sheriff rushed on, "Didn't know it was this late. You been home and cleaned up already?"

Jane nodded. "And I've been to Ma Henderson's to get a chicken for supper."

"Chicken?" The sheriff looked blank. "This ain't Sunday."

"I realize that," Jane said casually, "but just thought you might want something special for our guest."

"Guest?" Yarrow's bewilderment increased.

"You wouldn't want Mr. Jefferson to get the wrong idea of Torvo's hospitality. After all, the first day on a new job—"

"Jane!" The sheriff's face was crimson. "Do you realize where I got this—this—this new deputy? He ain't—"

"Of course I do," the girl laughed. "I was there when—when you met him at the train on his arrival." She hurried on, "I just dropped past to tell you supper will be a little later, this evening, with the chicken to clean and all. G'by, Uncle Matt." She nodded to Smoky and swept from view.

Yarrow sank back in his chair, glowering at his

deputy. "I not only appoint a bum, but I got to take him home to supper as well."

"I'll be eating on the county, of course," Smoky said gravely.

"You'll be eatin' on a cell floor," Yarrow fumed, "if you don't watch out. Just the leastest thing you do, and it's a cement job for you—oh hell! Let's go get a beer. I'm plumb parched with all this talkin'."

"On the county?" Smoky queried.

"No, by Gawd, you can spend that dollar I give you a spell back. Your sudden wealth has gone to your head."

7. Powder Smoke

At seven-thirty the following morning peace reigned in the small white cottage with its picket fence, which stood on the corner of Waco and First streets, in the shade of a spreading cottonwood tree. Jane Yarrow had already departed for the T. N. & A. S. depot, and the sheriff was lingering over his fourth cup of coffee in the small dining room, while he savored his morning cigar and perused various items in the Phoenix *Gazette*, which had arrived with other papers and some mail the previous day. The morning promised greater heat as the day progressed and Yarrow was reluctant to leave the house, much as his conscience continued to nag him about the advisability of leaving Smoky Jefferson in charge of the sheriff's office too long. But things had been quiet the previous evening. After a supper of fried chicken and dumplings, Smoky and the sheriff had returned to Main Street, the sheriff marveling at how well Jane and that—that bum—had got along. But Smoky had displayed certain manners, the sheriff had reflected. And things in town couldn't have been more peaceful. Smoky had remarked that it had been a long day and that he'd be glad when it came time to turn in. And with the remark that he could turn in any time, the sheriff had returned to his home and gone to bed. That had been last night; there was nothing apparent this morning that indicated any change.

At seven-thirty-one, just as Yarrow was reaching for the pot to see if it were possible to squeeze out another half cup of coffee to go with the last two inches of his cigar, there came a loud knocking at the front door, the noise resounding ominously through the house. The sheriff very deliberately replaced the pot and rose from the table. That knocking spelled trouble; no one making a neighborly call would knock that loud, the sheriff knew from long experience. He sighed and started for the door. Before he could reach it the pounding commenced again.

"All right, all right, I'm comin'!" Yarrow bawled. "No need for you to wreck the front of the house." He opened the door to confront the bulky figure of Luke Vaughn, owner of the Box-V. "What's up, Luke?"

Vaughn's thick black eyebrows drew apologetically together. "Sorry to bother you, Matt, but I can't talk any sense into that new deputy of yours—"

"Now what's that tramp done?"

"Reckon maybe his authority went to his head, last night—"

"Could be," Yarrow said shortly, and asked again, "What's he done?"

"Arrested Bart Fielding and Owney Powell on a charge of disturbin' the peace. Cracked his gun barrel over their heads—"

"T'hell you say! What caused the ruckus?"

"I can only give it to you as one of the boys told it to me. Seems Powell and Fielding were in the Sundown, last night, and got a mite liquored up. Your new deputy came in about the time Rittenhouse was tryin' to calm 'em down. There was some words, and your deputy give the two of 'em a gun whuppin'."

"Hmmm!" Yarrow tugged at his mustache. "You didn't see it, you say?"

Vaughn shook his head. "One of the boys brought the news out to the ranch last night. I came in this mornin' and asked your deputy to release Owney and Bart, but he refuses. Personally, Matt, if they were cuttin' up a fuss, they probably deserved what they got, and I'd let 'em stay in cells until the ants carried 'em out under the bars, but the fact is I got work to be done and I'm kind of short-handed, so if you could see your way clear to lettin' Owney and Bart go I'd be obliged to you."

The sheriff nodded. "I'll see what I can do, Luke. Just a minute until I get my hat."

The two men strolled down Waco Street, after the sheriff had closed his front door. At the corner of Waco and Main, Vaughn turned right, saying, "Tell them two I'll be waitin' in the Silver Spur Bar for 'em."

The sheriff nodded and continued on across Main. There weren't many people abroad yet. In front of the stores a few men could be seen sweeping the plank walks; cow ponies and wagons were sparsely scattered along the hitch rails. Dust kicked up in small clouds before Yarrow's feet, as he crossed to step to a plank sidewalk and thence to the small porch fronting his office, where Smoky Jefferson sat polishing his deputy's badge. Smoky said good morning. Yarrow nodded shortly and glanced within the office. The cot was neatly made up and the floor had been swept clear of cigarette butts.

The sheriff jerked one thumb toward the cell block. "I understand you got Powell and Fielding back there."

Smoky said, "You must have been talking to Luke Vaughn."

"Never mind where I heard it. What did you drag them two down to the jail for?"

Very deliberately Smoky pinned his badge back on his shirt. "Dragging was the only way I could get them here. They were in no condition to walk." He started to manufacture a cigarette while he continued. "Vaughn got sort of riled because I wouldn't turn 'em loose on his say-so. He claims it's always your policy to let drunks go the following morning. Now a little cement mixing—"

"That's whatever," the sheriff growled. "Get on with your story."

Smoky scratched a match on one thumbnail, held it to the end of the cigarette, and inhaled. Twin spirals of smoke curled from his nostrils as he resumed, "I told Vaughn I didn't think they deserved to get off so easy, but it was your say-so. That I always followed your orders."

"That's nice to know," Yarrow said dryly. "Exactly what happened last night?"

The deputy spoke in level tones. "After I left you I decided to take one more turn around town before I hopped into blankets. I heard loud talking in the Sundown and decided to investigate. Powell and Fielding were there, pretending to be drunk. Note, I say pretending. They were threatening to shoot the bottles off Hank's shelf. I suggested that they get out and hit the hay. They gave me an argument on that score and called a few names. I noticed 'em fannin' out, to get me between 'em, and their hands were mighty close to their hardware. Not wanting to waste the county's money by exploding shells, I rapped 'em both on the head with my gun barrel. Like I say, they had to be dragged down here."

Yarrow worried his gray-blond mustache. "Humph! You must've been almighty fast to get 'em both that way."

"I was fast enough," Smoky said shortly.

Yarrow sighed. "I don't like to do it, after what you've said, but—"

"If you doubt my word you can ask Hank Rittenhouse."

"Don't get proddy. Your word's good. What do you think should be done?"

Smoky's gray eyes twinkled. "Well, I wouldn't wish cement mixing on any man, but there's a J.P. in Torvo, isn't there?" Yarrow said there was. "Take 'em down to the justice and let him slap whatever fine he thinks is necessary on 'em. Fines might yet build that courthouse."

"You really figure they were out to gun you some?" Yarrow asked.

"I've no doubt of it."

"You don't want to bring a charge on that score?"

"I took 'em in on a charge of disturbing the peace. Let it stand that way. I'm satisfied."

Yarrow considered the matter. Finally, "An ordinary drunk is one thing; threatenin' with guns another. Mebbe I been too lax with some men in this town. You're right, Smoky. Fielding and Powell is due to go before the justice."

"I thought you'd see it that way," Jefferson said quietly. "When you plan to do it?"

"Judge Uhlmann will open court any time I request. I'll find him around town, someplace—likely in the hotel bar."

"When you round him up, let me know and I'll bring Fielding and Powell to court and give evidence."

"That's not needful. I'm capable of handlin' that pair, and Hoddy Uhlmann will take my word for what happened. If Powell or Fielding get obstrep'rous, I can always throw 'em back in a cell. But they won't. I'll put a bug in Luke Vaughn's ear and he'll talk turkey to 'em."

Smoky looked sharply at the sheriff. "You act like you didn't want me to have any part in the proceedings."

"That's exactly my idea. That Box-V outfit stick pretty close together. They ain't goin' to take kindly to you. I figure you'd best get outten town for a spell, until they've had a coolin'-down period. Four—five them fellers get the idea to gang up on you, and somebody might get hurt. Includin' you. Now you just take a *pasear* over to the Lone Star Livery and pick you out a bronc and rig—"

"Look here, Matt," Smoky protested, "I'm not figuring to run out on any trouble that might come—"

"—and don't let Andy Crockett put off any crow-baits on you," the sheriff said blandly. "He's got some nags in his stalls that's already overdue for the glue factory, so you look sharp when you take a hawss. And nobody's accusin' you of runnin' out of trouble. You're just obeyin' my orders."

"The same being?" Smoky asked resignedly.

"Ride out and get a look at the county you and I are coverin'. Ride west. I got deputies scattered around to the east in five towns. Keep your eyes open for any sign that might lead to Glendon gang activities—oh yes, 'bout eighteen miles from here you'll strike a dry wash. That's roughly the line between Mesquital and Bandinera counties, so don't cross that wash—"

"Any reason why I shouldn't?"

"Two reasons," Yarrow said grimly, "the first bein' that you won't have any authority, t'other side of that wash; the second, two of my deputies once disobeyed orders and were found dead between that wash and Jackpot. So you 'bide by your own territory, and don't attempt any explorin' on your own."

"Well, you've made that clear enough anyway." Smoky nodded. The sheriff failed to notice his deputy made no promises.

Twenty minutes later Smoky Jefferson, astride a wiry little roan gelding, left Main Street at the west end, crossed a plank bridge over the narrow Alamo Creek, and struck out for open country, the pony moving at an easy lope. For a time Smoky followed the cottonwood-lined stream as it cut through a gradually rising terrain. Then he swung on a slightly southwest course across an almost level stretch of sandy, gray earth, dotted with prickly pear, dry wispy sagebrush, cholla, and stunted mesquite; here and there an occasional paloverde tree rose above the tops of the brush, its delicate green fronds moving gracefully in the breeze that lifted across the range.

The sun climbed higher. Heat waves made shimmering, distorted patterns of plant growth and granite outcroppings. The way was somewhat undulating now, and became more rocky as Smoky progressed. From time to time he had recourse to the canteen on his saddle, taking each time only a slight sip of the lukewarm water. Now and then Smoky drew to a walk to "breathe" the roan pony.

It was drawing near noon when the deputy saw another rider approaching from the north. He drew rein and waited for the man to come even with him, noticing as the rider came near that he was Captain Chandler of the Border Rangers. The horse that Chandler pulled to a halt at Smoky's side was foam-flecked and streaked with sweat.

"By cripes"—Chandler smiled broadly—"I'm sure glad to see you. Ran out of makin's a while back. How about it?"

Smoky extended a partly filled sack of Durham and papers. "Keep it, Captain. I've got another sack." They talked while Chandler manufactured a cigarette. "Looks as though you'd been traveling," Smoky observed.

Chandler nodded. "This is just too damn much territory for one man to cover. I have to keep pushing."

"Without any luck, I take it."

"You take it correct, Smoky. I've not been able to uncover one damn thing that might lead to anything. How about you?"

"I've not been on this job long enough," Smoky laughed, "to even get started."

"I suppose not." Chandler removed the flat-topped black sombrero and mopped at his face with the blue bandanna about his neck. "Well, I've got to be getting on toward the border. You heading much farther west?"

Smoky shook his head. "There's a dry wash up ahead someplace. I figure to stop there and eat some sandwiches I brought along. I could wish there was water running in that wash."

"If you care to go on to Jackpot you'll find some water there."

"I can make out. I was thinking of my pony. I guess he'll have to make out too. Jackpot's out of my territory. You going back to Torvo?"

Chandler said, "No," and explained that he was headed toward the Mexican border.

"That's right." Smoky nodded. "You already told me that."

Chandler offered such water as was in his canteen,

but Smoky refused with thanks, saying there wouldn't be enough for the horse anyway. The men talked a few minutes longer, then Chandler took up his reins and touched spurs to his horse's ribs. The horse leaped ahead, sending up clouds of dust as it threaded a swift way through the desert growth. "That hombre sure pushes his horseflesh," Smoky mused, then urged his own pony on its way.

At noontime Smoky drew rein beside the dry wash and unpacked the sandwiches of beef and bread he'd brought, washing the food down with the remnants of liquid remaining in his canteen. He glanced longingly across the twisting wash with its rock-cluttered bottom, toward the low ridges, topped with brush, beyond. "Chandler said there was water to be had at Jackpot," he mused. "Of course Jackpot isn't in my territory, according to the sheriff. Just the same I'd sure like to get some water for this pony. I wouldn't want him to drop dead—not at county expense." He surveyed the pony, standing with loosened saddle and dropped reins. The wiry animal didn't appear to be suffering, much to Smoky's disappointment. "Can't never tell, though," he told himself. "That horse might be ready to drop any instant. I'd better not take chances. And Jackpot can't be more than another twelve or fifteen miles away. Yep, that pony should have water. That's as good an excuse as any." Rising to his feet, he tightened the saddle and mounted, then directed the roan across the rock-cluttered wash. Once on the other side, he kicked the pony in the ribs and commenced to make better time.

It was between two-thirty and three that afternoon when Smoky rode into Jackpot. On either side of a slightly curving dusty main thoroughfare, with semi-desert growth sprouting from ancient wheel ruts, was a miscellaneous collection of dilapidated, ramshackle buildings. Tie rails were down; doors were missing from sand-blasted frame buildings, or hung loosely from one hinge. Here and there roofs had caved in; windows had long since been shattered. Sagebrush and wiry grass thrust upward between the broken planks of rickety sidewalks. Smoky pulled his pony to a walk, his eye following the curving street to the open country, the foothills of the Torvo Mountains and the blue sky beyond. He shifted weight in the saddle, noting wide spaces between various buildings, where charred timbers, sole reminder of Jackpot's old fire, lifted their blackened lengths toward the wide expanse above. "Like rotting snags in a mouth of missing teeth," Smoky told himself. How many of the buildings had been rebuilt, or repaired, after the fire he had no way of knowing. The lumber of the remaining structures had been weathered to a pale grayish brown. There was one exception:

A two-story brick edifice, with paneless windows and a wide-open double doorway, bore a sun-faded sign, Jackpot Hotel. One corner of the brick structure was crumbling, and a long crack traced a jagged, diagonal course across the hotel's façade. Other signs were to be seen on the faces of various buildings: the Roan Pony Saloon; Faro Annie's Place, the Bronze Buffalo Bar; Paris Peggy's Shop—French Fashions; Miner's Rest Saloon; Horatio Brown—Assayer; Dance & Chance Parlor; Pat Runnel's Saloon; Gotham Bazaar—the list seemed extremely varied. A blocky squat structure of adobe and rock with rusted iron bars at the paneless windows proved to be not a jail but the Jackpot Bank. Still other signs advertised honky-tonks and business houses, the sun-bleached paint of the letters standing out cameolike from the surface of the wind- and sand-eroded bare wood. Mostly the buildings were one-story, with high false fronts. Cross streets had once existed, though these were now difficult to locate. Scattered back of the buildings lining the dusty roadway were small shacks, seemingly tossed down helter-skelter on the earth. A number of these showed blackened timbers and twisted bits of rusty metal; tin cans and rubbish were strewn about, nearly covered with drifted sand. Excepting Smoky, there was no human being in sight. A definite air of eerie desolation hovered over the decaying ghost town.

"Chandler said," Smoky remembered, "there was water to be had here. He should know. But I wonder where? Ah, that pump and watering trough up ahead, probably. *If* the pump works."

The pump had functioned recently, anyway, as Smoky discovered when he drew rein just beyond what had once been the Flying Hoofs Livery, a two-story building with one wide door sagging drunkenly against the front wall; the remaining door to the double entranceway was missing. On the second floor a huge square opening afforded a partial view of the loft, with sunlight glinting between warped wall boards. Smoky's gaze returned to the big wooden trough, and he saw a shallow layer of water covering the bottom. Anyway, he mused, the trough was watertight, or the water would have seeped out. That attested recent and frequent use. Tentatively Smoky tried the handle of the pump. From its inner workings came a cool gurgling sound, and a moment later fresh liquid gushed from the spout. "Must be considerable of a well below," Smoky decided. He took a long drink, splashed water on his face and neck, then pumped more water for the horse. "Damned if this trough isn't sizable," Smoky complained. "A man could spend a heap of time pumping it full." He paused. "Go ahead, pony, sluice down your tonsils."

While the horse was slaking its thirst Smoky rolled a cigarette and gazed about. There was considerable broken glass strewn along the sagging sidewalks. Across the street stood a two-story frame building which had formerly constituted the Golden Bull Rooming House. Rickety steps led to a doorless opening; there were three windows above and two below, none of which contained a whole pane of glass. Smoky speculated, "Jackpot must have been quite a town in its day. I expect prospectors drifted through here, frequent—say, come to think of it, the sheriff said somebody called the Cactus Man lived here. Must be out cactus-ing at present, or don't feel sociable enough to put in an appearance." The horse lifted its head, gazed at Smoky a moment, then again dipped its dripping nose into the trough. Smoky laughed. "Careful you don't fall in, horse. That trough's nigh big enough to drown you."

He concluded rolling his cigarette, ran the edge of the paper along the tip of his tongue, placed the brown paper cylinder between his lips, and reached for a match. Almost instantly the cigarette was torn violently from his mouth, and a split instant later Smoky caught the report of the rifle.

He whirled, right hand whipping out his six-shooter, eyes alert for the slightest movement that would indicate the source of the shot. "That was damn good shooting, if he'd been aiming at my cigarette," Smoky grunted, "only he wasn't—"

He broke off, noting a thin wisp of powder smoke drifting across the dark opening of the Flying Hoofs Livery loft. Instantly he sent a leaden slug winging upward, the report of the gun echoing flatly through the empty buildings along the street. There'd been no target in sight, but an answering shot should at least serve to keep the hidden assailant from becoming too bold.

Water splashed against Smoky's left hand as a bullet from a different direction thudded into the water trough. Smoky took two quick backward steps, eyes darting across the street. A haze of black powder smoke floated in the vicinity of one of the windows on the upper floor of the Golden Bull Rooming House. Smoky unleashed a second shot and heard the sudden crashing of glass. Instantly a hand bearing a six-shooter was thrust through the broken pane. The gun roared, kicking up dust at the side of the trough. Again the rifle cracked from the loft opening and Smoky felt the sombrero jerk on his head. Moving swiftly, he threw another shot in the direction of the loft, then scrambled back to crouch behind one end of the watering trough. Instantly firing broke out from each side of the street.

Smoky drew a deep breath and commenced to shove fresh cartridges into his gun. "Caught between fires, by cripes! But those scuts will have a hard time reaching me, so long as I stay ducked down here." A soft gurgling caught his ear and he heard water from the trough running from a bullet hole. "They may sieve hell out of this trough, though," he grunted. "Thank the Lord it's a big one." He risked a quick look toward the livery loft. There came the splintering noise of shattered wood, and a leaden missile plowed a furrow across a top board of the trough. Shooting at random, Smoky threw a return fire and had the satisfaction of hearing a sudden yelp of pain.

"Hit him!" Smoky exulted. "Talk about blind man's luck. Maybe I'll do better with my eyes closed." He raised his voice: "How about coming into the open, you two? I'll—"

Somebody pumped lead fast from the Golden Bull Rooming House. A bullet thudded into the trough. Two more slugs kicked up sand and gravel near by. After a few moments a shot from the livery loft flew wild overhead. No one replied to Smoky's challenge to come into the open.

"It's a fix," Smoky muttered. "So long as I stay behind this trough there's not much danger of being hit. But how long will I have to stay here? It would be just like the low-life bustards to kill my pony, then where would I be?" And the after-thought: "Right where I am now, I reckon." The pony had flinched slightly at the sound of each shot, but was now standing quietly enough a few yards away.

Smoky considered the angles from which his assailants' shots had come. He frowned. "No, they can't reach me here, so long as I stay down, but I don't dare stick my head up either. That fellow in the loft is in the best position to plug me, so I'd best watch that direction closest. But, dammit, I can't stay here all day. When dark comes I might make to slip off, but they might sneak up on me too.

Cripes! I've got to figure out some way of getting clear of this jam with a whole skin."

Crouched low at the end of the big trough, Smoky rolled a cigarette, while his mind pondered the problem. A circle of wet sand had formed below the trough, but water had ceased running from the bullet hole by this time; the slug must have entered fairly high in the side. While he was working on the cigarette, Smoky had kept his gaze cocked toward the opening in the livery loft, but there'd been no movement evident. Finally he swiveled slightly on his heels, the movement bringing the crown of his sombrero into view around the street edge of the watering trough.

Instantly from the rooming-house window came the reverberating explosion of a Colt's six-shooter.

For one brief moment Smoky's body appeared above the top of the trough, his desperately out-flung left hand releasing the cigarette it had held and scattering flakes of tobacco in the sun-baked dusty roadway. Then a loud groan parted his lips and he slumped, doubled up, to the earth, an instant before a second shot whined above his head. Seconds of silence ticked off. Flies buzzed madly above the huddled form. These and the hot wind and the quivering heat waves were the only moving things along the silent street. Then, from the rooming house across the way, came an exultant yell of triumph.

8. Back Trailing

Tucson Smith and his pardners guided their ponies at a walk through the foothills of the Torvo Mountains. There was considerable grass here, and a short time previously they'd spied a scattered bunch of Box-V white-faced Hereford steers. "I'm surprised," Lullaby commented, "there aren't more outfits over in these hills. The feed don't look bad a-tall."

"It's just in these foothills, though," Tucson replied. "Another half hour or so and you'll see this grass thin out. Those were Box-V cows we saw a spell back. As I remember it, when we passed through Torvo a few weeks ago somebody mentioned the Box-V as being within fair riding distance of the town. Probably those cows followed up that creek we crossed on our way to Yubaville."

"What ain't clear to me yet," Stony frowned, "is why we're riding back over the same trails. I always like to take a different way home, where there's a chance to find some *real* excitement. All we've found on this trip is one poor cuss who'd committed suicide—or maybe he wasn't a poor cuss, and maybe he deserved killing, like Tucson suspected. But there wasn't any fun in that. Always before we've tried to find trails that would show something new—"

"I've been wondering about that myself,

Tucson," Lullaby put in. "You just seem to be hell-bent to return by way of Torvo. How come?"

A rather sheepish smile crossed Tucson's weathered features. "To tell the truth," he admitted, "I'm just not sure myself why I wanted to come back this way. Fact is, however, I may have overlooked something important when we found that fellow dead. I've thought it over a heap and have come to the conclusion I maybe deserve a good strong boot applied to the portion of my anatomy that rests on my saddle."

"You hear that, Lullaby?" Stony asked. "You're not the only one who deserves a kick in the pants for not using your brains."

"You finally admit I got brains, eh?" Lullaby laughed.

"We-ell . . ." Stony hesitated. "That was what you might call a slip of the tongue. I didn't really mean you were smart—"

"Do you think you are?"

"There's no doubt of it," Stony asserted.

"Prove it, then."

"How'll I prove it?" Stony commenced.

"What a man!" Lullaby shook his head despairingly. "Doesn't know how to prove he's got brains. That's plumb idiotic. Well, I'll tell you, stupid. You can prove it by keeping your big mouth shut until I hear what Tucson started to say. You just run along and play with your string of spools. Now go ahead, Tucson, you were remarking which?"

Stony fell silent and Tucson continued: "That Jake Glendon that we found dead—whether it was suicide or murder doesn't greatly matter. The thing that keeps sticking in my craw is the way the face was blown off—"

"Buckshot will do that sometimes," Stony put in dryly.

"It will," Tucson agreed, "if a face is in front of it when the gun goes off. But how many suicides have you ever heard of who blew their own faces off? Vanity, if nothing else, generally prevents a man from killing himself that way. Much of the time a suicide will put a gun against his heart and pull the trigger. If he does shoot himself in the head, he usually puts the muzzle of the weapon against the side of his head, or thrusts the barrel down his throat—"

"So what's the answer?" Lullaby wanted to know.

"It's right difficult to identify a man with no face—"

"So help me Hanner, you're right!" Stony said. "And if letters with the name Jake Glendon were put in the dead man's pocket . . ."

"To make a long story short," Lullaby put in, "you don't think that dead man was Jake Glendon, Tucson."

"That's the way I've been figuring." Tucson nodded. "Also, I've been mentally kicking myself for not thinking of that, right off."

"But what would be the reason for Glendon wanting people to think he was dead?" Lullaby persisted.

Tucson shook his head. "I haven't the answer to that one. Maybe the law was closing in on Glendon, and he wanted to throw it off his track. Ten to one there was some letup in vigilance when the news got out that Glendon was dead. Nope, I just can't believe that corpse was Jake Glendon's, and that's why I want to go back to Torvo and learn if anything new has happened. If I'm wrong we haven't gone out of our way any."

The men discussed the improbability of Glendon's death at some length, then rode on in silence for a time. They were coming out of the foothills now and the terrain was flattening out to some extent, only gentle slopes lying before them, where hills and ridges had existed previously. Grass gave way before sandy patches of gray earth; cactus of various species, greasewood and catclaw dotted the landscape; there was a good deal of mesquite. Once, topping a rise of land, they saw, through the quivering heat waves, the undulating outlines of a small town, still some distance away. Lullaby made some comment, and Tucson shook his head. "No, that's not Torvo. More likely it's Jackpot, that town Sheriff Yarrow mentioned."

"Let's cut through it," Lullaby suggested. "It won't be much off our trail."

"Might as well," Tucson nodded.

Stony said, "All right, I'm stuck. I got to go where you two go, but why anybody should want to visit a ghost town is more than I can figure."

Lullaby drawled, "I'd expected a man with your drinking habits to be interested in ghost towns."

"What's ghost towns," Stony asked cautiously, "got to do with drinking?"

"Ghosts—spirits," Lullaby snickered. "If you wasn't dumb you'd seen the connection."

Stony said disgustedly, "Oh, for Gawd's sake. Is that a joke? I don't see anything to laugh about."

"*You* wouldn't." Lullaby grinned. "All you can think about is going to some town where there's a bar."

"That's where you're wrong," Stony said indignantly. "It's not just bars. I like to see the people in town, and there's generally girls around—"

"Girls!" Lullaby guffawed. "Why, you bow-legged, bronc-warped old ram, you! I—" He broke off, shaking his head. "Girls! Women! I thought you'd outgrown all that foolishness."

"Aw-w." Stony blushed. "You got me all wrong. I'm not interested the way you think. Can't a man look at a pretty girl without becoming involved? Hell! You know women are out where I'm concerned."

"You don't have to tell us that. One look at that physog of yours explains everything."

"I'm not denying it," Stony said cheerfully. "I never claimed to be any Adonis, but—"

"What's doughnuts got to do with it?" Lullaby interrupted.

"Not doughnuts. Adonis. Haven't you ever heard of him? He was a handsome cuss in history. Adonis is his name." Stony started to explain.

Lullaby was unimpressed. "Boasting of your book learning again, eh? Where did this Adonis ever swing his loop?"

"Over in Greece a long time ago—"

"Look here," Lullaby interposed, "you don't have to tell me doughnuts is made in grease—"

"Oh, my Gawd," Stony groaned, "how can you be so addle-pated? I said Greece, not grease. Greece—a country over in Europe. I'm trying to give you a mite of Greek mythology."

"Oh, sure." Lullaby winked at Tucson. "Missology. As long as you have to miss something, it might as well be your ology."

There was an air of speculation about the manner in which Stony drew his six-shooter and meditatively commenced slamming the barrel against the palm of his other hand. "I've heard of hombres having some sense knocked into their heads," he murmured. "It might be worth trying, if you—"

"No need to get proddy," Lullaby said. "I'll listen to your yarn, but I got a better one about a saddle salesman that stopped overnight at a ranch—"

"Button your lip, Lullaby," Tucson said, gravefaced. "I'd like to hear about this Greek pard of Stony's."

Stony looked reproachful. "You too, eh?" Impatiently he said, "Dammit, Adonis wasn't no pard of mine. This is Greek mythology—"

"You already explained that part," Lullaby sneered. "Go ahead with the rest of this windy you're spinning. Go on, air your erudition for the benefit of us poor benighted, uncultured souls that ain't even heard of this Roman emperor you're talking about—"

Stony burst out, "He wasn't Roman. He was Gr—"

"If he wasn't roamin', he must have got a job and settled down, then," Lullaby chuckled. "I should have known that. You just got through telling us that this Adonis hombre swung his rope in Greece. What comes next?"

Stony continued, "Well, this Adonis was one handsome hombre, as everybody admitted. I never saw a picture of him, but I imagine he wore hundred-dollar Stetsons and hand-tooled riding boots and concho-decorated chaps. Likely had a purple or canary-yellow silk bandanna too. I ain't quite sure about that last, not havin' read the story since I was knee-high to a yearlin'. Seems like Adonis must have had a silver-mounted saddle; he was a hell-roarin' bronc twister, as I remember, though I might have this mixed up with some other story."

"What's the best ride he ever made at Pendleton?" Lullaby asked.

Stony scratched his head. "I don't recollect the book givin' any rodeo records. But, like I tell you,

Adonis was sure hell for looks. All the girls was smitten with him, and when he dropped into a dance hall, I reckon he got his pick of the women."

Lullaby shook his head. "I never trusted that type overmuch. Adonis was probably one of these grandstand riders—a showoff."

"The hell he was!" Stony flew to the defense of his hero. "He was a right solid citizen and faithful to one girl he'd fell in with, in Dodge City, or Abilene—hell, no, I forgot. This happened in Greece. Anyhow he'd got acquainted with the girl someplace, and she wouldn't even look at any other cow hand. When Adonis came riding in off the range she always had his beans ready, and helped him to pull off his boots. Her name was Aphrodite. She was a Greek, too, though the Romans knew her as Venus."

Lullaby snorted. "And you claiming she was faithful of this Adonis hombre? I can't believe it. She was double-timing Adonis, that's what she was doing. I'll leave it to Tucson. Here she was playing around with Adonis, in Greece, where all the out-fits knew her as Afro-dity. Howsomever, when she goes repping to this Rome outfit, they all know her by a different moniker—Venus. If you ask me, I'll bet she was playing Adonis for a sucker, while this Rome outfit steals all the Adonis beef critters. Don't it look that-a-way?"

"It appears right suspicious, I'd say," Tucson said gravely.

A dubious frown crossed Stony's forehead. "We-ell, it just never occurred to me that way. I never thought of Aphrodite as that kind of a girl, and I don't remember the book mentioning the Flying-A—that being Adonis' iron—ever lost any stock. But here's the story as I got it: everything was going fine with the Flying-A. The herd was increasing and there was plenty of grass and water, and life looked right comfortable to Adonis and Aphrodite. They certainly made a smart-lookin' couple when they hit town in their buckboard to pick up the mail and get supplies." Stony paused. In effect, he wiped away an unbidden tear as he added sadly, "And then along came hard luck."

"Nesters—from Rome, I'll bet," Lullaby guessed.

"Drought?" Tucson chuckled.

"Afro-dity lost her nightie," Lullaby rhymed, and commenced to snicker.

Stony frowned indignantly. "Dammit, I already told you she was faithful to Adonis. Now here's what happened: Adonis was out lookin' for strays one morning. He'd pushed his pony through a tangle of mesquite or chaparral, or cactus—something like that—when all of a sudden he sees a bear blockin' his trail—"

"Bear?" Tucson broke in. "I've heard your story before, someplace, but as I recollect, it was a *boar* attacked Adonis—you know, a wild pig with tusks."

Stony was shaken by this contradiction, but stubbornly he stuck to his guns. "No, siree, Tucson, it was a big silvertip grizzly."

"You wouldn't be making this up as you go along, would you?" Tucson asked dryly.

A scornful laugh burst from Lullaby. "A swell cow hand this Adonis proves to be. Killed by a wild pig!"

Stony spoke with some heat. "I already told you it was a bear. Who's telling this, you or me? Anyhow, this bear comes bustin' out of the brush, gnashin' his teeth and claws. Adonis happened to be forkin' a young bronc that he was just in process of bustin', so the pony ain't too steady. It gets scary and rears, just as Adonis yanks his six-gun and starts unravelin' his lead. Owing to the horse sunfishin' around, Adonis gets spilled, but one foot sticks in the stirrup. Off goes the horse, hightailin' it to beat hell, dragging Adonis through the brush and over the rocks, which same spoils his handsome features considerable. And in addition he gets drug to death. So I maintain it was the bear was responsible for his death. No cow horse would run from a pig."

"What became of the bear?" Tucson asked amusedly.

Stony pondered. "Seems like," he fabricated, "Aphrodite must have took down the old Sharps buffalo gun and went out and finished it. But that's irrelevant."

"What's an elephant?" Lullaby demanded. "First it's a pig, then a bear, and now you claim—"

"I didn't say it was an elephant," Stony said defensively. "I meant that what happened to the bear don't make any difference."

"The hell it don't," Lullaby contradicted. "That's the most important part. The bear was responsible for rubbin' out Doughnuts, wasn't it?"

Stony waved one hand in exasperation. "All right, all right, I'll admit I don't remember what happened to the bear, but my guess is as good as any." He waited a moment and then resumed, "When Adonis didn't show up for his beans and bacon that evening, Aphrodite got to figuring that maybe he'd rode into town to get liquored up, which same made her plumb peevish, her having baked a fresh batch of sourdough biscuits that day. With blood in her eye, she heads down to the mess shanty where the hands were just sittin' down to their chow. 'Where's Adonis?' she asks the foreman. 'Last I see of him,' the rod replies cautious-like, 'he was ridin' down into Labyrinth Gulch to practice his bulldoggin' on Minotaur—"

"Hold up!" Lullaby interrupted. "You've been claimin' Doughnuts was true to Afro-dity. Who's this Minnie Tower?"

"If you ain't the damnedest to tell anything to!" Perspiration burst on Stony's face. "Minotaur isn't a girl—"

"Look here, pard," Tucson broke in, "you're not

getting your Greek mythology a mite scrambled up, are you?"

"Certainly not," Stony replied with some dignity, albeit he hurried to resume, "You see, this Minotaur was a man-killing bull that was raising hell every time he got into the herds."

"I thought you said Doughnuts was out hunting strays," Lullaby reminded.

Stony eyed his pardner with some consternation until he was struck by a sudden thought. "That's what I'm trying to make clear, Lullaby. He was hunting the strays that Minotaur had frightened into stampedin' off into the brush." He shot a triumphant glance in Tucson's direction and went on. "Well, Aphrodite rides out to see if the foreman was just stalling, or if he'd throwed a straight rope. And, sure enough, she found Doughnuts—dang you, Lullaby, you got me saying it—she found Adonis drug to death, his features mangled something terrific."

"What did she say then?" Lullaby asked.

"What would a woman say in a situation like that?"

"I'm waiting to hear," Lullaby persisted.

Stony wrinkled his forehead. "Let me think what the book said . . . Oh yeah, she dropped on her knees, and she sets up a wail, 'Great Jupiter! He's croaked. I told him he'd have trouble with them Mex *tapaderas*. They was always more ornamental than practicable. Why couldn't he have stuck to plain little old oxbow stirrups?' And then she gets to feelin' right sorry for herself when she realizes from now on she'll have the outfit to rod by herself. She thinks deep for a spell. Sudden it comes to her and she gets up off'n her knees and says, 'This is a case for Pluto.' "

Lullaby looked startled. "Pluto?"

"Pluto was the Lord of Darkness," Stony explained loftily. "He had the power of bringing the dead back to life. Well, Aphrodite sends a rider burning the trail to Pluto with a note, the same explaining how she was a lone widder woman now and there was still a mortgage to be paid off on the spread. And could Pluto give her the loan of his crew for a spell to help out on the Flying-A. Well, Pluto give the matter considerable thought, and he commenced to see Aphrodite's side of the problem. Finally to keep her from borrowing his outfit to use on the Flying-A, he allows how he'll fix it so Adonis can return to earth and rod his spread for six months out of every year. So that made everything fine, and Adonis always arranged his visit so he could be on hand for calf branding and beef roundup—"

"Which same left the winters for Afro-dity to play around with the Romans, I expect?" Lullaby said.

"All right, all right," Stony growled. "Here I've been trying to impart some knowledge to you hombres, but it 'pears like I've just been casting pearls before swine. If I—"

110

"Doughnuts before wild pigs, you mean, don't you?" Lullaby grinned.

Tucson eyed Stony with something of awe in his gray eyes. "My Lord," he breathed, "what your imagination can do with Greek mythology, when it gets started, is something scandalous—"

"You hinting I made that story up?" Stony demanded.

"No, he's not *hinting,*" Lullaby said shortly.

"You think I was lying?"

"Hush it!" Tucson said suddenly. "I thought I heard shooting."

Instantly serious, the three men drew rein and listened, their ears straining above the sound of the wind through the semidesert brush for the sound of reports.

"There! Hear that?" Tucson said. "Sounds like it might be coming from the direction of Jackpot. We should be nearly there by now."

"Dammit, horse, stand quiet!" Stony swore. "Yeah, I heard it."

"Sounded like a rifle and six-shooters," Lullaby put in.

"Reckon we'd best investigate a mite," Tucson nodded. "It might be somebody just shooting for practice. Again, it might not. C'mon, let's get going!"

They spurred the horses to swift movement and swept up a long gradual slope, thickly grown with sagebrush and greasewood. Gaining the top of the slope, they found themselves gazing down on the roofs of the supposedly deserted ghost town. Even while they momentarily drew rein, further shooting reached their ears.

"If you ask me," Lullaby snapped tersely, "that ain't nobody shooting for practice. Let's rattle our hocks, pards."

Gathering their reins, driving in spurs, the three flashed swiftly down the long gradual grade that led to Jackpot.

9. The Cactus Man

The first scattered shacks of Jackpot were passed in a blur of swiftly receding dust clouds when Tucson signaled his pardners to pull up. "We'd best not barge in on anything until we learn how the land lies. I've heard no more shots, but they might have been lost in the rush of wind. We'll take it at a walk from here on in."

They moved cautiously forward until, rounding the corner of an ancient frame structure, they found themselves looking along Jackpot's curving main street. Here they stopped, sharp eyes scrutinizing the empty thoroughfare and the weathered buildings on either side.

"There's a horse," Lullaby said. "No rider, though."

"No more shooting either," from Stony, "but maybe—"

Tucson said suddenly, "Let your eye follow along the right side of the street . . . see? Near that water trough . . ."

The distance of a long city block away, they spied a huddled figure lying in the dust at the near end of the watering trough. Lullaby said, "Looks like somebody caught a slug—"

"Hush it," Tucson said softly. "Look along the left side of the street."

A man with a red bandanna about his throat had appeared from the doorway of a two-story building and stepped warily to the sidewalk. Unaware of the Mesquiteers' proximity, his gaze intent on a point in the vicinity of the watering trough, he started to cross the street, moving in the direction of the huddled figure in the dust. In the middle of the street the man paused and raised the six-shooter he clutched in his right fist. Now he had a clear view of the end of the trough. He took a step nearer, while the wind whistled eerily through the empty buildings ranged along the street.

Tucson opened his mouth to yell out, when from the slumped form in the dust came an abrupt movement that ended in a lancelike streak of white fire. An expression of pain, shock, crossed the face of the man in the middle of the street. He managed to pull the trigger of his own weapon but the bullet flew harmlessly to one side. Now the man huddled at the end of the trough bounded catlike to his feet and fired again. A frantic cry of agony sounded along the street, and the man with the red bandanna spun twice around and then crashed down, the six-shooter flying from his grasp and coming to rest in a weed-grown rut ten feet away.

Without giving the fallen individual a second glance, the other man now moved swiftly out between the ruts, his gaze bent on the loft opening of the livery stable on the right. His voice carried clearly to the Three Mesquiteers: "Come down out of that loft, mister, or make your play from there!"

Stony exclaimed, "He was putting on an act, by Gawd! C'mon, let's see what this is all about."

The three moved forward as the man standing in the roadway either heard Stony's voice or sensed the approach of the three riders. He whirled suddenly and started to back toward the sidewalk on the left side of the street, his attention divided between the oncoming Mesquiteers and the loft opening opposite him. His six-gun traveled in a wide arc, back and forth, that covered both points, his eyes alert for the first hostile move. "You three stop where you are!" he shouted, backing another step.

"Take it easy, hombre," Tucson called back. "We're not taking any part in this squabble." He and his companions continued their advance. "We're not looking for trouble, but if you want any, I warn you you're outnumbered."

"Maybe so, but—" the man commenced, then paused to ask, "Who are you?"

"My name's Smith." The Mesquiteers were closer by this time. "These are my pardners, Joslin and Brooke."

"I'll be damned!" The man started to lower his gun, then thought better of it as his gaze quickly shifted back to the livery opening. "You're the Three Mesquiteers!"

"We've been called that," Tucson admitted. "Who are you?"

"Name's Jefferson—Smoky Jefferson. Deputy sheriff of Mesquital County." He took a step toward the three riders, then changed his mind. "I'll be right back," he announced and, leaping into a run, disappeared into the building whose sign proclaimed it the Flying Hoofs Livery.

"A man of few words, I'd say," Lullaby commented. They came up even with the watering trough and dismounted. Leaving the ponies to slake their thirst, the three strode out to the middle of the road where the man in the red bandanna lay silent in death. Stony knelt by his side, then again stood up. "Both shots through the heart, and not an inch apart. I'd call that smart shooting."

"So would anybody else." Tucson nodded. "I wonder what that deputy went into that old livery for?"

"He looked," Lullaby commented, "like he was heading for more trouble, but there hasn't been any shooting. Let's get a drink. If he's not back by then we'll investigate."

They returned to the tank and pumped water. Faces were washed. Stony ducked his head in the cooling depths of the trough and came up dripping. "This hot wind blowing all the time sure parches a fellow." They waited a few minutes longer, then Tucson said, "C'mon, let's go see what's keeping that deputy."

They entered the livery stable. Loose boards creaked beneath their feet. Within was a long line of stalls; nothing else was to be seen except a closed door at the rear of the livery. Footsteps sounded overhead and crossed the floor to one rear corner. Glancing up, Tucson saw a ladder leading to a small square opening in the board ceiling. A moment later Deputy Jefferson's booted feet appeared on the ladder. As he came into view they saw he carried over one shoulder the body of an unconscious man whose denim shirt was stained with blood. Tucson and his pardners hastened to Smoky's assistance, and a moment later the limp form was lowered to the livery floor.

"Damnedest thing I ever saw," Smoky was saying. "I just hit this hombre by chance—just threw a shot his way to scare him back. Got him plumb through the neck. Might be my bullet ricocheted and struck him. I heard him let out a yelp and noticed his next shot flew wild."

They'd been examining the unconscious man while Smoky talked. "That's a nasty wound," Tucson said at last, "and has bled more than a man can usually stand to lose. But he might pull through if we could get him to a doctor. I'll see what I can do." While Lullaby found a rusty tin can to hold water, Tucson ripped a clean bandanna into strips and commenced working over the wounded man. Finally everything had been accomplished that was possible. Tucson asked, "Know who he is, Jefferson?"

Smoky shook his head. "Never saw either of these fellows before."

"The one in the road's dead," Stony said. Smoky just nodded, as though he was already aware of that fact, and dropped a remark to the effect that he hadn't been shooting just for the fun of it.

"If you feel like telling us what happened . . ." Tucson hinted.

"Cripes, yes." Smoky nodded. "First, I've heard about you three. I'm glad to meet you." The four men shook hands. "There's not much to tell," Smoky went on. "I came into Jackpot to water my horse. While he was drinking the shooting started. The buzzards had me caught between fires." He added further details anent the shooting, concluding with, "Well, it looked like they'd keep me trapped forever, if I didn't do something. So I edged my head around the edge of the trough to draw fire—"

"You sure drew it, brother," Lullaby observed. "Your bonnet has got itself four holes."

"It was hit twice." Smoky nodded. "Anyway,

when the second bullet passed through I let out a
groan that must have been heard all the way to
Torvo and dropped in a heap, managing to keep my
body pretty well concealed behind the trough,
though. I figured that would draw somebody into
the open. The way I was laying I could keep one eye
on the loft, and I figured to hear anybody that came
out of the boardinghouse. Course, I didn't know the
hombre in the loft was already out of the fight.
And—well, you hombres know what happened."

"And you don't know who they are or why they
shot at you?" Tucson pursued.

"I haven't the least idea, unless . . ." Smoky hesitated. "There's no use speculating. Maybe if we
could get this hombre"—nodding toward the
unconscious man on the floor—"to a doctor, he
might be able to talk eventually, but the nearest
doctor is at Torvo and I'm damned if I know how
we can get him there, without—"

"One thing is certain," Tucson said, "he and his
pards must have come here on horses. The broncs
are maybe hidden out in one of the buildings. Let's
split up and take a look-see. We might find the
mounts."

Leaving the unconscious man on the floor of the
livery, the four men returned to the street. Tucson
and Smoky headed east along the sidewalks; Stony
and Lullaby took the opposite direction. While
Tucson took the left side of the street Smoky
entered the various buildings along the right.

The first place Tucson entered proved to be an ancient saloon. The floor was covered with dust, in which were several scuffed boot prints, though they appeared to have been made some time before. A bullet-scarred bar, some broken chairs, and a shattered mirror back of the bar went to make up the furniture. A glass, thick with dust, still stood on the bar and there were broken bottles about. He left the bar and entered the next building and the next. Bits of ragged blankets, old broken-down cots, and the inevitable dust met his eye wherever he went. Here and there discarded bits of clothing still hung from rusty hooks. The air of eerie desolation and the continual sighing of the wind through broken windowpanes were depressing. There was something uncanny in this business of entering building after building and never encountering a human being. And always there were broken boards underfoot and broken glass crunching beneath his boots. Now and then a rat scurried frantically from view to disappear beneath the ramshackle floors.

Tucson left a building which he judged, from the amount of broken crockery on the floor, had once been a restaurant, and stepped once more to the rickety sun-warped boards of the sidewalk. He glanced along the street toward the west; neither Lullaby nor Stony was in view. Across the way Smoky was just entering an old structure that bore a sign stating it had once been the Jackpot

Hardware Store. Tucson resumed his quest. The next building was smaller, and Tucson was about to pass it up when he noticed that the door, contrary to his past experience with Jackpot's doors, was tightly shut. Neither was there so much dust on the doorstep as he'd been accustomed to seeing. He tried the knob of the door and found it to be locked from the inside. Without thinking, he put his shoulder against the door and shoved—hard. There came a sudden splintering of wood as the bolt within gave way, and the door swung open.

Tucson had time to notice little more than that a doorway existed at the rear of the building and beyond the doorway was a small corral, when a crabbed voice at his right asked peevishly, "What in hell do ye want here, mister?"

Glancing quickly around, Tucson saw an elderly individual, with unshaven tobacco-stained beard and unkempt gray hair seated on a bunk, at one end of which were some rumpled, filthy blankets. The old man had a six-shooter in his hand and it was bearing directly on Tucson.

"Sorry," Tucson said, "I didn't realize anyone lived here."

"Goddammit, ye don't taken no thought 'bout bustin' in an old man's door," the fellow whined. He lowered the gun. "Can't a man have no peace?"

"I've told you I'm sorry." Tucson took a five-dollar bill from his pocket and extended it to the ancient. "This should cover the cost of getting your door fixed."

Somewhat mollified, the old man nodded. "It mought. Now if ye ain't no more business with me, ye can git out."

"Maybe I have business with you," Tucson said. He glanced around the room and saw cactus plants of various sizes and species stacked against one wall, earth still clinging to the roots. Most of the plants were what is known as the barrel cactus type, though a few of the long cereus variety were to be seen. Near the rear, where light came through a window and the open door, stood a bench holding a few small crates made from old wood, and three more barrel cactus, each of which was about a foot in diameter, though the roots had been cut from these and the bare flesh of the cactus showed where a gouge had been made.

Along the other wall of the room, beyond the bunk, was a stove, some cooking utensils hanging from hooks, and a pantry shelf, stacked with canned goods of various sorts. A soiled towel hung from a nail at the end of the pantry shelf. The floor was littered with old papers, bits of wire and rope, cigar butts, and dried chewing tobacco "cuds."

The old man spoke again, sarcastically. "Hope ye recognize my place, next time ye lay an eye on it."

"It's likely I will," Tucson returned pleasantly. "You seem to be interested in cactus. What's the idea?"

"No business of yourn, but I don't mind tellin' ye. I dig 'em from th' kentry hereabouts and sell 'em to fools who'll pay money for cactus. Thet's all ye can call 'em, fools! But I makes a livin'. Who mought ye be?"

"My name's Smith. And yours?"

"Joel Wyatt. Mostly, folks jest calls me th' Cactus Man." He spat an unerring brown stream at a small lizard which had stuck an unwary head through a crack in the floor, then cackled with a sort of maniacal glee when he scored a clean hit. "Thet'll teach them little skitterin' anamiles not to come intrudin' on Joel Wyatt's privacy. Lucky I didn't treat ye th' same way, mister."

"I reckon it is." Tucson smiled. His gaze strayed back to the bench where the cacti and crates lay. "I note you've removed the roots from those plants. What's the idea?"

"It jest goes to show ye don't know nary a thing 'bout cactus," Joel Wyatt stated scornfully. "Them plants diseased. They've started to rot. I cut out the rot and when them bar'l cactuses has dried out I plant 'em again. Then they sprouts new roots."

"That's amazing."

"It always is to fools." The Cactus Man cackled some more and shot another brown stream on the floor. "Ye ain't said yit whut ye want here?"

Before Tucson could reply Smoky Jefferson entered. "I thought I heard voices over here." He glanced at Wyatt and then ran his eyes quickly about the room. "The Cactus Man, eh? Sheriff Yarrow was telling me about him. Hi, Grandpaw. I'm the sheriff's deputy. Name's Jefferson."

"Ye're likely honest then," Wyatt grunted. "Yarrow's a good man, as good a shurf as Torvo's ever like to have. Don't see much o' him no more, though. Whut you fellers doin' here, anyhow?"

"There was some shooting a spell back," Tucson commenced, "and—"

"D'ye think I didn't hear it?" Wyatt demanded. "I ain't deef. And you, Deppity, I ain't yore gran'paw, nuther. You smart-alecky young squirts come snoopin' 'round—"

"If you heard the shooting," Tucson asked, "how come you didn't put in an appearance?"

"I ain't crazy," the Cactus Man sneered. "Mought be some o' thet Glendon gang I hearn tell 'bout. I don't stick my snout inter whut ain't my business, and other folks"—meaningly—"mought be better off did they do th' same."

"What do you know of the Glendon gang?" Smoky asked.

"Only whut I've heerd," Wyatt replied. "They don't bother me and I don't aim to give 'em no chance to, nuther. So if I hear firearms explodin', I keep my snoot indoors."

"Have you heard much shooting hereabouts?" Tucson asked.

Wyatt shook his head. "Fust time in my expurance was today. Course, I ain't to home only part

123

of th' time. Mostly I'm out in the hills diggin' plants or takin' 'em to be shipped."

"There's one man dead and another badly wounded," Tucson explained. "We'd like to get 'em to town. Have you seen any horses around here?"

"Ain't I told ye," Wyatt demanded irritably, "thet I don't know nuthin' and I don't see nuthin' whut ain't my business? No, I ain't seen no hosses. Now if ye'll git out—"

At that moment they heard Stony and Lullaby hailing them. Tucson stepped to the door and saw the two approaching. "Find any horses?" Tucson asked.

Lullaby nodded. "They were tethered down back of an old dance hall, the other end of town. What you doing in there?"

Tucson explained and Stony and Lullaby followed him into Wyatt's shack. The Cactus Man had risen from his bunk now, put away his gun, and was engaged in taking a drink from a partly filled bottle of whisky. Now that he was on his feet, Tucson saw that he was of medium height, though somewhat stooped, and that his denims were faded and dirty. The old man lowered the bottle indignantly upon seeing Stony and Lullaby. "Damned if my house ain't took to lookin' like a convention hall, with all you hombres crowdin' in here. Can't an old man have no privacy?"

"That's no way to talk to a guest," Stony said

reproachfully. "You might pass the bottle around and make us welcome."

A flow of obscene invective greeted the suggestion, and Wyatt hastily recorked the bottle and put it away. "I ain't passin' out free drinks to every passel o' bums whut feels privileged to come here. Saw you three when ye rode in, and figgered ye mought come 'round a-beggin'. Well, ye can jest be on yer way. I ain't havin' no truck with strangers. Get along now! Scat!"

Lullaby had wandered down to the far end of the room. Returning, his eye ran along the various cans and other food supplies. He sighed. "I'm getting hungrier every minute." He picked up a flat can from the shelf. "Sardines! My favorite fruit! Look, mister, how about letting me—"

"Put thet can down!" Wyatt shrilled angrily.

"But you got more sardines than anything else," Lullaby persisted. "They're the kind of fish I like best. Sell me a can, if you won't—"

"Put thet can down!" The ancient's voice quavered with rage. "I'm warnin' ye!" He started tugging at the six-shooter in his holster.

Quickly Lullaby returned the can of sardines to the shelf and moved toward the doorway. "That's what I call flint-hearted," he said. "Come on, let's get out of this den of penurious iniquity."

"Th' sooner the better," the Cactus Man snarled. "Go on along, now, all of ye, and leave an old man to his privacy."

"Never saw such a stubborn old bustard," Stony observed as they stepped through to the sidewalk and heard the door slammed behind them. "Stubborn as those two moth-eaten mules out in his corral—"

"Were there mules out there?" Lullaby said. "I didn't notice—"

"Now, Lullaby," Stony said reprovingly, "you're not that hungry. Besides, mule steak would make tough chawing—"

"Didn't want mule," Lullaby said disappointedly. "I wanted sardines. Dang that old fool."

Tucson said, "I noticed those mules. They were standing in the shadow at one side of the corral. Neither of 'em looked like it had enough life to travel far."

"Probably old Wyatt starves 'em to death and abuses 'em on top of that," Smoky commented.

"Well, that's neither here nor there," Tucson said. He eyed the two saddled horses that Stony and Lullaby had found. "I've got an idea," he went on, "that we could rig up some sort of sling with our blankets and ropes and carry that wounded cuss between the two horses. If I can get him to Torvo, we might save his life and hear what he has to say. C'mon, let's get busy."

10. Trouble Brewing

It was late that night when the four riders and the two extra horses, bearing the wounded man and the other grisly burden, drew to a halt before Sheriff Yarrow's office. Only a few lights shone along the street, and these mostly illuminated various saloons. Here and there drowsy cow ponies slumped on three legs at hitching rails; there weren't any pedestrians on the walks. A lighted lamp in the sheriff's office shed a rectangle of light that stretched to the dusty roadway.

Hardly had Tucson and his companions pulled to a stop before the door of the sheriff's office was flung open and Yarrow's form was silhouetted against the lighted opening. "That you, Smoky?" he asked anxiously, eyes narrowed against the darkness.

"It's me, Matt, and—"

"Thank God." They heard the sheriff's long-pent-up sigh of relief, which was instantly replaced by a sort of stored-up fury: "Goddammit, where you been? I been worried sick. I told you—"

"Save it until later, Matt," Smoky interposed. "We've got—"

"I don't know what in hell I should save anything for," the sheriff raged, in mingled anger and relief. "It's cement mixing for you, or I—" He broke off. "Who's with you? What you got there?"

127

"Look, Matt," Smoky said, "we've got a man here who's hit bad. He's still alive, but I don't know for how long. Where's the nearest doctor? We can talk later. Meanwhile, these are friends— you met them when they came through a few weeks back."

Yarrow had reached the sidewalk by this time and was peering at the riders and the burdens the horses carried. "Gawd, looks like you got a dead man there too." His gaze came back to the Mesquiteers, and he nodded and said something about being glad to see them again. Once more Smoky stated it was imperative to get the wounded man to a doctor.

"You said that before," Yarrow growled. "All right, *you'd* best stay here in the office. If one of you fellers will go along with me I'll show the way to Doc Arden's place. We can drop the dead man at the undertaker's later." Details were quickly settled. While Lullaby and Smoky remained at the sheriff's office, Tucson and Stony accompanied Yarrow and the extra horses with their burdens.

It was three quarters of an hour before they returned, by which time Lullaby had procured a large pot of coffee and a goodly supply of beef sandwiches from a neighboring all-night restaurant, and had the food spread out on the sheriff's desk. Tucson said as he entered, "I dropped off at the hotel, pards, and got us three rooms, then we took our broncs to the livery—"

"If I knew of a livery for mules," Yarrow interrupted hotly, "I'd send one deputy sheriff there, pronto. By the seven ring-tailed steers, I don't know why I always get deputies that can't obey orders. S'help me Hanner, I aim to—"

"Why, what's wrong, Matt?" Smoky asked innocently.

"What's wrong, what's wrong!" Yarrow swore a bitter oath. "You disobeyed orders, that's what's wrong. I told you and told you, distinctly, not to go out of the county, and here you had to go snoopin' around Jackpot—"

"I see Tucson has been talking." Smoky smiled.

"Certain he's been talking. Didn't I warn you I already lost two deputies by them not stayin' in their own county? Didn't I?"

"Seems like I do remember something of the sort," Smoky said apologetically. "I'm sorry, Matt, but my horse sure needed water bad. I didn't want you'd have to put a dead horse on your expense account for this month—"

"Bosh! Do you expect me to believe that? Only you had some luck, we'd have found your body layin' out on the range someplace, like with my other two deputies. Damn you, Smoky!"

"I've already said I was sorry," Smoky said, lips twitching, "but somehow your orders just sort of slipped my mind, when Rafe Chandler mentioned there was water to be had in Jackpot. And it was a mighty hot day, you'll recollect—"

"Rafe Chandler? Where'd you meet the Border Ranger?"

"Over towards the county line. He was headed south when he crossed my trail—"

"Riding hell out of a bronc, I suppose," Yarrow said in quieter tones.

Smoky nodded. "He only stopped long enough to borrow a sack of makin's."

Yarrow shook his head. "If I only had a deputy that would work as hard on a case as Chandler, instead of snoopin' all over the range, we might accomplish something in this office."

"Yeah, we might," Smoky agreed. "Anyway, I still have hopes. What did the doctor say about that wounded fellow, Matt?"

"Say, that's somethin' else," Yarrow cut in. "When we got to Doc Arden's I recognized that cuss. He's Jerky Trumble; works for the Box-V. Wait until I get a chance to talk to Luke Vaughn. If I don't ask him how come his hands is throwin' lead at my appointed officer—"

"Who's the other hombre?" Smoky asked.

"Never saw him before," the sheriff responded. "We dropped him at the undertaker's. I'll ask Vaughn about him, though. What? Oh, Trumble. Yeah, Doc Arden says he has a chance. He'll do what's possible to pull him through. Once Trumble is able to talk, if he is, I aim to do some investigatin'. Tucson here has told me somethin' of what happened, but I'd like to hear it first-

130

hand. Just exactly what did happen in Jackpot?"

Coffee was poured into thick china cups and sandwiches passed out. By the time the men had finished eating and were rolling cigarettes, Smoky had finished his story. At its conclusion Yarrow slowly shook his head. "I still can't see how you were so lucky, Smoky. It should teach you a lesson. After this you'll know enough to obey orders, I'm bettin'. If you'd just leave things to me—"

"I know, I know." Smoky grinned. "The Cactus Man said you used to be a good man, so—"

"Used to be!" Yarrow snorted. "I remember when Joel Wyatt was a good man, too, but he turned sort of cracked and bitter. Time was when he was workin' a claim over near Jackpot, then when the metal petered out and he saw he wouldn't get rich, he just turned sour on the world. I figure he's sort of cracked in his upper story. Cactus Man! Phaugh! I figure he just uses that as an excuse to go prospectin', and the fools who pay money for cactus supports him in such endeavors."

"Such things happen," Tucson commented.

Stony said, "Is there any more coffee in that pot?" There was and he refilled his cup. Lullaby dropped a wistful statement to the effect that he wished the sandwiches weren't all gone.

Smoky said, "Matt, I'm not alone in thinking that maybe wasn't Jake Glendon that was found with his face blown off. Tucson has ideas along the same line. We've talked matters over some, on the way here, and that's what brought him back this way."

"Fact is," Tucson said, "I feel as though I should have thought of that right off, only I didn't."

"Can't blame you none," Yarrow grunted. "It was me that stated positive it was Glendon. It wa'n't none of your affair. Still and all, I'm glad you've come back. T'tell the truth, I sort of suspicioned you fellers, until Smoky made me see I was way off'n the track."

"If it wasn't Glendon, where's Glendon now?" Lullaby wondered.

"That's something I'd give my right eye to know," Yarrow replied. "Whether or not it was Glendon, the Glendon gang is still operating. To tell the truth, there's an election coming up before too long, and I'd like to have the credit for bustin' up that gang." He sighed. "But I probably won't have no such luck. If anybody does it, I'm afeared it'll be Rafe Chandler, the way he's working on the case. Then the Border Rangers will get the credit, and folks will forget me when election time arrives."

"In other words," Tucson said, "you'd give a lot to beat the Border Rangers to it." Yarrow nodded. Tucson went on, "My pards and I are sort of interested in the business. We figure to stay around Torvo a spell until we see how things come out."

"I'd sure like to have your help," Yarrow said, pleasure tinging his tones. "From what Smoky tells me, you've had a lot of experience in law bustin'. But I can't give you any authority. My expenses for Mesquital County are loaded to the hilt right now."

"We're not asking any authority," Tucson replied. "We might be able to do more good just as friends of yours who've dropped into Torvo to see you awhile."

"In that way," Lullaby added, "our hands wouldn't be tied. We could ride where we liked, and you wouldn't be responsible for anything we might do."

"Responsible?" Yarrow frowned.

Stony said, "In case we were forced to do anything outside of the law. Not that we expect to, but you never know what might come up." He paused a moment. "To make it clear, we always like to work on our own, with any help the law can give us when necessary."

Yarrow nodded his comprehension and Smoky said, "Matt, it looks like luck has swung our way for a spell."

"In one way, yes," Yarrow conceded gloomily, "but things don't look any better for *you,* Smoky." Smoky asked the sheriff what he meant. Yarrow continued, "Immediately you left this mornin', I took Owney Powell and Bart Fielding before the justice of the peace, despite of Luke Vaughn's objections. Judge Uhlmann fined 'em each twenty-five dollars for disturbin' the peace. They're both sore as boils. Vaughn was awfully mad and the minute he'd paid the fines he tore out of Torvo like he was never coming back. When you didn't show up by sundown I figured maybe him and his crew had jumped you somewhere. You had me worried, son."

"Thanks, Matt, but you can see your worrying was for nothing."

"I ain't so sure. There's trouble brewing. The Box-V is out to square matters with you. It puts me in a fix: if I send you out of town to avoid trouble, they might ambush you out in the brush. Fact is, you'd be better off, maybe, if you resigned and caught the first train out of town."

"Look here, Matt," Smoky said earnestly, "you've got to admit I've taken care of myself so far."

"Yeah. But you ain't been ganged up on yet—not with guns."

"What do you figure happened in Jackpot? Those hombres had guns. Shucks! I'm still not worried." Smoky smiled.

Tucson offered a suggestion: "Perhaps it might be wise for one of us to stay close to Smoky's trail when he moves."

"You see, Matt," Smoky said, "things are looking up."

Tucson went on, "It might even be a good idea for one of us to sleep in this office with Smoky, until we see how things are going to turn out."

"That won't be necessary," Smoky said quickly.

"I'll have the door locked when I'm asleep. By the time anybody tried to break in, I'd have taken care of 'em or help could arrive."

"Just as you say." Yarrow nodded. "Well, I'd best get along home and let Jane know you arrived back safe."

"Was Jane—Miss Yarrow concerned?" Smoky began eagerly.

The sheriff said tartly, "No. You know any reason she should be?"

"You said you'd better get home and tell her—"

Yarrow glowered. "I just happened to get careless at supper and mention that I might need a new deputy soon—"

"Listen!" Tucson said abruptly. "That sounded like a shot—"

"And there's another!" Stony exclaimed.

11. Destroyed Evidence

The men were on their feet now and followed Yarrow outside when he flung open the door. They glanced along the darkened street. Clouds moved overhead, partly obscuring the moon. Yarrow swore. "Those shots sounded like they come from over near First and Deming Street. Reckon I'd best go investigate."

"We'll all go," Tucson said. Yarrow slammed the office door and the men set off at a run, the sheriff giving directions as they moved. At the first corner to the west they turned on Deming, then, as they approached First Street, steps were heard pounding along the walk toward them. From nearby came the sounds of doors banging and windows being flung open. A man's head appeared in a doorway and wanted to know what the shooting was about. Tucson and his companions didn't reply.

In the half-light from the moon they now saw a man approaching, running. "It's Doc Arden!" Yarrow exclaimed.

A spare gray-haired individual, hatless, and with his nightshirt tucked in trousers and his suspenders hanging behind, said, "Is that you, Matt?"

"It's me, Doc. What's the trouble?"

"Somebody," Dr. Arden panted, "shot through my window—twice. They got that fellow you brought in a while back—Jerky Trumble."

"He's dead?" Yarrow snapped.

"If he ain't, he should be. I didn't make an examination, but I saw where the slugs entered his head—"

"Get back and check up," Yarrow said. "We'll investigate around the house."

By this time there was a small knot of men gathered before the doctor's residence, a sprawling wooden structure on the northwest corner of Deming and First streets. Yarrow asked various questions. No, no one had seen the gunman. One fellow insisted he had heard a horse galloping fast, a moment after the shot had been fired. Tucson said, "In what direction?" West, straight out of town, was the reply.

Light shone through a broken pane of glass on the Deming Street side of Arden's house. A moment later the doctor raised the window. A loose section of glass shattered to the ground. The doctor's head was thrust through the opening. He said, "Matt, it's murder all right."

Yarrow said, "I was afraid it might be." He turned on the men standing curiously about. "You hombres had best go back to bed. You're just scuffin' up any sign we might see. What?" in answer to a question put by one of the bystanders. "Feller by the name of Trumble—worked for the Box-V. No, I don't know anything more to tell you. Now all you hombres cut along home."

Reluctantly the crowd dispersed. Tucson and the others scattered, looking over the earth, but the dirt road was so chopped with boot and hoof prints that there was little to be learned. Tucson stooped once and picked something up which he thrust into a pocket. "Looks like," he commented, running sensitive fingers over the earth and squinting in the half-light from the moon, a few yards from the doctor's broken window, "a horse might have waited here, though we can't be certain it was the murderer's horse. I'd like to check the angle at which the shot would have to enter . . ."

Yarrow led the way around to the doctor's front door, with Smoky and the Mesquiteers following.

A slight white-haired woman in a wrapper, whom Yarrow introduced as the doctor's wife, met them at the door. Then Arden emerged from an inner room and showed the way to the bedroom where Jerky Trumble lay still in death. Tucson shot a quick glance around the chamber and at the lamp burning near the bed. "Hmmm . . . yes, a rider could have waited outside for an opportunity—by the way, Doctor, where were you when the shots were fired?"

"I was undressed and just about to go to bed," the doctor replied, indicating another bedroom across a small hall, "when I decided to take a final look at Trumble before I put out the light. I came in here, carrying my lamp. There seemed nothing more I could do. Trumble was still unconscious, of course. I set my lamp on that table there, while I took his pulse, and in that moment the shots came—"

"No question of the shots being meant for you?" Smoky asked.

"I doubt it. I've no enemies I know of. No, you can see both shots were meant for Trumble and found their marks in his head. I was too shocked to do anything but just stand here for a moment, then I got my wits about me, quieted my wife down, and pulled on my pants and boots. Meanwhile I'd been hearing a rider leaving like a bat out of hell, out Deming Street. Then I set out to find Matt . . ."

The men talked a few minutes longer. "When we get back to Main, Doc," Yarrow said, "I'll let the undertaker know he's got two stiffs to prepare, 'stead of just one. I reckon we can hold the inquest on both tomorrow mornin', can't we?"

Dr. Arden nodded. "I'll round up a coroner's jury, early. And ask Spade Jenkins to come pick up Trumble's body, soon's possible. I'd like to get some sleep tonight."

"I'll take care of it, Doc."

Tucson, Yarrow, and the three others returned to Main Street, where a stop was made at the undertaker's. That taken care of, the five men stood talking on the sidewalk a few minutes. Yarrow sighed. "How do you figure it? Why should anybody want to kill Jerky Trumble when he was already half dead?"

"Maybe," Tucson speculated, "Trumble had knowledge of something that would involve other people in trouble, said other people being fearful Trumble might talk out of turn. And so an execution was decided on."

"A matter of killing off evidence, eh?" Smoky commented. Tucson nodded. Smoky went on, "Somebody must have seen us bringing Trumble and that dead man into Torvo—"

"Look here," Lullaby broke in. "It was too dark for anyone to recognize Trumble, and none of us had talked to anybody. That makes it appear that somebody was aware of what happened in Jackpot and hurried here with the news." He paused. "That's just guesswork, of course. All we know is that someone got word to rub Trumble out. I wonder if there was someone in Jackpot watching our movements—"

"What about the Cactus Man?" Stony asked.

Lullaby shook his head. "I can't imagine that old coot moving fast enough to beat us to town—not on those mules of his."

"That means," Tucson resumed, "that there must have been somebody hidden in Jackpot, or near there, we never did lay eyes on. But whoever it was spied us."

Yarrow didn't say anything for a minute. He glanced along the street, then stated, "I see a light still burnin' in the Silver Spur Bar. That's the usual hangout for the Box-V outfit."

Smoky asked, "You figuring that the Box-V had something to do with Trumble's murder?"

"I didn't say that," Yarrow replied testily. "I just keep remembering that Jerky Trumble works— worked—for Luke Vaughn. I reckon I'll take a *pasear* down that way."

He didn't ask the others to accompany him, but when he started off Tucson was at his side, with Lullaby, Smoky, and Stony close behind, their heels clumping hollowly on the boardwalks in the silent town. A single light burned in the Silver Spur which proved, when they entered, to be a typical cow-town type saloon: there was a scarred bar with brass rail along the right side of the low-ceilinged room, with behind the counter a back bar and flyspecked mirror which reflected but dully the rows of bottles and stacked glasses. A few round-topped board tables and straight-backed chairs were scattered about. A door at the rear was closed. There were pictures of burlesque actresses, race horses, and prize fighters tacked to the walls. Excepting Abe Kincaid, the proprietor of the Silver Spur, a beetle-browed man with a soiled white apron lashed about his bulging waist, Luke Vaughn, standing at the far end of the bar, was the only man in the room. Kincaid glanced up as Yarrow and his companions pushed through the swinging doors.

"Sorry, Matt," Kincaid said. "I was just closing up. Of course, if you and your friends want to take a couple of bottles—"

"We didn't come in for a drink, Abe—" Yarrow commenced.

"Probably," Luke Vaughn cut in sourly, "you're looking for somebody else to frame with a twenty-five dollar fine."

"Now, Luke," Yarrow said soothingly, "no use you holdin' a grudge about that. You know your boys were in the wrong—"

"T'hell I do," Vaughn snorted.

"All right, we'll just disagree and let it go at that," Yarrow said shortly. "Fact is, I come here hoping to find somebody from the Box-V. I suppose you heard there was a man killed at Doc Arden's tonight, Luke."

"Yeah?" Vaughn assumed a surprised look and

Abe Kincaid made the appropriate remarks. Vaughn resumed, "I did hear a couple of shots, but figured somebody was just shooting off steam or something. Didn't pay any attention. Who was killed?"

"One of your men," Yarrow said bluntly. "Jerky Trumble."

"Trumble! Jerky Trumble? I'll be damned! But you're wrong about him being one of my men, Matt. Hell's bells! I fired Jerky nearly three weeks back. Paid him off. Never could get him to stay around the ranch. I don't know where he went, but he was always ridin' off someplace—say, who shot him? Why?"

"You say Trumble wasn't on your pay roll any more?" Yarrow asked skeptically.

"That's what I'm telling you." Vaughn paused. "You look like you don't believe me. Say, what's this all about? I'd like to know."

"I'll ask the questions, Luke," Yarrow said heavily. "Which of your men was in town tonight?"

"Gesis, I don't know—let me see. Owney Powell and Bart Fielding I sent out to the ranch right after the justice fined 'em, this morning. Port Osborn was in for a time, so was Gabe Lindley and Gene Merker. But they left right after supper a short spell. I can't think of anybody else. Say, you're not suspecting any of my boys?"

"Was Tulsa Nash in town?" Yarrow interrupted. "He never seems to get very far from you."

"Tulsa? Oh, sure, Tulsa was in for a spell. He left

142

town quite a while back." Vaughn turned to Abe Kincaid. "Must have been three-four hours ago Tulsa left, wa'n't it, Abe?" The two exchanged meaning glances.

"Just about," Kincaid grunted.

Vaughn shrugged his shoulders. "Y'see how it is, Matt. I can't think of any reason why you should be checking on my outfit. Trumble was never any good, but he didn't have any enemies among my boys. I should think"—casting a meaning glance at the Three Mesquiteers—"you'd be checking around to see if any strangers hit Torvo recent."

"I get your meaning exactly, Luke," Yarrow said heavily. He jerked one thumb in the direction of Tucson and his pardners. "These are friends of mine named Smith, Joslin, and Brooke. Meet Luke Vaughn."

Vaughn and Tucson and his companions exchanged cool nods. Tucson took up the conversation. "I examined the ground some in the vicinity of the window where Trumble was killed. I found something I figure the killer dropped, while he was waiting for a chance to shoot. Maybe he lost it by accident, maybe he just tossed it away in a hurry when his chance came—"

"What did you find, Smith?" Vaughn asked, trying to keep the eagerness from his tones.

Tucson drew from his pocket a partially consumed plug of chewing tobacco. "This"—extending the section of plug for Vaughn's inspection. The others gathered close, Yarrow looking at Tucson with new respect.

"Dammit," the sheriff blurted, "I looked over that ground—"

"Don't mean a thing," Vaughn interposed. "There's a hell of a lot of hombres in Torvo use eatin' tobacco."

"But only one man," Tucson pointed out, "would leave teeth marks like this—mighty crooked teeth, looks like. A pair of buck teeth in front; those on either side are slanted in and out or sideways—"

"Tulsa Nash, by God!" Yarrow exclaimed.

"Don't talk like a fool, Matt," Vaughn snapped. "Sure, Tulsa's teeth are crooked as hell, but there's other hombres with crooked teeth."

"It might be a smart idea to fit this plug to Tulsa's teeth," Smoky suggested.

"I agree with that idea." Tucson nodded. He handed the section of tobacco to Yarrow. "You'd better keep this bit of evidence, Sheriff." Yarrow took the plug.

"Even if it was Tulsa's plug," Vaughn persisted, "it's no sign that he did that shooting. You got to have more proof than that. Come to think of it, that's not even Tulsa's brand, if I remember correct. Let me see that plug a second, Matt."

Unsuspecting, the sheriff handed over the plug, without noticing that Vaughn already had his clasp knife out of his pocket and opened. "I'll pry off this tin advertisin' tag in the surface of the plug,"

Vaughn said, indicating the small enameled tin tag stuck into the tobacco, "and show you—"

Too late Tucson put out one hand to stop Vaughn. Vaughn jerked away and in doing so drew the blade of the knife across the teeth marks in the tobacco, destroying, as though through accident, the jagged teeth incisions which might have proved to be important evidence.

"Hey, what you trying to do, Smith?" Vaughn protested, and there was a mocking look in his eyes. "One of us might have been cut."

"Something worse than that is likely to happen to one of us, someday too," Tucson said softly. "You think fast, Mr. Vaughn, awfully fast, but there'll come a time when you won't think fast enough—"

"Dammit, Luke!" Yarrow protested. "You've spoiled the marks on that plug—"

"Not my fault," Vaughn replied, his black eyebrows lifting in a sort of amused protest. "Smith, here, grabbed at my hand and made the knife slip. All I was aiming to do was pry off this tag—see?"—indicating the plug with the tag still intact. "Anyway, I reckon it won't be necessary to pry it off. Anybody can see that this is Red Indian Plug. Tulsa always chews Pine Tree brand—you know, that kind that comes wrapped in tinfoil—"

"Oh hell, give me that tobacco," Yarrow growled.

"Let him keep it, Matt," Tucson said quietly. "We'll get other evidence. Come on, let's get out of here."

Vaughn laughed. "No sense in going away mad, gents. Might be I could persuade Abe to open up his bar so I can buy a drink."

"Sure." Kincaid nodded, a contemptuous look in his eyes. "I'm not in any particular hurry to close up—"

"You see, we can all be friends," Vaughn pursued. "I don't want any hard feelings, and I'd like to know more about Trumble's killing. Just what happened, Matt?"

"You show up at the inquest in the morning," Yarrow said heavily, "and you'll hear the story."

"But you wouldn't make me wait that long, Matt. Just give me the details—"

But he found himself talking to the empty air as the swinging doors banged behind Tucson and his companions. They strode along the sidewalk without speaking for a few minutes. Abruptly, in an angry fit of self-condemnation, Yarrow halted, jerked his hat from his head, and flung it angrily at his feet. "Damn me for a dumb, unthinkin' buzzard," he raged. "Only a fool would have handed that plug over to Vaughn, like I done! Why don't you hombres kick me to hell and back? I got a notion to go back to the Silver Spur and arrest Vaughn for obstructin' justice—"

"Forget it, Matt," Tucson said quietly. "You couldn't prove a thing against Vaughn. He just outfoxed us, that's all, and I'm as much to blame as you for falling in with his plan. He knew I'd make a grab for his knife. I wasn't thinking as fast as I should have, either."

"You couldn't be expected to," Yarrow mourned. "But I know Vaughn, and I should have been on guard."

Stony said, "Tucson is right, though. There's no use crying over spilt milk—not with cows all over the range."

"Whoever heard of a range cow being milked?" Lullaby said.

"There's a heap of calves do a good job at it," Stony retorted.

Smoky laughed and the tension was relieved somewhat. Lullaby went on, "I don't know this Tulsa Nash hombre, but it's my opinion that Vaughn's actions sort of tied the killing to Nash."

"Yes"—Smoky nodded—"but like Tucson says, we can't prove a thing now—"

"I should have my head examined by a doctor," Yarrow groaned. "I ain't no business to be a sheriff—"

"Maybe," Smoky ventured, grinning, "we can both go to work on that cement job."

Yarrow smiled ruefully. "Nope, just me." He stopped, picking up his hat where he'd flung it to the sidewalk, and the men strode on, while the sheriff explained Smoky's allusion to cement to Tucson and his pardners. "So maybe there's two of us bums now," he finished disgustedly.

The others told him to forget it. They reached the

sheriff's office, and Yarrow told Smoky to turn in. "I'm going along home to find my blankets too," he said. "There's nothing more we can do tonight."

"You're right." Tucson nodded. "I'm sort of anxious to learn what those hotel beds are like myself. Just as soon as my pards and I have walked over to your house, with you, Sheriff, we'll be getting into the hay—"

"With me?" Yarrow said quickly. "What's the idea?"

Tucson evaded. "We-ell, we might want to know where we can find you in a hurry sometime, Matt."

"I can't swallow that, Tucson," Yarrow protested.

"All right," Tucson said frankly, "it's like this. You mentioned tonight that trouble was brewing. We've seen some of it. More may be coming to a boil right now. We'd just like to make sure you get home safe tonight so you can be sure of testifying at that coroner's inquest in the morning. That Vaughn hombre is smart, and Lord only knows what he might be cooking up, right this minute. So let's all get to bed—only let's make sure we get there."

"All right, if you want it that way," Yarrow grunted. They said good night to Smoky, who entered the sheriff's office, then sauntered along the board sidewalks, spurs clinking musically in the silent street. Half an hour later Tucson and his pardners were sound asleep in the hotel beds.

12. Inquest

By nine o'clock the following morning the inquest was well under way. Dr. Arden as coroner had quickly rounded up his six-man jury, which viewed the corpse of the unknown man and that of Jerky Trumble at the local undertaker's before adjourning to the big barnlike courthouse on the corner of Main and Deming streets. Previous to this a great many other people, mainly out of curiosity, had visited the undertaker's, and the unknown man was still, so far as Arden knew, unidentified. Once the coroner and his jury arrived at the courthouse, already packed with townspeople, the inquest went quickly forward, after Dr. Arden had thumped his gavel for quiet. He explained that while this inquest was simply an inquiry to determine, if possible, the cause of death and to fix blame, still any and all witnesses called were under oath to speak the truth. Failure to give truthful testimony, if discovered, rendered a witness liable to a charge of perjury, and any such person could be prosecuted under the law.

Sheriff Yarrow, Smoky Jefferson, Tucson, and his pardners had seats near the front of the room. Luke Vaughn, accompanied by some ten or eleven of his Box-V crew—a hard-bitten-looking outfit which was a bit inclined to be noisy—sat at the rear. Arden spoke first, mentioning the bullets that had brought death to the two deceased men, and his findings in that phase of the matter. Then he called Smoky Jefferson to the stand. Smoky related in clear concise sentences how he had been trapped between fires while in Jackpot and the defense he had put up. No, he had no idea why they had opened fire on him; he simply had defended himself to the best of his ability.

"A damn good defense," yelled a man in the audience.

"If that tramp deputy is speakin' truth," one of the Box-V crew cried out.

Arden rapped for silence. "If anyone has any testimony to offer, his time will come," he said sternly. "Otherwise remain silent, or I shall have to ask Sheriff Yarrow to place him in a cell until such time as these proceedings are finished." The crowd fell silent.

Next Tucson Smith and his pardners were called to testify as to their arrival at Jackpot and the scene they had witnessed. Their testimony backed up, to some extent, the story Smoky had told. Sheriff Yarrow's testimony came next; he told how Smoky and Tucson Smith and his pardners arrived in Torvo with the body of the unidentified dead man and the unconscious Jerky Trumble, and of the removal of Trumble to Arden's home. The doctor broke in at this point:

"I feel sure that I could have brought Trumble to recovery, so in considering what happened to him next, it is my opinion that Deputy Jefferson should in no way be held responsible for Trumble's death. I wish to make it clear that this is only my firm belief, and is not intended in any way to sway this jury in its decision." He continued with the story of the shots being fired through his window and what followed. Yarrow, Tucson, Smoky, Lullaby, and Stony gave their stories on this point. Two townsmen were called who testified they had heard a horseman leaving the vicinity of Arden's house, directly after the firing of the shots. Next came the testimony telling of the finding of the partly consumed plug of tobacco and what had happened to it. Several people in the audience directed suspicious glances in Luke Vaughn's direction, and received in reply only broad, confident grins from the Box-V crew.

Luke Vaughn was called to the stand, sworn, and asked by Dr. Arden if he knew either of the dead men on which the inquiry was being held. Vaughn replied casually, "I knew Jerky Trumble. He used to work for me."

"And hasn't recently?" Arden asked.

"I gave him the sack three weeks ago," Vaughn replied.

"Why?" from Arden.

"He was no good," Vaughn replied promptly. "He was always saddling up and riding off—God only knows why. So I let him go."

"Why," Arden asked next, "did you destroy what

151

might have been evidence on that plug of tobacco?"

"That wa'n't my fault," Vaughn said. "I was merely going to pry off the tin tag, when Smith made a grab at my hand and the knife slipped."

"You're sure it didn't slip intentionally?" Arden asked.

"Hell—er—certainly not, Doc. Any fool knows when you—"

"We are not," Arden said testily, "fools conducting this inquiry. You will conduct yourself in a proper manner and speak accordingly."

"All right." Vaughn nodded. "It happened through accident. I'm sorry, but there you are." His manner indicated a "and what do you intend to do about it?" insolence.

Abe Kincaid was called to the witness stand and gave it as his opinion that the destroying of teeth marks on the tobacco plug had been unavoidable. Tulsa Nash was called next.

"Where were you last night?" Arden asked.

"In Torvo, until around eight or a mite after," Nash replied coldly, his thin wiry frame and washy blue eyes expressing an unspoken resentment that he even had to testify as to his whereabouts.

"You left Torvo at that hour?" Arden pursued.

"Ain't I just told you?" Nash sneered. "I was back at the Box-V long before them shots was fired."

"You have proof you arrived at the Box-V within a reasonable time after your departure from town?"

"Ask any of the boys who were there when I

152

arrived—say about nine-thirty or a mite later—ten o'clock at most."

Arden said tartly, "I intend to ask them. Now, Mr. Nash, the bullets I removed from Trumble's head were of .45 caliber. You carry a .45-caliber six-shooter, do you not?"

Nash nodded coolly. "And so does nigh every other man in this section, Doc. So you can't hang nothin' on me there."

Arden considered a moment before shooting his next question: "You chew Red Indian Plug tobacco, don't you?"

Tulsa Nash started to speak, checked his words, and then, half snarling, replied, "I don't fall in that trap neither, Doc. Everybody that knows me knows I chew Pine Tree brand. Hell! I got a plug right in my pocket now." He started to draw out a tinfoil-wrapped rectangle of tobacco, but Arden stopped him and said that was all and that Nash could step down from the stand.

One by one the Box-V men were called. All testified either that Nash had left town around eight or that he had arrived at the Box-V at nine or a little later; one stated he thought it was nearer ten that Nash had arrived at the ranch. As the murder of Jerky Trumble hadn't occurred until around midnight it seemed, on the face of the evidence, that Nash was innocent of the shooting. Apparently Luke Vaughn had his crew well rehearsed in what they were to say, or the Box-V members had had nothing at all to do with Trumble's death. A few other minor witnesses were called to the stand; some witnesses were recalled, but Arden could produce nothing more than the information that had already been given. Arden made one more try: he looked over the group of Box-V hands and then recalled Port Osborn to the stand. Osborn was a sandy-complexioned man with bulging eyes and thick lips. His mouth was always open, as though he existed in a state of continual surprise, and he was probably the least intelligent man in the Box-V outfit.

"Mr. Osborn," Arden commenced quietly—and the "Mr." brought certain snickers of amusement from those who knew Osborn well—"exactly how long have you worked for Luke Vaughn?"

"Uh-uh," Osborn said dumbly, " 'bout two years, I reckon."

"I see." Arden nodded. "What kind of tobacco do you chew, Mr. Osborn?"

"Uh—uh—me? I don't chew no tobacco, Doc."

"You smoke, though?"

"Oh—uh—uh—yeah, I smoke."

"Bull Durham, I expect."

"Oh, sure. I like seegars too, Doc."

"What brand?"

Luke Vaughn was frowning now, wondering what this line of questioning was leading to. The questions had nothing, apparently, to do with the killing of Jerky Trumble.

"What brand, Doc? Uh—uh—any kind what sells for a nickel." Port Osborn cast a rather vapid smile around the room, proud at the importance he thought his testimony was lending the inquiry.

"Well"—Arden smiled friendlily—"a lot of us smoke nickel cigars, and I think you show fine judgment, Mr. Osborn, in not spending more." His voice didn't change but the next question came with disarming suddenness: "Just why was Jerky Trumble killed?"

"Uh—uh—that's easy. They was afeared he'd talk too much—"

"Who was afraid he'd talk too much?" Arden flashed.

"Don't answer, Port, don't answer!" Luke Vaughn shouted from the back of the room. "You don't have to answer that. Doc's trying to incriminate you—"

"And just why doesn't he have to answer?" Arden demanded angrily.

"You're trying to tangle the Box-V in this killing," Vaughn said furiously.

"You'll keep silent or I'll have you placed under arrest," Arden snapped. He turned back to the witness. "Now, Mr. Osborn, just who was it was afraid Trumble would talk too much?"

"Oh—uh—uh—" Osborn looked helplessly toward Vaughn, then back to the doctor. "Uh—I reckon I don't know what you mean, Doc. I—uh—uh—wouldn't know exactly. I reckon I guess he must have had an enemy."

155

Arden tried further questions but could make no headway with Osborn. Finally the witness was dismissed. A few more details were attended to, then the jury retired to reach its verdict. The crowd left the courthouse to gather in small knots along either side of the street. The Box-V men headed in the direction of the Silver Spur Bar, while the sheriff and his deputy, accompanied by Tucson and his pardners, went to Rittenhouse's Sundown Saloon in quest of cold beer.

"Well, Doc Arden made a good try with that Osborn hombre," Stony commented. "Led up to the question real slick like."

Yarrow nodded. "Yes, if Vaughn hadn't butted in we might have learned something. I always figured Port was lacking in some of his wits, and Doc nigh proved it. But I reckon this inquest won't prove anything beyond what we already know."

"They're a right smart outfit, aside from Osborn, though," Tucson said. "Without Vaughn to lead 'em, they might not be so smart, but he's a pretty shrewd customer."

Smoky said, "He certainly had Tulsa Nash fixed with what to say on that plug tobacco question. Doc's trap didn't work there either."

Lullaby put in as he replaced his empty beer glass on the bar, "It might have been smart for us to inquire around town and see what the stores have to say about Nash's habits in plug tobacco."

"I did that this morning," Smoky said. "I reckon

I covered every place in town that handles eating tobacco. Nobody remembered what brand Nash used, though one or two stores thought it was Red Indian Plug. Five stores were sure it was Pine Tree brand—for the simple reason he'd purchased a plug of Pine Tree at each of those five places—this morning."

Tucson whistled softly. "No wonder he had a plug of Pine Tree on him. He was sure prepared. He'd figured—or Vaughn had done the figuring ahead—that somebody might be checking up on him—"

"Five plugs?" Lullaby snorted. "Five! Cripes A'mighty. He must eat tobacco the way that Cactus Man devours sardines. That reminds me: I'm hungry."

"That's nothing unusual," Stony said, then to the barkeeper, "Hank, how about another beer all around?"

They had finished the second round of drinks when a messenger arrived from Dr. Arden with word that the coroner's jury had reached its verdict, so they hastened back to the courthouse, pushing their way through the crowd, now making its way into the big room, where Arden waited.

The verdict, when it came, was about what Arden had expected. That the unknown man had been killed by Deputy Jefferson there was, of course, no doubt; Smoky himself had admitted that. However, the deputy had acted in self-defense and was, therefore, held blameless for the death. The jury awarded Smoky complete exoneration. Jerky Trumble, it was decided, had met his end at the hand of "some person or persons unknown," and Sheriff Yarrow was directed to take the necessary steps to apprehend the murderer, or murderers, when and if discovered. With the verdict in, Dr. Arden thanked the jury and discharged it, and the courthouse emptied swiftly. It was past dinnertime, and Torvo's citizens now hastened about their usual affairs.

Yarrow, Smoky, Tucson, and his pardners paused on the corner a moment to talk over the inquest. It was decided that very little had been accomplished. While they were standing there Smoky glanced across the street just in time to see Jane Yarrow entering the hotel. When next Yarrow turned to speak to Smoky the deputy had vanished.

Ascending the steps leading to the hotel porch, Smoky had crossed the small lobby and entered the dining room of the hotel, where he saw Jane's taffy-colored hair at a table in the far corner. He gave an assumed start of surprise, then hastened toward the girl. "Never dreamed of seeing you in here," Smoky said glibly. He drew out a chair and seated himself across from her. "May I sit here?"

Jane's dark violet eyes surveyed him with some amusement. "Do I have anything to say about it?"

"Far more than you realize," Smoky said fervently. "And of course you'll let me buy your dinner."

"I seem to remember," Jane said, laughing, "that

Uncle Matt told me he gave you a dollar. Or do you intend to charge this to the county under the head of official business?"

"Important business," Smoky corrected her. "As to that dollar—we-ell, I have some of it left, and it just happens I have a little change of my own—"

"I'll bet Uncle Matt didn't know that."

"I'll bet he didn't either." Smoky grinned.

A waitress came and took an order for roast beef, fried potatoes, coffee, and pie. The two chatted while the food was consumed. Smoky asked Jane about her work at the depot. ". . . it's more or less of a fill-in job," Jane explained. "At present I'm taking the place of a man who has been ill. He'll be back in a few days. Meanwhile, the salary comes in convenient to pay my taxes."

"Taxes?"

"On the hotel."

Smoky's eyes widened. "You own this place?"

Jane laughed, shaking her head. "Not a chance. I'm talking of the hotel in Jackpot."

"Cripes! Why . . . what . . . ?"

"I'd better explain, I guess. You see, when the ore petered out over there, people left Jackpot. Buildings were put up for sale at auction. I had some money my mother had left me and on impulse I made a bid for the hotel which brought me the property. The amount was unbelievably low."

"But what the deuce did you want with a hotel in a ghost town?"

159

"Sometimes I'm not sure in my own mind," Jane replied. "But if the mines had come to life again I'd have had a valuable property. I own rangeland just north of Jackpot. There's good grass there and water. Someday there'll be stock raising over there, and Jackpot will live again—" She stopped. "Or will it? I like to think so, anyway. Meanwhile, I pay taxes on the property to hold it. It's foolish, of course—"

"I'm not so sure it is," Smoky said seriously. "When I was over that way it looked like there'd be good grazing in the foothills of the Torvo Mountains."

"You're not the only one thinks that. Two years ago several men talked of starting ranches over that way, then this Glendon gang business cropped up, and most folks feel it's good country to stay away from now. Uncle Matt lost two deputies, my father was found dead. Only yesterday you were shot at—"

"In short," Smoky said, "it's not healthy country over that way."

"That's the general idea." Jane nodded. She took a swallow of coffee. "For a time I had the idea I'd start a ranch of my own over there, but there were difficulties—"

"You needed a man to run the place, of course," Smoky cut in, "one with knowledge of cows and grazing conditions; one who knew how to work herds—"

"Pshaw!" Jane smiled at him. "You seem to think I know nothing of ranch life—"

"I could teach you far more than you ever dreamed," Smoky interrupted. "Before I joined—that is, before I took up a life of roaming, I was probably the best cow hand in my section of the country. There isn't a thing I don't know about cattle."

"Modest, aren't you?" Something akin to a giggle escaped Jane's lips. "And now you're being held down by a job of law enforcing."

"This is only temporary," Smoky said airily. "I always did want a ranch of my own. You and I could really make a go of it—"

"Seems to me you're going rather fast already," Jane commented.

"Strike-while-the-iron's-hot Smoky they call me. When do we start?"

"Just how"—Jane tried to keep her tones severe—"do you figure you and I could run a ranch together?"

"I think we could run it fine together. Of course we'd have to make a visit to the minister first, and there's details like getting a license, and then loading a buckboard with supplies to last us—"

"Your imagination is running away with you, Smoky Jefferson. Let's see, exactly how long have you known me?"

"Forever," Smoky said warmly. "I've seen you in my dreams—hair like soft spun taffy, eyes like violets brushed with stardust—"

161

"Nonsense!" Color crept into Jane's face. "You'd better drink your coffee before it gets cold. Besides, I remember reading words like that in a book. You must have read the same story—"

"I probably wrote it," Smoky chuckled.

"You better stick to your deputy-sheriffing. Do you realize we're the last diners left in here? Everybody's finished and gone—"

The waitress appeared at that moment to ask if they wanted more coffee. Jane said, "I hate to keep you here, Millie—"

"It's all right, Miss Yarrow. I'll have to be here to clean up the other tables anyway. Just you take your time."

More coffee was brought, but now Jane refused to let Smoky return to his former conversation. She asked questions relative to the inquest, which Smoky answered, adding, "You seem interested."

"Naturally I am. I'd like to see the mystery that exists in the vicinity of Jackpot cleared up."

"You're convinced there is a mystery then?"

Jane nodded. "So are a lot of other people. Why have three men been killed over there, and a suicide found? Why were you shot at? I'll bet if Jackpot were in Mesquital County, Uncle Matt would have had an explanation by this time."

"Has he asked the sheriff over there to look into things?"

"Numerous times. But there's been considerable

rustling west of the Torvo Range, and I think the Bandinera sheriff has been kept busy."

Smoky considered, a serious expression on his tanned features. Finally, "I'm wondering if you could be trusted to send a telegram for me?"

"Certainly. When I go back to the depot, you come along—"

"I'd just as soon no one saw me over there, if you'll send it for me—and keep a secret." Jane asked curiously to what secret he referred. Smoky didn't reply at once. Producing a small notebook and stub of lead pencil, he scribbled rapidly for a few moments, tore out a sheet of paper, and passed it to Jane. "I'll be obliged if you'll send this and not mention it to anyone. . . ."

Frowning, Jane scrutinized the written words. "But—but"—raising her eyes to Smoky's—"this doesn't make sense."

"Code rarely does," Smoky replied quietly, "unless you happen to know the code. And I definitely do not want anyone to know I'm in touch with—with the man to whom this telegram's addressed."

"I can take care of it." Jane nodded. She glanced again at the signature to the telegram. "Will he—the man this goes to—know who 'Smoky' is?" The deputy said his friends had known him by that name for a great many years. Jane said, "Apparently you're not the tramp everyone thinks you are."

"Tramp?" Smoky's eyes danced. "That was a

name your uncle and the town tacked on me. Maybe they jumped to conclusions."

"It looks that way. Are you going to let Uncle Matt know?"

Smoky shook his head. "There's always the chance he might, inadvertently, drop something that would be heard by the wrong ears. What he don't know won't hurt him, or anyone else—and now, speaking of that ranch we're going to start—"

"I'd an idea we'd finished speaking of it." Jane smiled. "Besides, I've an important telegram to send off and I must be on my way."

"Don't say 'finished,'" Smoky begged. "'Postponed' is a better word."

"I'll agree to anything, just so we can get out of here—"

"Anything?" Smoky brightened.

"Anything sensible," Jane amended, rising to her feet. Smoky left some money on the table and followed her from the dining room.

They encountered Sheriff Yarrow on the hotel porch as they stepped from the lobby. Jane nodded and continued on her way when Yarrow caught at Smoky's sleeve. "I puzzled over where you'd vanished to," the sheriff growled. "What was you doin' in there?"

"Eating my dinner," Smoky replied meekly.

"With Jane?"

"We each had a dinner of our own—"

"Dammit, you know what I mean." The sheriff

looked his exasperation. "I suppose that was on the county too?"

"Oh no," Smoky said innocently. "She paid for both dinners."

"Bosh!" the sheriff said, and added an oath. "I know that ain't true."

"What did you ask for, then?" And before the sheriff could frame a suitable reply Smoky continued, "Where's Tucson and the others?"

"They drifted over to the Kansas City Restaurant to get their dinners, and I figure to do likewise now that I've located you. I already told them the hotel dining room was just suitable for women and dudes and city folks—"

"Anyway, I ain't a woman," Smoky put in.

"I ain't sure what you are sometimes," Yarrow grunted. "You don't obey orders, you get into trouble—"

"And out."

"Your good luck can't last."

"Never mind, Matt, if things go right I figure to resign someday soon."

"You aimin' to go back to bummin'?"

Smoky shook his head, only half conscious of the sheriff's words, completely lost in a world constructed from his own dreaming. "Nope, I'm getting interested in cattle raising . . . cattle . . . taffy-colored hair and eyes like dusty violets . . . there's good water and feed—"

"What in hell are you talkin' about? You gone

165

haywire?" the sheriff snorted. "Cattle with taffy hair and violet eyes! And rings on their fingers and bells on their toes, I suppose—"

"That's it, a ring!" Smoky exclaimed. "I got to get—" He broke off, his face crimsoning. "What were you saying, Matt?"

"It doesn't make no difference," Yarrow said disgustedly. "You don't pay no attention anyway. I'm going to get a bite. Try to keep out of trouble while you're out of my sight, will you?"

"Sure, Matt. Should I run into any of the Box-V crew, I'll apologize for any wrong thoughts I might have had concernin' 'em, and buy 'em a drink—"

"Not at county expense, you won't," Yarrow said heavily. "And you won't encounter none of the Box-V crowd. Vaughn herded his waddies out of town, a short spell after the inquest was finished. I've got a hunch he wa'n't in a mood to answer any questions that might come up."

"You could be right, Matt." Smoky nodded. "But I'll bet a plugged peso they'll be back just as soon as they've figured out some new brand of deviltry to pull. I've a feeling we should brace ourselves for trouble."

"Humph!" Yarrow grunted. "I can't remember as I ever seen you when you was unbraced."

"Whatever that means," Smoky chuckled as he watched the sheriff striding off in the direction of the Kansas City Restaurant.

13. Bad Medicine

Contrary to Smoky's feelings in the matter, trouble failed to eventuate. The next three days passed with no untoward incidents of any sort. Luke Vaughn was the only member of the Box-V crowd who had come to Torvo, and he had remained only long enough to pick up his mail and some supplies before leaving for his ranch. He had passed Smoky on the street on his way out and had nodded civilly enough. Matt Yarrow occupied himself with clerical duties in his office, and commenced to feel that he was at long last beginning to catch up with his paper work. Jane Yarrow had had the sheriff bring Tucson and his pardners to supper one evening and as a matter of course Smoky had been included in the invitation.

Stony was commencing to chafe at the inactivity, as was Lullaby, though Tucson was inclined to take a more cautious view of matters.

"I've a hunch, pards," Tucson said, "there'll be ruckus aplenty before too long. This is only the calm before the storm breaks."

Smoky had accompanied Tucson and his pardners to Hank Rittenhouse's Sundown Saloon one evening after supper for a cold bottle of beer. The sheriff had promised to join them later, after he had concluded checking over a proof of a reward bill (prepared by the local printer) which was to be distributed in the hope that it would lead to the apprehension of Jerky Trumble's murderer. There'd been a number of customers in the Sundown when they entered, so the men had taken up a position at the far end of the bar where they'd have some degree of privacy.

"Trouble is," Stony was saying, "I never did like calms—before a storm or any other time."

"It's just something you'll have to put up with, Stony," Tucson replied. He glanced meditatively along the bar where the light from the overhead oil lamp shone on the faces of several of Torvo's citizens and a couple of cow hands from the Rafter-H outfit. Tobacco smoke made a floating gray-blue haze through the barroom. Perspiration beaded Hank Rittenhouse's round face as he hustled to meet the demands of thirsty customers. Tucson's attention came back to Stony. "You know," he said, "there's not one dang thing we can do until the other side makes a move, or at least until something gets our interest enough to warrant us moving. So long as the enemy lays low—"

"And the sooner we lay 'em low the better," Lullaby put in.

"—there's very little we can do," Tucson finished.

"Patience is a virtue," Smoky added.

"Cripes! Who wants to be virtuous?" Stony grunted. "I'd like to see some *real* excitement."

"If we move without knowing where we're going," Tucson said, "we might blunder into something we won't like. Maybe that's what the enemy's waiting for. Eventually the other side will get impatient and make a move. That's what we're waiting for."

"And we're not even sure yet who the enemy is," Lullaby said.

"The Jake Glendon gang," Stony said promptly.

Smoky asked, "But who, exactly, is the Jake Glendon gang?"

"I've got a hunch," Stony said, "that you could go to the Box-V and find most of the members—"

"But we've no actual proof of that," Tucson pointed out.

"Look, Tucson," Stony suggested, "why don't we take a ride over toward the Box-V someday? No telling what we might find out—"

He broke off at a low exclamation from Lullaby. Entering through the swinging doors of the Sundown were Luke Vaughn and Tulsa Nash. Apparently the two men had been having a slight disagreement over the quality of liquor served at the Silver Spur Bar. "I tell you, Luke," Nash was saying as they entered, "I'm sick of that hogwash Abe Kincaid slops over his bar. No, I don't give a good goddam if you do own an interest in the Silver Spur. That's all the more reason for you to see he buys good whisky instead of rotgut."

"That's all your imagination, Tulsa," Vaughn said. What else he said was lost to hearing as the two men bellied up to the bar and ordered drinks,

forcing their way roughly between a couple of citizens, entirely disregarding the other men in the
saloon. Tucson surveyed the pair while he sipped
his beer—the bulky-shouldered Vaughn with
heavy black eyebrows and Tulsa Nash, wiry, thin,
with quick nervous movements and shifty, pale
blue eyes. As though realizing he was under
inspection, Nash suddenly turned his head. A slow
angry flush crept into his narrow triangular face as
he spied Tucson and his companions. Almost too
ostentatiously he drew from one pocket a plug of
tobacco, peeled back the tinfoil covering, and took
a bite from the plug. He said something to Vaughn,
who swung around, nodded coolly in Tucson's
direction, and again gave his attention to his drink.

"I wonder," Lullaby said softly, "if I was to yell
'Jake Glendon,' right out loud, if either of those
two would come to attention."

"I doubt it," Smoky said in a low voice. "If either
of 'em is smart enough to be Glendon, he's too
smart to be caught off guard."

"There's something in that—" Tucson commenced, then broke off.

Nash and Vaughn were arguing again: Vaughn
had announced his intention of going to the Silver
Spur Bar, and Nash was refusing to accompany
him. "I like it here," Nash snapped. "Give me
another shot, Hank."

"All right, suit yourself," Vaughn said testily.
"I'll be at the Silver Spur when you get ready to

leave town." He swung away from the bar and an instant later the swinging doors banged behind him.

"I like it here," Nash repeated to the room at large, "and I like the whisky." Picking up the fresh tumbler Rittenhouse had set on the bar, he threw back his head and lifted his drink. The splash at the back of his throat could almost be heard as he emptied the glass at a gulp.

"Like it almost as much as you like Pine Tree chewin', eh, Tulsa?" laughed a man who had been at the coroner's inquest.

Very carefully Tulsa Nash replaced the glass on the bar, then he turned slowly to look at the man who had spoken. He didn't say anything, he just looked the hate that had abruptly possessed his whole being. The man commenced to back away, his face pale, a frightened look in his eyes. "Look here, Tulsa," he quavered, "I didn't mean nothing—"

"Don't pull that gun, Nash!" Moving lightly, swiftly, along the bar, Smoky's left hand closed suddenly over Nash's wrist as the man's fingers closed on the butt of his holstered .45. For a full half minute Nash and Smoky just looked at each other, before Smoky said softly, "I wouldn't want to have to arrest you, Nash."

Nash laughed harshly. "Meanin' there's other ways?"

"One way would be enough," Smoky said quietly.

171

"You think you're man enough?" Nash demanded.

"That's for you to learn," Smoky replied.

Nash relaxed. "All right, Mister Tramp Deputy. We'll let it pass. You can be brave with your friends to back you up. I didn't come here for trouble, but dam'd if I have to listen to a blab-mouth that thinks he's got free to say what he likes to me."

"You might be right on that point." Smoky nodded. He turned to the object of Nash's wrath of a minute before. "You'd better think before you start throwing talk around loose, after this."

"Gesis, I didn't mean a thing," the man protested. "I was just joking—"

"Some men never learn to take a joke, mister," Smoky said easily. "If I was you, I'd go someplace else to do my drinking for the rest of the evening."

"Anything you say." The man turned and hurriedly left the barroom.

Smoky looked at the barkeeper. "Sorry if I'm the cause of you losing some trade, Hank."

Rittenhouse wiped cold perspiration from his brow. "Anything is better than a fight in here, Smoky." He forced a laugh. "Fights is too hard on my mirror."

Nash glared at Smoky. "You orderin' me to leave too?" He asked.

"I'm not ordering anybody to leave," Smoky said quietly. "I just make suggestions. I've not made *that sort* of suggestion to you."

Nash said, "Oh hell," and turned back to the bar. "Give me another drink, Hank."

Smoky rejoined his companions at the far end of the counter. Tucson said, "You handled that right well."

"Just so it was handled, that's the main thing," Smoky replied. "I'm not sure yet it's all finished. And I won't be until Nash leaves." He poured the remainder of beer from his bottle and rolled a cigarette. The others lighted smokes, while they watched Nash farther along the bar. Conversation had started up again and the situation was rapidly returning to normal. Nash was lingering over his drink, gazing moodily into the contents of his glass and now and then taking a small sip. When it was finished he called for another drink, and treated it as he had the previous one.

Smoky said finally, "I wonder why Matt hasn't joined us? He should be here by this time. Maybe somebody dropped into the office to detain him."

"Probably." Tucson nodded.

At that moment Tulsa Nash swung abruptly away from the bar and came swaggering toward the rear of the room, as though he had reached some sudden decision. "You, Smith," he snapped, coming to a stop in front of Tucson, "I want a word with you."

Tucson eyed him steadily a moment. "I've had words with better men than you, Nash"—he smiled—"so let's hear what's on your mind."

"You accused me of killing Jerky Trumble," Nash said angrily.

Tucson shook his head. "You're wrong. I haven't yet. I will, if it will make you feel any better."

"You ain't no proof of that," Nash snarled.

"That's why I haven't accused you."

Nash said, "Christ Jesus! I'm sick of all this talk and hintin' around. I'm askin' you to quit it."

Tucson said, "I don't hint, Nash, when I have anything to say, and I'm repeating, I've not yet accused you of killing Trumble."

Smoky took a step forward, but Tucson raised one hand to detain him. "Let be a minute, Smoky. I want to see what this hombre has to say. Nash, get it off your mind."

Nash glanced defiantly at Lullaby, Smoky, and Stony, then switched his gaze back to Tucson. "I don't want no truck with any deputy sheriff, and there's no reason for him to cut in. My business is with you, Smith. I ain't sayin' you actually accused me, but you claimed it was my plug tobacco you found near Doc Arden's—"

"Wrong again, Nash," Tucson pointed out. "I found the tobacco, and it looked like it was your teeth that made the marks in it—but up to the time I found it I didn't even know a Tulsa Nash existed."

"I think you're a liar," Nash said bluntly.

Tucson's eyes narrowed slightly, though his voice didn't rise above normal. "You've got a gun in your holster," he said. "Do you care to back up that statement?"

Nash shook his head, flinging his arms wide from his body. "You'd like to start something, now, wouldn't you, when you've got your pals and the deputy on your side? Hell, yes, I'll back it up, but not now. My time will come and when it does—"

"Thought you said you were sick of talk," Tucson reminded him. "You seem to be the one making it. Let me warn you, Nash, you're brewing bad medicine."

"All right, I'm brewing bad medicine," Nash flashed. "The sort of bad medicine you won't like."

"Maybe I've got an antidote for your brew." Tucson smiled thinly. "Let me tell you about 'em. They're little lead capsules cased in brass. One dose to the patient usually does the trick, and I find he usually shakes well before taking. They're manufactured for the firm of Samuel Colt and are a well-known cure for what seems to be ailing you. Just say the word and you can try one—"

"Now look here, Smith," Nash blustered, his pale blue eyes baleful, "you can't scare me—"

"I don't stop at scaring." Tucson's voice had gone suddenly stern. "You called me a liar, Nash. Either you retract that or go for your gun."

For just a second Nash hesitated, then he slowly backed away, shaking his head. "Not while you got your pals with you. I don't aim to be ganged up on—"

"So I'm to take it I'm not a liar?" Tucson persisted.

Nash backed another step and then another. Suddenly, without another word he turned and ran from the saloon, the swinging doors banging after him. Tucson laughed softly, eyes still intent on the swinging doors. "I guess I'm not a liar after all," he chuckled.

14. Ranger Man

A long sigh ascended through the barroom. The swinging doors had almost ceased their motion by this time. Lullaby swore angrily. "Dammit, pard," he said, "you should have yanked your iron and had a showdown the minute he called you a liar."

"Under some circumstances I might have"— Tucson nodded—"but I wanted to learn what he was up to. He knows damn well I never accused him of murdering Trumble. I'd like to know what his reason was for saying that. And he wasn't trying to promote a fight. You saw how he acted."

"Maybe he lost his nerve when he saw he was in over his depth," Stony suggested.

"That could be," Tucson admitted thoughtfully.

Hank Rittenhouse clattered four bottles of beer on the bar. "On the house," he announced, removing the stoppers, his hands shaking so he could scarcely hold the bottles. "That's twice it looked like I'd have a shooting in here. I don't like it." He looked resentfully at Smoky. "What kind of a deputy don't act when he sees a fight shaping up? Sure, I know, you acted quick enough before. Why didn't you—"

"I just got too interested," Smoky said sheepishly, "in watching Tucson handle the business. You couldn't ask any more than that, Hank. Cripes! I wasn't even necessary."

"I reckon you are right, Smoky. But if a Box-V man never comes in here again, it will be too soon. Those lowlifes make for trouble." He passed out drinks on the house all along the bar, and the other customers resumed the various subjects that had been occupying them previous to Tulsa Nash's abrupt display of anger and cowardice—if cowardice it really were.

Rittenhouse went along the bar, reaching and turning up the wicks of the three hanging oil lamps suspended above the customers' heads. Tobacco smoke floated lazily in the room, swirling in violent spirals near the swinging doors when customers departed or new drinkers arrived. Four men left the bar after getting a pack of cards from Hank Rittenhouse and settled to a game of seven-up at one of the round wooden tables. Voices drifted in from the doorway now and then as men clumped along the plank sidewalk beyond the entrance. Occasionally the creaking of saddle leather and the clumping of ponies' hoofs were heard from the dusty roadway outside, as some rider passed.

Smoky put down his empty beer glass. "I reckon I'd better drift back to the office and see what's happened to Matt. It might be I could help him on something—"

He abruptly stopped speaking, cocking his head toward the entrance as had everyone else in the Sundown. Some sort of altercation was taking place on the saloon porch, just the other side of the entrance. There were loud voices, one of which belonged to Tulsa Nash, and the sounds of a short sharp struggle. The next instant the swinging doors banged apart and Tulsa Nash appeared, hatless, his shirt collar torn and his knotted neckerchief riding high below one ear. Behind, propelling him forward with a firm hand, was Rafe Chandler, and drawing up in the rear was Sheriff Yarrow. In his right hand Tulsa Nash still clutched his six-shooter.

Smoky moved swiftly forward, one hand covering Nash's gun, keeping the barrel pushed toward the floor. "I'd hate to have that gun go off accidently," he exclaimed.

"It's all right, Smoky," Chandler said. "I don't figure he'll start anything now."

Questions and answers flew back and forth, and through it all was Tulsa Nash's voice proclaiming his innocence of any wrong intent. ". . . and just as Matt and I left the office across the street," Chandler was saying, "I saw this fellow skulking near the doorway, peering over the swinging doors at someone inside, here. He already had his gun out. Has anyone here had any trouble with this man?"

". . . Rafe and I had been chewin' the fat in my office"—Sheriff Yarrow's words were superimposed on Chandler's—"and about the time we left, I see Rafe cross the street like a bat out of hell. Sufferin' rattlers! I hadn't even noticed Nash standin' in the shadow of Hank's porch. Before Nash knew what had happened, Rafe had closed in—"

". . . it certainly looked as though this Nash hombre was set to bushwack somebody in here"— Chandler talking again.

"I tell you you're crazy!" Nash's eyes shifted uneasily from side to side, something venomous in their expression, like those of a cornered rattlesnake. "I wasn't intendin' nothin'. You Border Rangers think you're Gawd A'mighty—"

"We still have authority in this section," Chandler snapped. "When I see a man look like he's intent on murder I aim to stop him. That's all there is to it."

"Aw, hell . . ." Nash slid his gun into its holster. "You're just tryin' to put on a show to make folks think—"

"Has Nash had any trouble in here recently?" Chandler interrupted.

"He and I had a few words a spell back," Tucson said quietly.

Chandler's eyes shifted to Tucson's. Yarrow said, "Rafe, this is Tucson Smith, Lullaby Joslin, and

Stony Brooke." The men shook hands. Yarrow went on, "Rafe Chandler's in the Border Rangers—I should say Captain Rafe Chandler."

"I'd guessed as much"—Tucson nodded—"from the outfit—dark blue corduroys, blue neckerchief, black shirt and flat-topped sombrero. Even over in my country we've heard of the Border Rangers."

"We're able to accomplish some good now and then." Chandler nodded. "And I hope I've maintained our reputation just now. If you had words with Nash, Smith, it may be he was out to take a pot shot at you. That's the way it looks to me. He was sneaking around that entrance, with his gun out—"

"All right, I had my gun out," Nash snarled. "There ain't no law against drawing a gun. I didn't shoot it. Anybody claims I did, don't know what he's talkin' about—"

"A man don't usually pull a gun less'n he intends to use it," Yarrow pointed out heavily.

"In this case I did," Nash said defiantly, "and I wa'n't figuring to use it a-tall. And I wa'n't sneakin' around that entrance, neither—"

"What were you doing, then?" Chandler asked sternly.

"I was comin' here for a drink and to get straightened out with Smith here. We'd had some words, and I got to thinkin' maybe I was wrong. On the way here, walkin' along, I'd taken out my gun, like a feller will sometimes, and was spinnin' it on my finger. Like this, see." He drew the gun, forefinger thrust through the trigger guard, spun the weapon in the air, letting the butt drop into his palm at every third revolution. "What th' hell! You've seen fellers do that hundreds of times—"

"Put the gun away, Nash," Yarrow grunted. "Accidents could still happen." His words had been prompted by the sudden scattering, on the appearance of the gun, of the Sundown's customers, who were gathered about Nash, the Mesquiteers, and their companions.

Nash slid the gun back in his holster. "And that's all there was to it, see? And just as I was about to step in here, Chandler overtakes me from the rear and damn nigh knocked the breath outten me. Natural, I put up a fight. Who wouldn't, bein' took by suprise that way? And natural, I didn't have much chance, bein' outweighed some forty pounds like I was. And that's the whole story. And anybody says different is crazy."

"I still think," Chandler said tersely, "you were out to get Tucson Smith."

"I ain't responsible for what you think," Nash snarled defiantly. "Ain't I said I come here to get things straightened out with him? You just jumped to conclusions."

"Tulsa," Yarrow grunted, "I ought to put you in a cell."

"On what charge?" Nash said swiftly. "You ain't—"

"On suspicion of plannin' murder," Yarrow said. "How you goin' to prove it?"

Yarrow paused and looked helplessly about. Smoky said, "Ranger Chandler's word might go a long way as evidence."

Nash spat, "You still ain't no *proof.* It's all circumstantial evidence. All right, Matt, throw me in your hoosegow. What have you got when I come up before the J.P.? Sure, I might have a fine thrun at me, but is that square? I ain't harmed nobody. Speak truth, now, did you see me in a threatenin' position, like I was goin' to shoot Smith?"

Yarrow swallowed hard. "No, can't say I did. The Sundown porch is in shadow. I don't see how Rafe saw you, exceptin' his eyes is younger then mine."

"There y'are," Nash pointed out triumphantly. "Chandler is your only witness, and it would be his word against mine. But it's up to you, Matt; you're the sheriff."

The helpless look was still in the gaze Yarrow bent on Tucson. Tucson said, "If it's up to me, Matt, I'm making no charges. There's a limit to how long you could keep him locked up, just on suspicion. He'd be bound to get out before long, and if he has any plans against me, he would carry 'em out then."

"But I ain't no plans against you," Nash protested. "Ain't I said I come here to—"

"Oh hell," Yarrow voiced his exasperation, "get out of here, Tulsa, and watch your actions from now on. If you'd practice spinnin' a rope and do some work, instead of twirlin' that hawg leg of yours, you'd be better off. But whatever you spin, you'd better spin it at the Box-V. My patience is growin' damn short."

Nash showed his crooked teeth in a wide grin. "Thought you'd see the sense of it, Matt," he said and, turning, went swiftly from the Sundown.

The customers moved back to the bar. "Never a dull moment in the Sundown," Rittenhouse commented as he started taking orders. The sheriff and Chandler joined Tucson and his friends at the far end of the long counter.

Chandler shook his head. "I'm not sure I can agree with what you did, Matt," he said seriously. "A vicious sidewinder like Nash should be in a cell—or better still, under six feet of desert earth. I still think he was planning to shoot Tucson."

"If that's so," Tucson said, "I owe you my thanks, Captain, for a piece of quick acting."

"That comes under the head of Border Ranger duty, Tucson, and requires no thanks. And just forget my rank; my friends call me Rafe." He paused. "I hadn't even figured to run into any trouble here. I just dropped in to get a change of ponies and pay Smoky for what I borrowed a few days back." He handed Smoky a sack of Bull Durham. "Hear you had a little trouble over in Jackpot that day you met me. Matt's been telling me about it, and what happened after you got to

Torvo. I can't understand it. I've never seen anyone around Jackpot, except that old coot, the Cactus Man, and a prospector passing through now and then. You haven't any idea why those hombres picked you for a target?"

"Not the slightest," Smoky replied, "unless they figured I might stumble on something they didn't want known."

"And what could that be?" Chandler wondered.

"That's exactly what I'd like to find out," Smoky replied.

"From now on you'll stay in this county," Yarrow said, "so there ain't much likelihood you'll learn nothin' more in Jackpot."

"I was afraid of that," Smoky said meekly. "It's bad news; I was getting right interested in Jackpot."

"There's other bad news to think about." Yarrow scowled. "Rafe tells me his headquarters got word of another shipment of dope landin' in Frisco. The authorities captured some dope peddler there, and they grilled him—"

"And learned it came from this part of the country?" Smoky asked.

Yarrow nodded. "But more than that the peddler didn't know—or leastwise didn't say."

"What was it," Tucson asked, "opium?"

The lips above Chandler's sinewy jaw curved in a rueful smile. "Opium." He nodded. "The police in Frisco captured this fellow and over two hundred five-tael cakes of the stuff—"

"Five tails?" Stony asked. "I saw a calf once with two tails, but—"

"You've got the wrong word, Stony," Chandler laughed. "This is spelled t-a-e-l. It's an oriental unit of weight, something over an ounce. You see, the Chinese and other oriental countries have different names for such things—there's the liang, and the catty—"

"That's what Stony was thinking of," Lullaby put in, grinning, "a five-tailed catty, or should I say 'kitty'?"

"Don't let Stony and Lullaby throw you with their tomfoolery, Rafe," Tucson advised. "Best thing is to just ignore 'em. What's a tael of opium worth in our money?"

Chandler considered, his brow wrinkling. "It's difficult to say, definitely. The price varies with the locality and depends on the demand. Say, oh, somewhere from ten to fifteen dollars a tael."

"Roughly, a five-tael cake should bring around sixty or seventy dollars, then," Tucson said. "And two hundred cakes would be worth twelve or thirteen thousand dollars. Whew! There's money in dope."

"That," Chandler commented grimly, "is why it's so difficult to stop the smuggling. There are always men willing to take chances for big money, regardless how much misery they bring to the world."

"Does all the opium come from China?" Smoky asked.

Chandler shook his head. "A lot comes from India, the East Indies, Turkey—wherever poppies will grow. I've a hunch there's a lot of the stuff grown right down in Mexico. The Mexican Government have found some of the fields already, but it's a business that's hard to stamp out. Some peon will start growing the stuff off in a little hidden canyon someplace. A dope agent will come and give him seeds and tell him how to grow the poppies, though he doesn't realize what he's growing. All he knows is that he's raising a crop of pretty flowers that produce seed pods, which the Señor Stranger will pay money for."

"You figure," Tucson asked, "that the opium that is being smuggled through this country is grown in Mexico?"

"That I don't know," Chandler said. "We just know it comes up from Mexico. It may arrive by ship at Baja California, from the Orient."

"I should think," Stony put in, "the Mexican Government could check every ship that arrives."

"That's a bigger job than you think," Chandler pointed out. "All the ships don't go to regular ports. A ship might not even stop. Somebody aboard could throw a supply of opium overboard in a watertight container and float it ashore, or there might be someone in a smaller ship alert for somebody to throw the stuff overboard—"

"I never knew before," Lullaby put in, "that opium was from the seed pods of poppies."

"Opium"—Chandler warmed to the subject—"is made from the sun-dried juice of poppy pods. There's a certain time of year those pods have to be picked. Of course, you probably know opium has to be cooked before it can be smoked. A victim of the habit will pick up a small bit of the opium—it looks like a brownish sort of damp mud when ready for smoking—as I say, the addict picks up some of this sticky brown stuff on the end of a needlelike instrument, and twists it around and round until he gets a small ball, which he cooks over the flame of a peanut-oil lamp, then places on the small hole of his opium pipe and inhales. It only lasts for a few drags, but that's enough. Of course, there are other ways of preparing the stuff for smoking, but that's the common method."

"I've seen hombres that smoked marijuana," Lullaby said. "Is opium anything like that?"

"There's quite a difference in the two," Chandler explained. "In the first place marijuana can be grown most anyplace. It's just a plant from which hemp is made. It's not so habit-forming as opium, but it can sure drive a man to do the most ungodly things. On the other hand, opium just makes a man listless as a rule; he reaches the point where he just loses all ambition. The two drugs act differently, too. Marijuana will dilate an addict's eye pupils; under the influence of opium, the pupils contract—"

Stony broke in to ask, "If opium just causes a

man to lose his ambition, why do folks get so excited about it? Of course, I can understand that it's not good to go shiftless, but—"

"It's not just the opium," Chandler said, "it's the derivatives of opium, morphine and heroin, that create so much trouble. They act completely different on a victim, and he reaches the point where he has to have more and more each day, until he's willing to kill and steal to get the drug—" He broke off suddenly, smiling. "I seem to have got wound up in the subject. I'd better let somebody else talk for a while."

Tucson laughed. "All you've been saying is mighty revealing to us poor ignorant cowpunchers, Rafe. It's been interesting."

"I've talked too much," Chandler said, "when I should be catching up on my sleep. I've got a room at the hotel for the night and I think I'll head there, right now. What's more, I won't need any opium to put me to sleep." He offered to buy a drink all around, which offer was refused with thanks, then said good night and headed for the doorway, tossing back over one shoulder, "Glad to have made your acquaintance, fellows. I'll see you again sometime—only God only knows when."

They watched the swinging doors slowly come to a stop. Yarrow said suddenly, "Dang it, I meant to mention to Rafe our suspicions regarding that suicide."

"What suicide?" Smoky asked. "Oh, you mean that Glendon—if it was Glendon's corpse—that Tucson found."

"Yeah." Yarrow nodded. "He'd be interested in our theory that maybe that wa'n't Glendon a-tall."

"He probably would," Smoky agreed.

"He's one smart hombre, that Ranger man," Yarrow went on. "You should have seen him when he spied Tulsa Nash, waitin' outside that doorway with his gun drawn. Like a cat in his movements, Rafe was. Dammit, maybe I should have put Tulsa in a cell."

"You'd best forget it, Matt," Tucson said. "I'm not worried. In case Nash is looking for trouble, he'll have no trouble finding it." He changed the subject: "Anyway, we're certain of one thing: dope is passing through this country. How does it leave, Matt?"

"That's something a hell of a lot of people would like to know, Tucson."

"It's an interesting subject," Tucson stated meditatively. "I'll have to give it some thought."

15. Tucson's Hunch

It was still early the following morning when Tucson, accompanied by Lullaby and Stony, stepped into the Kansas City Restaurant for breakfast, and found Smoky Jefferson just completing his meal. "I can recommend the pancakes and

189

coffee," Smoky stated, waving a greeting. "Have a seat at the banquet table, gents."

The Mesquiteers found stools at the long counter and gave their orders to the combination waiter and proprietor. Coffee was promptly set before them and they rolled and lighted cigarettes while awaiting the arrival of food. Smoky grinned. "Can't understand anybody getting up this early unless he has a job to do. You must have something in mind."

"I wanted to talk to Matt," Tucson replied.

"He'll be around by eight or so," Smoky said. "I can slip over to his house and get him, if you want."

"Let it go for the moment," Tucson said. "Anything doing around town?"

"Everything quiet," Smoky replied. "Tulsa Nash and Luke Vaughn left for the Box-V around midnight last night. Leastwise, Abe Kincaid claims they started for the Box-V, though I can't say I'd believe Kincaid if he swore to it on a stack of Bibles. You think you're up early. Cripes! When I came in here Captain Chandler was just finishing his breakfast and his horse was waiting outside."

"Where'd he leave for?"

The door banged open and Matt Yarrow stepped into the restaurant. "Couldn't sleep," he grumbled. "Got to dreamin' about tons of dope passin' through my county. Figured I might just as well get out as to lay there, wide awake, thinkin' about what

I'd been dreamin'. I'll swear, this dope business is wearin' me down."

"Early as we are," Lullaby put in, "Smoky was just remarking that Chandler had already hit the trail. I'd just asked where he'd headed for when you came in."

"Never no tellin' where Rafe is operatin'," Yarrow grunted, sliding his haunches across a stool next to Tucson. "He's ridin' like a madman, day and night, hopin' to find some clue, or to run across somebody smugglin'." He stopped to give an order to the counterman.

Tucson said, "Matt, we know the dope is smuggled into this county. Now how does it get out?"

"You tell me and I'll tell you," Yarrow grumbled.

Platters of food were placed on the counter and the men commenced to eat. Nothing more was said until they'd all finished and were standing on the sidewalk before the restaurant. In the east the sun was just edging above the horizon of low hills. Tucson said, "Matt, could that dope be shipped on the T. N. & A. S. from Torvo?"

"Don't know how it could be," the sheriff said. "I thought of that too. I've even had freight packages inspected, and got myself in bad because I held up the shipping."

"Does the Box-V do much shipping out of packages?"

Yarrow shook his head. "They receive freight shipments now and again—saddles, maybe some blankets—I remember once they got a buckboard by freight."

"That's not what I mean. You don't know of 'em shipping anything?"

"Not a damn thing I can think of."

"Somehow," Tucson said, "I've a hunch Jackpot has something to do with the smuggling. What's the first stop the T. N. & A. S. train makes after it leaves here, headed west?"

Yarrow's eyes widened. "Hell, the next town it stops at is Corona del Monte, way over other side of the Torvo Range."

"What sort of town is Corona del Monte?"

"'Bout the size of Torvo; cow town. More ranches over that way than around here. It's the county seat of Bandinera County."

"And there's no stops between the two towns?"

"Not one." Yarrow hesitated. "We-ell, wait a minute. There's Cyclone, but you can't rightly call that a regular stop. It's a flag station, I reckon—"

"Where's Cyclone?"

"Over in the foothills of the Torvo Range. Like I say, it's more or less a flag station. Trains heading west stop at the water tank in Cyclone to take on water before startin' the climb over Escarpado Pass. The eastbound trains will stop on signal, if anybody over that way was ever there to get on, but I reckon there ain't. Nope, Cyclone ain't what you could call a town."

Tucson considered. "I'm getting interested in

Jackpot. I think it might be a good idea to ride over that way and look around."

"At least we'd be on the move," Stony said. "That's better than just loafing away our time in Torvo."

"Suits me." Lullaby nodded. "I'll get some grub to take along." He vanished into the restaurant.

"I'd better get my horse too and go with—" Smoky commenced.

"You'll do nothin' of the sort," Yarrow said tartly. "That's Bandinera County and out of our jurisdiction. How many times I got to tell you that, Smoky?"

"The first time was enough, but I didn't think there was any harm in trying." Smoky turned to Tucson. "Take a good look at the hotel over there, Tucson—"

"Now why," Yarrow demanded, "should Tucson be interested in that ramshackle—"

"I might be interested in it myself, someday," Smoky said placidly. "Jane is still paying taxes on it, and some other land, near Jackpot."

"Seems to me," Yarrow grunted, "you know a heap about Jane and her doin's. Probably been tellin' you she hopes to start a cow outfit over that way sometime."

"Now you mention it," Smoky said casually, "I believe there was something said to that effect."

"I don't know why that's any of your business," Yarrow snapped.

"It ain't my business," Smoky replied, and added under his breath: "yet."

Ten minutes later the Mesquiteers had procured their horses from the Lone Star Livery Stable, saddled up, and were on their way out of Torvo. Smoky stood on the sidewalk, looking wistfully after them. Yarrow darted a penetrating look at his deputy. "If I'd knowed you was goin' to take it that hard," he relented, "I might've busted a rule and let you go with them."

"I could catch up in nothin' flat," Smoky said eagerly.

Yarrow shook his head. "You'd best stay here. I happen to know Jane is expectin' you to eat with us tonight—though Gawd knows why I should feed you, when the county stands that expense. There ain't never no tellin', though, what a woman will get in her mind. I give up tryin' to figure her out long ago."

"And I'm just starting." Smoky grinned. "Someday I'll bet you and I will have something in common."

It was nearly noon by the time Tucson and his pardners approached Jackpot. They hadn't pushed the horses hard; already the sandwiches Lullaby had brought had vanished. Even now Lullaby and Stony were arguing the matter of food and drink and any other topic which entered their heads. Tucson seemed lost in thought, and had said but little. The horses picked their way past clumps of prickly pear, mesquite, and soapweed. Overhead, fleecy wisps of clouds formed white patterns against the turquoise sky as they scudded swiftly before the hot wind lifting across the range. Before long the riders came within view of the first shacks of Jackpot with, towering beyond, the high rugged peaks of the Torvo Mountains, now sharply etched against the blue in the dazzling noon sunlight.

As Tucson and his pardners entered the curving street between the deserted buildings they became sharply alert for the first hostile shot or movement, but the street seemed dead, lifeless, the eerie silence pierced only by wind whistling between buildings and brushing the stunted sagebrush where it grew between the ruts of the dusty thoroughfare. They rode straight to the watering trough, past the Cactus Man's place with its closed door, and commenced to pump water. Once men and beasts had slaked their thirsts, Lullaby said, "What next?"

"I can't say I'm certain what I'm looking for," Tucson said. "Smoky asked us to take a look at the hotel. We might as well, I suppose, so we can tell him it's still standing."

They left the horses at the trough and walked along the rickety sidewalk with its broken boards. Occasionally a horned toad darted from beneath their feet to disappear between wide cracks in the walk. At one point a gila monster, sunning its beaded orange-and-black length at the edge of the sidewalk, moved sluggishly away at the men's approach, its fat stubby tail leaving a crooked trail in the sand. Stony kicked a small bit of rock toward the reptile, which immediately stopped, raised the forepart of its vividly colored body on its short legs, and began to emit hissing sounds, its ugly jaw snapping venomously the while.

"If he was thinner," Stony commented, "that lizard would remind me of Tulsa Nash."

"You think those gilas are more poisonous than rattlers?" Lullaby asked.

"I don't reckon so," Stony replied. "I've heard of folks taming 'em for pets, and I never heard of no man keeping a rattler for a pet. Still, I wouldn't want to get bit by one. They make a heap nastier wound than a rattler."

They went on, arriving before the brick hotel. The boards of the steps sagged as they approached to the porch and thence through the wide-open doorway to what had once been the hotel lobby. The floor was covered with dust, and while there were several footprints nothing could be made of them, nor was there any way of telling how long ago they'd been made. A great deal of broken furniture lay about. At the right, as they entered, was a short reception desk standing chest-high. An ancient ledger with rumpled leaves lay face down, and near by a faded stain on the wood surface of the desk showed where a bottle of ink had been tipped over. The bottle still lay on its side, now forming a cobwebby home for a nest of spiders.

Stony stepped quickly behind the desk. "Good day, gentlemen. I can give you a room and bawth."

"You can't give me any bath," Lullaby said. "I'll take my own, and I don't know where you got one to give anyway. You never had one. That's why I always give *you* plenty room."

"Is that so," Stony sneered. "You wouldn't be taking that attitude if I'd showed you the way to the dining room."

"Can I help it if I'm always hungry?" Lullaby complained. "I wonder what sort of dining room they had here?"

He and Stony passed through a doorway in a partitioned wall, while Tucson ascended a creaking stairway to the second floor. Ten minutes later they met again in the lobby. "Broken dishes in the dining room and a broken mirror in the bar," Stony lamented. "What did you see upstairs, pard?"

"A lot of dusty bedrooms, broken-down beds, and rusty springs. Rats living in rotting mattresses," Tucson replied.

"I'll bet this hotel is on the downgrade," Lullaby said seriously. "No wonder they don't get any business—"

"Listen!" Tucson said sharply. They listened. Nothing could be heard but the wind blowing through the street.

"What did you hear?" Lullaby asked.

"I don't know." Tucson frowned. "Sounded like a boot scraping against wood or something. Reckon I'm wrong. Probably a rat moving through the woodwork."

"Just the same," Stony said, "there's something queer about this place. I got a feeling like somebody was watching us all the time."

"Well, there's nobody here, anyway," Lullaby replied. "We've been through this dilapidated hostelry from top to bottom. What say we get out?"

They emerged onto the street once more. Everything looked as it had before they'd entered the hotel. The sun blazed down as hot as ever, making black shadows between buildings; the wind raised a small twirling dust devil at one far end of the street. And over all was the same eerie atmosphere of desolation and decay. Tucson said, "Let's go visit the Cactus Man."

They crossed the roadway to the weathered gray shack with its false front and sun-bleached sign which showed the place had once housed the Gotham Chop House. A blanket hung over the paneless front window on one side of the door. The other window had been boarded up. The door stood slightly ajar, but this time Tucson took the precaution of knocking. There was no reply from within. Tucson cautiously pushed open the door after knocking a second time. The door creaked on rusty hinges as it swung back. Tucson glanced quickly toward the bunk at his right. It was empty, though a couple of rumpled blankets lay at one end. "Reckon old Wyatt is out digging cactus," Tucson commented.

Lullaby and Stony followed him through the open rear doorway and stepped into a small corral, where two mangy mules slumped listlessly against one side of the bars. There was a barred opening at the back of the corral, and beyond stood a light wagon, its oaken tongue resting on the sandy earth. Tucson stepped outside the corral and looked over the earth. "I'd say he's had this wagon out fairly recent, judging from the sign on the ground. The ruts haven't sanded over yet." He returned to the corral and replaced the bars.

"Probably why those mules don't show more life," Stony observed. "Likely Wyatt's been drivin' 'em to death." The mules surveyed the men idly and switched lazy tails at the buzzing flies.

"But where's Wyatt?" Lullaby wanted to know. "If his mules is here, he can't be out digging cactus."

"There's enough cactus growing around so maybe it's not necessary to go far," Stony said. "Maybe he didn't take the mules."

"There's his spade and pick leaning against the wall," Tucson pointed out. "So maybe this isn't his day for digging."

Lullaby chuckled. "Might be we'd find him around town in one of the bars."

They re-entered the building and looked around. "One thing's certain," Tucson observed. "He's got rid of most of his cactus plants." There were no barrel cacti at all in sight. Three of the long slender cereus variety stood against the wall, their spreading roots, caked with clinging earth, resting on the littered floor. "Even those plants he told me were diseased, the ones he'd been gouging with a knife, are missing."

"Maybe he's already took them out and replanted 'em," Stony suggested. "Might be that's where he is now."

"Hell's bells," Tucson said. "He wouldn't have to take them far away, and I can't imagine him packing 'em in his arms."

"All I got to say," Lullaby commented, "is an awful lot of those plants must have been diseased." His pointing finger indicated various pale green pulpy masses scattered about the vicinity of the bench standing against the wall. "If that stuff isn't cactus innards he's been digging out, I miss my guess. I should think he'd move to some spot where the cactus is healthier."

Tucson frowned. "It's dang queer," he said slowly. "I—" A sudden exclamation from Lullaby interrupted the words. Tucson said, "What's the matter?"

"Here's something queerer." Lullaby pointed to the shelves of canned food built against the opposite wall. "Remember when we were here the other day, and I wanted sardines, and he wouldn't give me any?" Tucson and Stony said they remembered.

"Look," Lullaby went on. "He had more sardines than any other canned food—dozens of cans. Now where are they?" He strode resentfully to the shelves and picked up two small flat cans. "Only two cans left."

"Talk about opium addicts," Stony said. "The Cactus Man must be a sardine fiend. Probably gets a fit of the shakes and wants to murder folks if he don't have his sardines regular. Goes all a-tremble if he don't get 'em every meal."

"But how could a man eat so many sardines?" Tucson began.

"Maybe he had company for supper one night," Lullaby suggested.

"And fed 'em nothing but sardines, I suppose," Stony said scornfully.

"Why not?" from Lullaby. "I like sardines."

"Faugh!" Stony said disgustedly. "Sardines! Fishes' puppies!"

"Say"—Lullaby looked excited—"we were out back. I didn't see a lot of sardine cans layin' around, did you?"

"That is a finny situation," Stony snickered.

Lullaby looked his reproach and turned his attention to Tucson. "I remember seeing peach cans and tomato cans and bean cans—but no sardine cans. What do you suppose Wyatt done with those empty cans?"

"Probably uses 'em to plant diseased cactus in," Stony jeered.

"That's out," Tucson said. "All those cactus I saw were at least a foot through—the barrel cactus, that is."

Lullaby still held in his hand the two cans of sardines he'd taken from the shelf. He studied the red-and-yellow label on the cans, which was printed in Spanish, and slowly translated his findings: "'Atzec Brand Sardines,'" he read. "'Packed in Olive Oil.'" There was further information on the face of the can, stating that the sardines had been netted off the coast of Baja California and that they had been packed in Mexico, though the exact location wasn't given.

"I sure wish," Lullaby said slowly, "that I had some soda crackers and beer to go with these."

"Hey, those aren't your cans," Stony protested.

"I'm one of those sardine addicts you mentioned," Lullaby grinned. "I just don't have any will power where sardines are concerned."

"But that's stealing," Stony said indignantly.

Lullaby shook his head and took from his pocket a silver dollar, which he placed on the canned-goods shelf. "There"—virtuously—"I'm paying for the cans. More than they're worth."

"You'd best not let old Wyatt come in and catch you," Tucson chuckled.

"If he wants to catch me he'll have to come home awfully soon." Slipping one can into a pocket "for a snack later on," Lullaby drew from another pocket his clasp knife and opened a blade.

Inserting the point of the knife into the remaining can, he quickly cut around the edge and bent back the top. Oil dripped from the can, within which lay the tightly packed, neatly arrayed forms of the small fish. Employing the knife blade to fork one of the sardines into his mouth, Lullaby chewed with evident relish and extended the can to his pardners, who refused.

"You're not going to make me party to your crimes," Stony said.

Lullaby shrugged off their pious admonitions and continued eating until the can was empty. Then he went to the rear doorway and sent it sailing over the top bars of the corral to drop from view in a clump of sagebrush. Tucson said, "Now that we've violated the Cactus Man's hospitality, I figure we'd better get out before he comes in and murders Lullaby. There's nothing outrages a man like stealing his sardines."

"Aw-w," Lullaby protested, "you saw me leave money to pay for those two cans. Maybe it will teach him to be more generous. If he'd give things, he wouldn't have 'em taken."

They hesitated a few minutes longer, looking over the room. There were partly built crates standing about, built from lumber ripped from Jackpot's deserted buildings. On the bench were several lengths of coiled wire, a number of burlap sacks, and a quantity of long thin nails. "Dam'd if this isn't the dirtiest place I ever saw," Tucson commented. "I'll bet he don't sweep it out once a year. C'mon, let's get out of here before Lullaby gets ravenous again and attacks some more canned goods."

They left the building, closing the door behind them, and headed back toward the trough where they'd left the horses. "I still got a feeling we're being spied on," Stony said as they strode along the broken sidewalk.

"It's your imagination," Lullaby said. "All ghost towns have this same sort of uncanny air about 'em. You feel you should be seeing people where there's a town, and when you don't, you get so you imagine everybody's inside the houses."

"The Cactus Man still isn't accounted for," Tucson said. "Maybe he's dodging in and out of these empty buildings, keeping an eye on us."

"I doubt that," Lullaby said. "An ornery old cuss like Wyatt would have been on our necks the minute he saw us go in his place."

They reached the horses and climbed into saddles. Stony asked, "Where now?"

"My hunch is still working," Tucson replied, "though I don't know why. But it keeps suggesting that we take a look at Cyclone."

"Shucks, Cyclone's just a water tank," Stony protested.

"If it was anything stronger than water, you'd be halfway there by this time," Lullaby sneered.

And that started another argument that was going strong even before the riders loped their ponies out of the west end of Jackpot, dust from the weed-grown street boiling up from beneath the animals' flying hoofs.

16. Cyclone

By two-thirty in the afternoon they found themselves getting into the foothills of the Torvo Mountains. Both grass and mesquite grew higher here; occasionally they saw low piñons and small scrub oak trees. There were canyons choked with catclaw and manzanita. Now and then yuccas—the Lord's candles of Mexico—would be seen, their withered stalks of last spring's blossoms still intact, though now the delicate white flowers had turned brown and sere. Before long they spied sun-light glistening on the twin rails of the T. N. & A. S. Railroad and followed the tracks until, rounding the rocky shoulder of a high hill where dynamite blasting had blazed a path for progress, a strong wind immediately struck them with considerable force as it flowed down through the high mountain pass and whipped violently the manes and tails of the ponies bracing themselves against the strength of the blast. Lullaby clutched at his sombrero. "Must be we're nearing Cyclone," he cried. Tucson nodded and raised one arm to point to the water tank a hundred yards beyond.

The wind eased somewhat as the ponies picked their path along the rock-littered railroad right of way. On either side rose a jagged escarpment of reddish granite spotted here and there with straggling bits of plant life which had fastened its roots among cracks. Within a few minutes the riders were passing almost beneath the reddish-brown water tank on its trestlelike support. Water dripped from the tank's sides, furnishing a certain nourishment to the wiry grass and sagebrush that had sprung up there. A short distance away stood a blocky building of rock and adobe constructure, across the front of which was painted in the same reddish-brown paint: CYCLONE.

"Some depot," Lullaby commented as he and his pardners dismounted before the building.

"It ain't intended to be no depot," came a cheerful voice from beyond the open doorway, "but come right in anyway, gents."

They passed inside and found the interior pleasant after the sunlight and hot wind. There was a cot, table, and chairs at one side. Along the back wall was a shelf holding various canned and packaged foods; at the right, as they entered, was a short bar constructed from two planks resting on a pair of barrels, and sitting on the bar was a smiling middle-aged man with a bald head and spectacles resting on the end of his long nose. "It's sure welcome to see somebody," the man said. "You want I should flag down the Limited for you?"

Tucson shook his head. "No, we were just passing through and stopped off to rest our saddles."

"That's to the good. The engineer of the Limited allus gets riled when I flag him. He likes to ball the jack when he hits that east downgrade. I don't keep much of a stock here, but you're welcome to what I can serve you." The man slid down from the top of his bar.

Tucson and his pardners seated themselves at the table and learned that the bottled beer was warm, the crackers and cookies stale, and the cheese dried out. Some corned beef from a can augmented the meal. The stationman, proprietor, whatever he was, also seated himself at the table. "Gawd, it's good to see a human face," he stated. "I'm Joe Grimse." The Mesquiteers gave their names, and hands were gravely shaken. "This ain't a regular bar and restaurant," Grimse said apologetically, "or I'd be able to offer somethin' better. It's my job to stay here and tend that tank. Now and again somebody comes around that wants to get on a train and I flag it down. I put in a few supplies for them that wants nourishment, but it don't pay to carry much of a stock. Course, if you figger to stay to supper, I can open a lot of different cans—"

"Now there's the real symbol of civilization—the can opener," Lullaby commented.

"You should know," Stony jeered. "Talk about castin' the first stone! People what live in glass houses—" He paused. "I can't seem to remember the rest of it. What shouldn't people do that live in glass houses?"

"Change their underwear in the daylight?" Lullaby suggested hopefully, stuffing into his mouth a chunk of cheese that any self-respecting mouse would have turned up its nose at. He immediately withdrew it and muttered, "Speaking of rocks—" He broke off. "Say, Grimse, you got any sardines?"

"You got me there, pardner. I don't know as I ever before had any call for sardines."

"There's a good brand on the market, packed down in Mexico, called Atzec Sardines."

Grimse shook his head. "Only thing I get, packed in Mexico, is prickly-pear pads. You know, they slice 'em in long strips and when you fix 'em with salt and pepper and butter, they taste a heap like pole beans."

"I've heard of folks eating those prickly-pear cactus pads," Tucson nodded.

"I don't reckon I could go for eating cactus," Stony said.

"It don't sound natural," Grimse agreed. "But I can tell you somethin' crazier than that. Imagine folks growin' cactus in gardens, city gardens and parks and such. F'r'fact!"

"Who does that?" Tucson asked in disbelieving tones.

"I know you won't believe it, but it's so," Grimse insisted. "Just plain everyday little old barrel cactus like grows wild all over. Can you imagine folks payin' money for such?"

"You mean," Stony asked curiously, "that somebody digs up them barrel cactus and ships 'em off to cities?"

"Hope I may die if I ain't speakin' truth. With one exception, I don't see the same face on this job twice in six months. But that exception is an old coot that lives a spell from here"—Grimse jerked one thumb over his shoulder in a vague indication of distance—"in a ghost town named Jackpot. Ornery old cuss, he is. Wyatt's his moniker. Well, this Wyatt, you'd never in the world guess how he makes a livin'."

"Something to do with cactus, I suppose," Tucson said.

The garrulous Grimse looked disappointed. "How'd you guess? Well, it's so. He digs up them barrel cactuses, some of 'em more'n a foot in diameter, wraps 'em in burlap, nails 'em into a crate, then brings 'em over here in his wagon so's I can flag down the freight trains when they come through. Many a crate I've helped him lift into a boxcar. He always ships collect, of course."

"Where do you suppose they go?" Tucson asked idly.

"Like I said, to parks and such. I hear they grow 'em in big glass houses, where the climate's cold, and city folks come to look at 'em. Craziest thing I ever hear of."

"Do you mean," Tucson asked, "that he addresses these crates to people in all different cities?"

Grimse shook his head. "There's just two cities they go to," he replied. "San Francisco and Denver, Colorado."

Tucson shook his head. "Imagine it! You think of folks in those towns as being smart. Now who do you suppose, in cities like those, would be paying out hard-earned cash for cactus plants?"

"It's plumb diff'cult to believe, aint it?" Grimse said. "But it's the truth. Big companies buy 'em. One of 'em is called the Dagert Plant Nursery. The other in Denver is the Janus Horticulture Company."

"It's amazing," Tucson said, repeating, "the Dagert Plant Nursery of Frisco, and the Janus Horticulture Company of Denver, eh? I don't see how you remember names like that, Mr. Grimse."

"I don't forget things easy." Grimse added modestly, "Course, it ain't no credit to me; I been seein' those two addresses at least once a month for over two years now."

"I suppose not," Tucson said casually. "I reckon the little plants that are sent out go to the nursery company to raise, eh? Seems like it would be up to a nursery to grow big ones from little ones."

Grimse shook his head. "No, I don't think old Wyatt ever sends out any small plants. Now you mention it, you'd think folks crazy enough to want to see cactus in a garden would likewise want to see what they look like when little. But Wyatt always sends the big barrel type, some of 'em a foot through and three feet high. And then he sends the other kind of barrels too—them with the fishhook spines that are shaped like a ball, ten or fifteen inches through and about the same high."

"I got stuck on one of them fishhook cactus once," Lullaby put in. "You want to be careful, Grimse, next time you help Wyatt put his shipment aboard a freight car."

"No need to be careful," Grimse said. "Wyatt always wraps 'em in burlap and then wires 'em secure to the crate, so they don't jounce around."

"Don't he ever send any yucca or ocotillo or dasylirions?" Stony asked.

"Nope. Reckon folks ain't interested in them. But Wyatt told me there was a prime market for the barrel cactus he sends out."

"When did he send off his last shipment?" Tucson asked.

"He was just here yesterday, with some crates to go to the Denver Company. We put 'em aboard the four-ten freight when it rolled through."

"It must be getting around that time now, isn't it?" Tucson asked.

Grimse nodded. "If you gents will stay to supper I can fix you a real bang-up meal."

"Thanks just the same, Mr. Grimse. I think we'd better be pushing along. It's been nice to make

211

your acquaintance." He paid for the food and beer they'd consumed, then the Mesquiteers left the building and got into saddles. They rode off, with the hot wind pushing at their backs and the memory of Joe Grimse standing in his doorway and looking wistfully after them.

None of the riders spoke until they'd rounded the blasted hill shoulder and were once more out of the wind.

"It's my belief that following a hunch is sure to pay off," Tucson opened the conversation as the three jogged their ponies through the high foothill grass. "I think we've uncovered something, pards."

"It sure looks that way." Stony nodded. "The Cactus Man never ships out any small cactus plants. Always the big barrel type."

"And the first time we were at his place he was hollowing them out," Lullaby remembered. "That dang old liar! Telling us he was just cutting out the diseased portions, so he could plant 'em again. If we'd come a day later he'd probably had them all hollowed out. Once he's put the stuff inside of 'em he wires 'em together again—"

"Wait," Tucson said. "You remember those long thin nails we saw at his place. I had a feeling then they wouldn't do for buildin' crates."

"What would he use 'em for?" Stony asked.

"I'm not sure, but I figure he could use 'em to hold the bottoms on the hollowed cactus, after he'd put the dope inside 'em. Then he wraps 'em in burlap and wires 'em secure inside his crates. Anyway, we know how he gets dope out of this section. Those long slim cereus cactus we saw at his place are just kept there for show. I thought they looked older, drier, than the other cactus we saw that first day."

They paused a moment, listening to the long-drawn-out whistle of a locomotive, some distance to their rear, as the four-ten freight rushed down the east grade from the mountain pass.

"I reckon we'd best push on to Torvo as fast as we can," Tucson said. "We can have Sheriff Yarrow send out telegrams to the proper authorities, tellin' 'em to seize any shipments of cactus that arrive at the Dagert Plant Nursery, in Frisco, and the Janus Horticulture Company at Denver."

"It might be a good idea, too," Stony suggested, "to advise the T. N. & A. S. to refuse to accept any more shipments of cactus at Cyclone."

"Think that might make old Wyatt suspicious?" Lullaby queried.

"I don't know as it makes much difference," Tucson said. "For that matter, it's not likely he'll be making any shipments again for a couple of weeks, at least. He's got to go out now and dig up some more cactus. We haven't proof, of course, but I'm right sure we've figured out his part of the business. The only thing we don't know is just how the dope is brought to Jackpot."

"That's something we'll learn before we're

213

through with this game," Lullaby said confidently.

Conversation lagged as they put spurs to their ponies and pushed steadily on toward Torvo. The sun swung west, touched the peaks of the Torvos with golden flame, then dipped swiftly out of sight, as night spread from the east. It was almost dark and the way had flattened out considerably when they again pulled the ponies to a walk to rest them.

"Do you reckon," Stony suggested, "that we should swing over to Jackpot and grab the Cactus Man right now? We could take him to Torvo and—"

"I don't think so," Tucson said slowly. "In the first place he might not be there, and we'd just be wasting time getting our news to Sheriff Yarrow. In the second place we haven't any authority to make arrests—though that wouldn't bother me if I wanted to throw a loop on old Wyatt. But I think we'd better tell Yarrow what we know and then let him act as he sees fit. He's so anxious to beat the Border Rangers to making an arrest and settling the business, that I'd sort of like to see him get the credit."

"I guess that's the best plan," Stony agreed. "Boy! When he hears our story it will certainly give him food for thought—"

"I'm hungry," Lullaby cut in.

"I should have known better than to mention food," Stony said disgustedly.

"Can't blame a man for getting hungry, can

you?" Lullaby said indignantly. "We haven't had any real food since breakfast, and that stuff that Grimse fed us wa'n't what you'd call palatable—"

"Cripes!" Stony said. "What do you call real food? You certainly acted like those sardines you ate at the Cactus Man's were palatable."

"Sardines!" A slow grin spread over Lullaby's face. "I'd plumb forgot I stuck that second can in my pocket. You see, my instinct just naturally provides for these little snacks that's so needful to a healthy growing body like mine. I might even share 'em with you hombres."

He produced the tin of sardines from his pocket, then drew out his clasp knife and opened it.

"You'd best be careful how that oil drips," Stony warned hastily as Lullaby stuck the point of his blade into the can. "You get that fish-smelling oil on your saddle or your pants, and you'll stink up the atmosphere even worse than you do now."

Lullaby smiled placidly. "Was I the type that angered easy, I'd say you was trying to insult me." He ran his blade quickly round the edge of the can. "At that, I think I'll demand that you retract that slanderous statement."

"All right, I'll retract," Stony snickered. "I was wrong. Where you're concerned, maybe that fishy oil will act as a perfume."

"Aw-w, you go to hell," Lullaby said goodnaturedly. "Anyway, this can don't drip oil." He peeled back the top of the tin and exposed the contents. Then his face fell. "Say-y-y, what the hell!" he exclaimed, gazing in perplexity at the can.

Tucson asked, "What's the matter?"

"Somebody's filled this can with tar," Lullaby grumbled. "No, it ain't black enough for tar—more like a stick brown adobe mud. If this is a joke, and me hungry—"

He broke off as Tucson reached over to take the can from him. Their eyes met in sudden comprehension. Tucson frowned, and touched one finger to the dampish brown mess that filled the can. Stony craned his neck to see what was going on, and swore suddenly as he got the idea.

"So that's how they bring it into this country," Stony said.

"That's how they bring it in." Tucson nodded. "Lullaby, I reckon you won't get to eat your sardines after all, but if you had the right sort of pipe, you could try dragging a few whiffs of opium. Because, unless I'm throwing my guess a mile wide of the mark, that's exactly what this can contains."

17. Canned Goods

Early afternoon of that same day found Luke Vaughn talking to his crew in the Box-V bunkhouse, a long narrow building of adobe construction, with a double tier of bunks along one side, and near the entrance a scarred desk and chair.

Small windows let in light, and at one far end a doorway led to the kitchen and mess shanty. The men sat on bunks and chairs. Saddles and other gear were scattered about the long room, hazy with the blue drifting smoke from cigarettes. Present were Tulsa Nash, Owney Powell, Port Osborn, the narrow-eyed Bart Fielding, two hard-bitten individuals named Gene Merker and Gabe Lindley, and four recent additions to the Box-V crew named Jigs Drubber, Herb Jahn, Turtle Cochrane, and Kent Roover. Most of Vaughn's remarks were directed to still another slim-hipped, broad-shouldered fellow, with dark hair and an ugly knife scar along one cheekbone, named Steve Demaret.

"I don't think you got no call, Luke," Tulsa Nash broke in, "to bawl out Steve. He done what was possible to the best of his ability."

"Which same wasn't too good," Vaughn growled. "I sent Steve to do a job, picked him because he can handle a Winchester better than any of us. And he didn't do that job."

"No use you gettin' riled, Luke," Demaret said, his long fingers carressing the old scar on his cheek. "How in hell could I kill Smith if he wasn't there? I did the next best thing, as I saw it."

"Where was Smith?" Vaughn demanded.

"I ain't the slightest idea. Didn't see him nor his pards in Torvo. I climbed up to the roof of the Silver Spur Bar, thinkin' them three would be down to the depot when the noon train arrived. But they wasn't, so I let drive at Yarrow. I thought you'd be glad. You been wanting to see the opposition whittled down—"

"Yeah, and what did you do?" Vaughn said savagely. "Right away you left town and come here. That was a mistake. You should have stayed in Torvo. You leaving that way is enough to make folks suspicious. How do you know somebody didn't see you leaving town, and think—"

"Hell, practically everybody's down to the train when it pulls in," Demaret said. "You know that. And what if somebody did see me, or happen to notice me, particular? That ain't no sign I'd be suspected. Hell, it was a chance not to be missed. With the train makin' so much noise and—"

"The very fact that a Box-V man is seen leaving town is enough to start people thinking. Yarrow already has suspicions about us. And you didn't even do a good job of it."

"All right, I didn't," Demaret said sullenly. "But that's a hell of a long shot to make. Is it my fault that Yarrow moved, just as I pulled trigger?"

Vaughn swore an oath and turned to Bart Fielding and Owney Powell. "Just how bad was he hit?"

Fielding said, "Damned bad, I'd say."

"It'll be a hell of a long while before the sheriff moves around again"—Powell nodded—"if he ever does."

"You sure of that?" Vaughn asked.

"Hell," Powell replied, "Bart and I were down at the depot, wasn't we? We hung around town a spell after Yarrow was took to Doc Arden's, picked up such talk as was going around. You know, Luke, I've been thinking that maybe Steve didn't do such a bad job at that."

"How you figuring?" Vaughn demanded.

"In the first place," Powell pointed out, "Yarrow is the key man in law enforcing. Without him to give orders, who is there?"

"That tramp deputy, Jefferson," Vaughn said.

Powell smiled scornfully. "What does he know about the setup around here? Sure, he's a scrapper and can handle a gun—"

"You should know about his scrappin'," Herb Jahn interposed with a nasty grin.

"Damn you, Herb—" Powell commenced, his face darkening.

"Shut up, Herb," Vaughn rasped. "Go on, Owney. You were saying?"

"Just that Jefferson wouldn't know what to do if anything serious came up, I'm betting. Yarrow wouldn't be fool enough to put much confidence in him—not a hobo that was kicked off a train and only got the deputy job because Yarrow was desperate. I got a hunch that we've crippled Torvo's law enforcement real bad."

"There's still Smith and his pals," Vaughn pointed out.

"Hell," Powell said, "they've no authority, even

if they saw a spot to use authority. I don't know what in hell they're even hanging around Torvo for, do you?"

"I wish I did," Vaughn said gloomily.

"If they weren't in town today," Kent Roover pointed out, "maybe they've left."

"It'd be a break for us if they have," Vaughn said. "I've an idea if it came to a showdown they might side with the law."

"What if they did?" Tulsa Nash growled. "I don't understand what you're afraid of, Luke. All we've heard from you is 'Get Smith, get Smith,' from morning until night. I don't see nothing to fear from those three cow pokes—"

"Oh, you don't?" Vaughn snarled, suddenly losing his temper. "Well, I'll tell you something you don't know, then. And this goes for all you dumb bustards! Smith and his pards aren't just ordinary cow pokes. They own a damned prosperous cow ranch—a good many hundred miles from here—but do they stay there? No! They got a bad habit of riding around the country and snooping into other people's legitimate business, and of raising merry hell with other folks' plans. They might just as well be connected with some law-enforcin' office—"

"Where'd you hear all this?" Nash asked dubiously.

"The same place I pick up a lot of my information. You should know better than ask. If you'd learn to keep your eyes open and read the papers now and then—but no, the outside world doesn't interest you, so long as you can swagger around Torvo and act tough." Vaughn's voice calmed slightly. "My God, Tulsa, it shouldn't be necessary for me to explain all this to *you*."

"Maybe not," Nash said sulkily, "but nobody ever tells me the why of things. I'm just told what to do and I obey orders. And I still don't see why you're so edgy of late."

"For the simple reason," Vaughn said, "that in a month to six weeks from now there'll be the biggest shipment of canned goods coming through that's been brought in yet. And I don't want anything to go wrong. And that's why I want all the law in Torvo whittled down until it doesn't exist. Does that make sense to you?"

"Certain." Nash nodded and looked around the room, then back to Vaughn. "It makes enough sense so I realize I've already wasted enough time throwing words at Smith. Now I'm going to act."

"Do you think you're fast enough?" Vaughn asked.

Nash laughed contemptuously. "The fact that I'm alive shows I'm fast enough—and I've stopped some awfully fast guns in my time."

"You put Smith out of the way and you'll get a bonus, Tulsa."

"It's as good as in my pocket right now," Nash bragged.

"How do you figure to do it?"

"It's not necessary to figure that far ahead. I'll do as I've generally done, I reckon—work him into an argument, which shouldn't be hard, and then invite him to pull his iron."

"You make it sound simple," Vaughn said ironically. "And when that's done, all you have to do is face his pardners."

"They'll be easier," Nash said confidently.

"Look here, Tulsa"—Vaughn's eyes narrowed—"just because Smith and his pards weren't in town today is no sign they've left, you know, so it won't do you any good to do a lot of bragging that you won't have to back up. It might be they've been called back to their outfit for a few days, but they'll return, I'm betting."

"You ever know me to do any bragging I couldn't back up?" Nash demanded. "If they come back I'll take care of 'em. If they don't we're so much the better off, to your way of thinking."

"I'd still like to know where they are." Vaughn frowned.

Turtle Cochrane said, "I managed to drop into the Sundown and make a few careless inquiries. Hank Rittenhouse said he didn't know where they were, hadn't seen 'em all morning."

"I did better than that," Owney Powell put in. "I asked that tramp deputy if his three friends had left town."

"What did Jefferson say?" Vaughn asked.

Powell flushed. "He got damn fresh. He told me

he guessed they'd left Torvo—because Torvo was where it had always been. I laughed that off, and he finally admitted he didn't know where they were; so far as he knew they were still sleepin' in the hotel beds."

"All this was before Steve plugged Yarrow, I take it," Vaughn said.

Powell said, "Hell, yes. Later was no time to be asking that deputy nosy questions. I don't want no more trouble with him—yet."

"No, I reckon it wasn't," Vaughn agreed.

"What's our next move?" Powell asked.

Vaughn didn't reply at once. He strode up and down the room a few times with the eyes of the other men following his movements. Finally he stopped in the doorway of the bunkhouse, seeing, without realizing that fact, the other ranch buildings, the cottonwood tree standing near the clanking windmill, and the corral with the saddlers standing near the bars at one side. Eventually, he turned back into the room.

"As I get it," Vaughn said, "Steve Demaret was the only Box-V man in town who wasn't down to the depot when Yarrow was shot."

"That's right." Tulsa Nash nodded.

"That being the case," Vaughn went on, "if anybody saw Steve leaving town, right after the sheriff had been downed, Steve's the one who might fall under suspicion—"

"I ain't so sure," Demaret said. "If that deputy

suspected me, why hasn't he come out here to make an arrest?"

"Maybe he's been kept too busy, staying with Yarrow, if Yarrow is still alive," Vaughn said. "If there was a chance of Yarrow hanging onto life for a few hours, it would be natural for the deputy to wait. On the other hand, I'm not sure you are suspected, Steve, and I don't want you to be. So you'd best get back to Torvo and hang around there for the evening, just like you hadn't a worry in the world—"

"Alone?" Demaret asked.

"Some of the boys will accompany you back. You won't be alone."

"But suppose the deputy did suspect me. He'd try to make an arrest."

"He couldn't prove anything if he did. No one saw you shoot Yarrow. You brought your rifle back here, didn't you? Well, you ain't nothing to fret over, then."

"I don't like the idea of staying in a jail, waiting for a hearing," Demaret protested.

"You wouldn't stay in the jail long," Vaughn promised. "I'd get you out on bail, which would be easy, so long as there's no actual proof against you—or if worse came to worst, we'd just take the goddam jail apart and release you."

Bart Fielding laughed. "Luke, you talk like you'd about reached the end of your patience."

"Maybe I have," Vaughn growled. "With Yarrow

out of the way, and plans made for Smith and his pards, I don't think it will be much more difficult to take care of that tramp deputy. Once that's done, we'll run Torvo to suit ourselves and put into office law men who will take our orders. I've got awful sick the past few weeks, pretendin' to be friendly to Sheriff Yarrow, especially when he throws out hints that maybe I know more than I pretend to know. Eventually the time will come when this country will have to realize who's boss in these parts—and that time ain't far off. You'll see, one of these days, that the profits we've made so far are just pocket money compared to what lies ahead, once we get things running the way they should be. Like I say, that time ain't far off—but I'm getting awful impatient. From now on we'll start hitting—and we'll hit hard."

Late in the afternoon a rider on a lathered horse came tearing into the Box-V. Vaughn and Tulsa Nash met him at the corral when he dismounted. "What's up, Waco? Something wrong?" Vaughn asked.

Waco Camden removed his hat and mopped his perspiring forehead. "Don't know for sure if any-thin's wrong, boss," he said. "Just thought you ought to know that Smith and his pards were in Jackpot today."

"The hell they were!" Vaughn exclaimed. "What happened?"

"I don't guess nothing in particular did. They

come in and snooped some. Went into the hotel, then went to Wyatt's place, then they got their horses and rode off—"

"Where were you?"

"Brose and I were hid out in one of the buildin's where we had a clear view of the street—"

"Did they see Wyatt?"

Waco Camden grinned. "They wa'n't far from him, but they never saw him. He was hid out, in the hotel—you know where. I was afraid as hell they'd catch him, but he heard 'em comin' and—"

"You're sure they didn't see you?"

"Sure as shootin'. Brose wanted to take a shot at them, but there was three of them and only two of us, and I kept remembering what happened to Jerky Trumble and Whittaker that day they closed in on that tramp deputy."

"You played it right, Waco. What did Smith and his pards do at Wyatt's place?"

"That's something I can't rightly tell you, boss. Soon as they left town I went out to the brush where the horses was hid and come on in to tell you about it. Thought you ought to know right off."

"They didn't spy you, did they?" Vaughn asked sharply.

"Not a chance with them going one way and me the other."

Tulsa Nash said, "You mean they didn't come back to Torvo?"

Camden shook his head. "They were riding due west when they left Jackpot."

Nash and Vaughn exchanged glances. Vaughn breathed a long sigh of relief. "I guess," he said, "they didn't find anything to arouse their suspicions in Wyatt's place, or they'd have headed back to Torvo."

"Looks that way," Nash agreed. "I wonder if they're pulling out of the country, Luke—heading west that way?"

"I wouldn't be a-tall surprised," Vaughn said. "And to be in Jackpot today means they must have left Torvo before Yarrow got plugged—"

"Somebody plug the sheriff?" Camden wanted to know, spitting a long stream of tobacco juice.

"So we hear," Vaughn said shortly. "The less you know about it the better, Waco. All right, go get a fresh pony and ride back to Jackpot. I don't like to leave Brose there alone too long. And I'm glad you rode in to tell me about Smith and his pals. If they headed west, it sure sounds like good news."

"And there goes my bonus," Nash growled.

"Don't fret about it too much," Vaughn laughed. "You'll have plenty money before long."

"What the hell!" Nash exclaimed. "Money ain't everythin'. I wanted a chance to notch my gun butt for that Smith hombre."

"Maybe you're lucky and don't know it," Vaughn said. "I guess Smith must have thought life in Torvo was too dull and it was time to shove on. Good riddance to nosy rubbish, says I."

Directly after supper Steve Demaret, accompanied by Tulsa Nash, Owney Powell, Bart Fielding, Gene Merker, and Gabe Lindley, saddled their ponies and rode in the direction of Torvo.

18. Eavesdropper

It was around eleven o'clock that night when Tucson and his pardners arrived in Torvo. Lights shone from saloons along the main street; the majority of the other buildings were dark. A few cow ponies waited at tie rails; now and then the sound of high heels clumping along the plank walks disturbed the quiet. Clouds drifted in the indigo sky, obscuring what light was offered by the moon.

Even before the Mesquiteers reached the sheriff's office they spied Smoky Jefferson hastening toward them along the sidewalk, every line of his slim muscular figure expressing grim determination. Tucson lifted his voice: "Smoky!"

The deputy halted, then stepped out to the road. "God, I'm glad to see you back," he greeted them. His voice shook a little with anger.

Tucson said, "Why, anything wrong?"

"Matt Yarrow was shot today."

"T'hell you say!" from Stony. Lullaby added similar words.

Tucson asked, "Matt dead?"

Smoky shook his head. "He may pull through. I was just on the way to make an arrest—"

"You know who did it, then?"

"Not for certain. I'm arresting on suspicion."

"Tell us about it," Tucson said. He and his pardners stepped down to the road. The men and horses made a dark blur against the faint gray of the dim thoroughfare. Smoky held his voice low while he talked:

"It happened while the train was pulling into the depot, about noontime. There was the usual crowd waiting to see it come in. The locomotive was making as much noise as usual with its steam blowing off and the chuffing and the clanking and so on. We never did hear the shot. I was standing a spell back of Matt, just sort of keeping an eye on some of the Box-V hands who were at the depot. I saw Matt take a step forward, and then sudden he went down in a heap. I thought for a minute he'd had a heart attack or something, then I saw the blood on his pant leg—"

"Got him in the leg, eh?"

"Just below the hip. Trouble is, the lousy bustard that threw the shot must have cut a notch in the end of his bullet, and it spread when it struck bone. Tore the hell out of Matt's thigh. Broke the bone, of course."

"You must have seen who shot him—somebody must've," Lullaby broke in on the story.

Smoky shook his head. "A lot of time was wasted

there. I couldn't see anybody near by in a position to shoot him. Finally I figured somebody with a rifle must have done it. But the first thing was to get Matt to the doctor's. He'd lost a hell of a lot of blood and the shock had just about made him unconscious. Doc had to operate and get the bullet out at once. While Doc was getting prepared, I came back to the center of town and looked around a mite. I found a man who said he'd seen Steve Demaret riding out of town, right after the time Matt was shot, and not losing any time getting away. What's more, Demaret was carrying some-thing wrapped in a blanket, which the man guessed might be a Winchester rifle."

"That's still not conclusive proof," Tucson pointed out.

"I'll get to something else in a minute. I went back to Doc Arden's and waited while he operated. Matt lost a hell of a lot of blood. Jane acted as nurse, and Doc Arden's wife and I helped where we could. We got the slug out, or Doc did. It was pretty much battered, but there was no doubt about it being from a .38-55 Winchester."

"That's a hefty slug," Lullaby said.

Smoky nodded and continued, "By the time the operation was over and Doc Arden had given Matt something to put him to sleep, so he'd regain some strength, it was late this afternoon. By then, all the Box-V men had left town. I knew the angle at which the slug had entered Matt's leg and I went

230

back to the depot and stood about where he'd been standing when he was shot. I studied over the situation for a spell and it looked to me like the shot had been fired from the flat roof of the Silver Spur Bar—"

"That's where the Box-V crew generally hang out," Stony interrupted.

"It's just one more link in the chain," Smoky agreed. "It'd take a good shot to hit Matt from there, but there's plenty men good enough to do it. Next I went down to see Eb Kenyon—he's the gunsmith here, you know—and asked him how many folks in these parts owns Winchester .38-55s. At first he said none that he knew of—that most men around here used .30-30s. Then he remembered that about a year back one man had brought in a .38-55 to have some work done on the trigger action. That man was Steve Demaret."

"You seem to be getting close," Tucson remarked.

"There's one more thing," Smoky said. "I went down back of the Silver Spur Bar. Somebody— maybe it was Abe Kincaid—had thrown some water out the back door, earlier in the day. The water had run down into a hollow, near the wall, and washed mud with it, against one side of a ladder which lay there. There was a mark in the mud that proved the ladder had been moved. I lifted it and climbed to the roof. There were a couple of chunks of mud near the edge of the flat roof, that had stuck to the ladder and then fallen off. From the roof I had a clear view to the vicinity of the depot where Matt had stood when he was shot."

"The picture's getting clearer every minute," Lullaby commented.

Smoky went on. "I had just climbed down the ladder when the back door of the Silver Spur opened. Kincaid had heard me on the roof and come to investigate. I asked him what time Demaret had left town. First he said he didn't remember, and then he couldn't even remember if Demaret had come to Torvo this morning. Asked if I'd seen him around the depot with the other Box-V men. I knew he was stalling, lying to beat hell. He knew something all right, but I couldn't prove it. He said he'd not heard anybody climbing to his roof, before Matt was shot. I asked, then, how he had happened to hear me when I climbed up. He explained there was no locomotive making a racket when I used the ladder. I had to admit he had something on that point. However, he refused to say positively if Demaret had been in town or not. Claimed he couldn't remember."

Smoky drew a deep breath. "I had a notion to ride out to the Box-V, but I hated to leave the town. For all I knew, they wanted to draw me away for some reason, and with Matt helpless, I didn't dare leave. I explained the situation to Hank Rittenhouse and then went back to Doc Arden's to see how Matt was. Jane is going to stay there until Matt is out of danger and help Mrs. Arden nurse him. Doc says he has better than a fifty-fifty chance to recover, if no infection sets in, and he doesn't think it will. Just a short time ago Hank Rittenhouse sent word that Steve Demaret and five other Box-V men, Tusla Nash among them, were in town. They'd dropped into Hank's bar and after one drink departed for the Silver Spur. What do you make of that, Tucson?"

Tucson considered. "It looks," he said shrewdly, "as though Demaret figures—or somebody figured for him—that he made a mistake in ducking out of town right after the shooting. Now he's come back to play innocent and brazen out any accusations that might be directed his way."

"And the other Box-V men," Stony added, "came in to intimidate you, in case you tried to make an arrest."

Smoky nodded grimly. "Exactly as I figure it. Well, I was on my way to the Silver Spur to arrest Demaret on suspicion when I met you. I'll get going again—"

"Wait," Tucson said, "maybe there's something more important comes first."

"More important?" Smoky showed his surprise.

Tucson said, "I think you're right in your suspicions of Demaret. But so long as he's come back here of his own free will, he's not likely to leave for a time. Let's go down to your office. We've got something to tell you about a discovery we made today."

Reluctantly Smoky turned back toward the sheriff's office, the other three following and leading the horses behind. At the office Smoky opened the door and, stepping inside, lighted the oil lamp that swung above the sheriff's desk. The other men came in and shut the door. Tucson placed on the desk the second sardine can that Lullaby had opened, and asked quietly, "What do you think of this, Smoky?"

The deputy seized the can, examined it, then raised his eyes to Tucson's. "Opium, by God," he exclaimed, "and in a sardine can."

"Considering you're just a tramp deputy," Tucson observed dryly, "you recognized that stuff awfully fast—about as fast as I might expect that Border Ranger, Chandler, to recognize it."

Smoky said shortly, "Maybe Chandler and I have had more experience with such mud than most folks."

"That's possible," Tucson conceded. "Now don't get the idea that all sardine cans of that brand contain opium. We've looked that can over mighty careful, and if you do the same, you'll find a tiny x mark scratched in the bottom of the tin. I've a hunch that when those cans come across the border there are sardines in the top of the load in case somebody gets nosy and insists on opening one or two of them. Cans of opium could be placed underneath and scratched with an *x* so those in the know would find the opium without trouble. That sound reasonable?"

"Very reasonable." Smoky nodded. "But tell me how you learned about this."

Tucson told him, told him the whole story of their trip to Jackpot, their visit to the hotel and the Cactus Man's place, and of what they had learned from Joe Grimse, of Cyclone.

"I'll be damned," Smoky said at the conclusion of the story. "So they smuggle it out in hollowed-out cactus. . . . You're right, Tucson, this is more important. Demaret can wait a little while. The faster we work on this, the better."

"Trouble is," Tucson pointed out, "with Matt unconscious, we won't know which authorities he'd want informed—"

"Leave that to me," Smoky said tersely. "There'll be word to be got down to the Mexican Government authorities, so they can check into the Atzec Sardine Company and make the necessary arrests. Telegrams should be sent off to the right people, so the Dagert Plant Nursery and the Janus Horticulture Company will be taken care of when the next shipment of barrel cactus comes in."

"You'll have to move fast and keep everything pretty secret," Tucson warned. "If word of what you intend gets out, the crooks could escape and start business in some other section."

"I can take care of the whole thing in a single

telegram to one man, who'll pass the necessary words to the right places. I can send it in code, too—"

Lullaby laughed softly. "Exactly what was your job before you became a tramp, Smoky?"

"I'd just as soon tell you fellows," Smoky said, "only I've been sworn to secrecy until this whole business is cleaned up. I can't reveal anything I may discover—" He broke off. "That's neither here nor there. I've got to get a telegram sent off. Code is likely to arouse people's suspicions, and it would require valuable time to write out, with so much to say. While the night telegraph operator, at the depot, is probably honest, I don't know a thing about him. There's always the slim chance that he might be in the pay of the dope ring. The day operator returned to his job today, so Jane won't be at the depot for a time—wait, I still think Jane could send the telegram I want. She could pretend she was sending word to some relative of Matt's about him being shot. The night operator wouldn't refuse her the use of the instrument. That's the ticket." Smoky got to his feet. "You fellows wait here for me. I'll be back before long." He hurried to the door, slammed it behind him. They heard his booted steps moving fast along the sidewalk. After a minute Lullaby got up. "That restaurant across the street is still open. You fellows want to get a bait?"

"Surely you're not hungry," Stony said mockingly.

"I think we'd better wait here as we told Smoky

we'd do," Tucson said. "Bring us back some grub and coffee."

Fifteen minutes passed before Lullaby returned with packages of bread and meat, cups and a pot of coffee which he placed on the desk. Stony said, "I suppose you've been stuffing yourself while this food was being got ready, too."

"As a matter of fact I haven't," Lullaby said seriously. "Just as I entered the restaurant that Tulsa Nash was coming out—"

"Did he say anything?" Tucson asked.

Lullaby shook his head. "He looked surprised, then sort of nodded and brushed on past. As soon as I'd give my order, I sauntered down to the Silver Spur. I could hear his voice inside, but couldn't make out the words."

"Does all this mean anything in particular?" Stony asked.

"I don't know," Lullaby replied, "only I noticed that there wasn't any laughs coming out of the Silver Spur, like you usually hear around a saloon."

They commenced eating and by the time they'd finished, Smoky entered. He dropped into a chair with a sigh of relief. "Well, that's taken care of."

"Jane send the telegram for you?" Tucson asked.

Smoky nodded. "I walked over to the depot with her. While she was getting ready I wrote out the message in code, just to be on the safe side. At the depot she explained to the night operator that she wanted to send off a message about Matt to some relatives. The fellow let her have the instrument. I stood at the ticket window, engaging him in conversation so his ears wouldn't pick up what was being said. The man's probably honest, but I didn't want to take a chance. Then I took Jane home, or rather back to Doc Arden's."

"How's Matt doing?" Stony asked.

"Doc figures he's going to be all right." Smoky looked up suddenly as the slight squeaking of saddle leather was heard outside, then relaxed. "Somebody riding past, I reckon."

"You think that telegram will do the trick?" Tucson asked.

Smoky smiled grimly. "Tomorrow morning a couple of plant companies and the Atzec Sardine Company are due to be raided, and the T. N. & A. S. will get orders not to pick up any more cactus shipments at Cyclone. We'll have the lousy dope merchants stopped to that extent, anyway." He paused to roll and light a cigarette. "Well, there's still a job to be done tonight."

"Putting Steve Demaret under arrest?" Tucson asked. Smoky nodded. Tucson went on, "Smoky, Demaret's got his pals with him. I figure you'd better take us along for moral backing, if nothing else."

Smoky considered. "I don't want to pull you fellows into—"

Tucson growled: "Don't talk like a fool. You need us and you know it. You're sheriff now, aren't you?"

"Pro tem." Smoky nodded.

"Swear us in as deputies."

Smoky thought it over a moment. "I think you've got an idea," he agreed. "Frankly, I'll be glad of your help." He glanced at their holstered guns. "I reckon you won't need to draw on the county for weapons or ammunition—"

"Just food." Lullaby grinned.

Smoky rose. "All right, stand and raise your right hands while I administer the oath of office."

They stood up, right hands raised in the air, but just as Smoky commenced to speak Tucson whirled away, reaching toward the closed door. There came the clattering of swift steps on the small porch outside, as Tucson flung open the door. In the light shining from the office he saw Tulsa Nash backing swiftly away across the sidewalk, then leaping the hitch rack to vault into the saddle of his waiting horse.

"Hold up, Nash!" Tucson yelled. "I want to talk to you."

19. Gunfire!

By the partial light from the moon and in the yellow rectangle of illumination from the open doorway, Tucson saw Tulsa Nash backing the horse swiftly away from the tie rail. Nash was crouched low behind the horse's head, gathering the reins into his left hand. "Me?" Nash stalled.

"What you want to talk to me about—"

The words were never quite completed, as Nash plunged in his spurs and swung the pony around. Tucson caught the man's sudden movement and the bright orange flash of the gun explosion from beneath Nash's lifted left arm. Tucson threw himself to one side an instant before a bullet thudded into the front of the building, and from the vicinity of his right hip ran two lancelike streams of flame and smoke.

Nash swayed in the saddle, the pony already in full flight down the street. Again he fired, as Tucson leaped to the center of the road, the bullet flying high overhead. Tucson unleashed a third slug from his .45.

By this time Lullaby, Smoky, and Stony had crowded out of the office doorway and followed Tucson to the middle of the street. "Nash!" Tucson replied to their hurried questions. "He was eavesdropping on us and Lord only knows how much he heard—"

The pony's hoofs drummed along the dusty road. Tucson lifted his six-shooter, took steady aim as he triggered a fourth shot from the weapon. "Missed, I reckon," he said disappointedly.

The rider was nearly a block and a half away now, approaching the Silver Spur Bar. In the light cast from the saloon windows they saw Nash jerk suddenly to one side and nearly tumble from the saddle, his sudden movement yanking the pony's head violently around. The animal stumbled, then went down, striking the roadway on head and right shoulder, its hoofs flying into the air. Nash went hurtling from the saddle.

"Maybe you didn't miss after all," Lullaby said grimly.

The four men started at a run toward the Silver Spur, Tucson plugging out empty shells from his gun and reloading as he moved. "Looks like this is it," Stony exclaimed, "and you never did finish giving us that oath, Smoky."

"T'hell with that!" Smoky jerked back. "Those formalities can be taken care of later." They pounded on, spurs ringing along the plank side-walk.

By this time the pony Nash had been riding was up again, and as Tucson and his companions drew nearer they saw Nash stagger to his feet and, crossing the sidewalk, reel through the swinging doors of the Silver Spur, to vanish from view. Doors banged along Main Street. Somewhere a man yelled questions to which no one paid any attention.

Approaching the Silver Spur, Smoky and the Mesquiteers slowed to a walk to catch their breath. They could hear agitated voices from within the saloon as they neared the entrance, then suddenly everything was silent. Without any hesitation Smoky pushed his way between the swinging doors, followed by Tucson and his pardners. Just within the entrance they paused to take stock of the situation.

At the left side of the room Tulsa Nash was slumped on a chair and sagging against a round-topped wooden table. A streak of blood shone wetly down his right cheekbone; the remainder of his features were the color of dirty ashes. He groaned and kept one hand pressed to his left side, where a dark stain was spreading through his shirt. A six-shooter, muzzle down, dangled from his right hand. His clothing, where it wasn't blood-smeared, was matted with dust. Near by stood Owney Powell and Bart Fielding, the latter holding a drink of whisky for Nash.

Demaret, Gene Merker, and Gabe Lindley were strung along the bar, on which stood three bottles and some half-consumed glasses of liquor. Abe Kincaid, a look of fright on his beetle-browed face, stood nervously behind the bar. As Smoky and his companions entered, Demaret commenced to back toward the closed door at the rear of the building.

"Stop right where you are, Demaret," Smoky ordered sternly.

Demaret stopped, though he swung half away, his right hand dropping near the holstered gun at his side.

Owney Powell snarled, "You've gone too far this time, Mr. Deputy. If Matt was able to take care of things—"

"Too far?" Smoky laughed harshly. "I haven't even started yet!"

"Somebody shot Tulsa—if not you, one of your pals—"

"Tulsa never had a chance," Bart Fielding put in. "He—"

"I seem to remember"—Tucson's voice cut through the room—"that Nash threw the first shot. If he couldn't make it good, that's his hard luck."

"Tulsa don't miss his shots," Gene Merker commenced. "He—"

"That's neither here nor there," Smoky interposed coldly. "We didn't come here to talk. Demaret, you're under arrest!"

"Me?" Steve Demaret assumed an injured expression. "What did I do? For Christ's sake! I ain't been into Tulsa's trouble."

"You're under arrest for the attempted murder of Sheriff Yarrow. Are you going to come along quietly, or do you want to make a fight of it? I don't give a damn one way or the other what you do, but make up your mind—fast!"

"You're crazy, Jefferson! Why should I try to kill Yarrow?"

"That's something you're going to have a chance to explain to me, if I have to beat it out of you with a gun barrel. Come on!"

Demaret backed another step, his tongue sliding nervously over dry lips. "Now look here, Jefferson, let's talk this over—"

A croaked oath from Tulsa Nash's pallid lips interrupted the words. "What in hell's the matter with you Box-V bustards? Cut out the palaver and make a fight of it. We got 'em out-numbered—"

With one final fleeting remnant of strength, Nash lifted his gun and fired a single shot which flew wide of whatever mark it was intended for, then toppled from the chair to the floor, dragging the table over with him as he went down.

The sudden shot, the noise made by the table crashing on its side, the tenseness of the situation proved too much for the pent-up fears and ragged nerves of the Box-V men. Like cornered rats they decided to make a last desperate attempt to escape the enfolding net of the law. Their hands swung to gun butts. Gunfire rolled through the barroom, shaking the rafters of the building, the thundering detonations of the guns making the flames dance in the oil lamps suspended above the bar. The acrid tang of burnt powder stung eyes and throats and nostrils, as the jarring concussions drummed through the Silver Spur barroom.

A bullet from Tucson's six-shooter reached Owney Powell an instant before he ducked behind the overturned table, firing wildly as he moved. The impact of the shot swung him half around, upsetting his aim and causing one of his slugs to strike the glass of whisky Fielding still held, splashing the fiery liquor in Fielding's eyes just as he threw down on Stony.

Smoky had directed his first shot at Demaret, then whirled and threw a second bullet in Merker's direction. Lindley, in the act of leveling his gun at Tucson, received a slug in the chest from Lullaby's weapon, and went sliding to the floor, one nerveless hand gripping futilely at the top of the bar.

Cursing loudly, Bart Fielding wiped liquor from his eyes with his left hand while his right tried again for a shot at Stony. Abruptly his legs sagged beneath him and he crashed, face down, on the saloon floor, as a shot from Smoky's gun found its mark.

From behind the overturned table Powell was still firing, though the wound he'd received had unsettled his aim. Tucson leaped over the table as a leaden slug whined past his ear, and directing his gun barrel downward, thumbed one swift shot.

Demaret, braced against the back wall, blood trickling from his open mouth, was bringing his gun to bear on Tucson, when a slug from Stony's six-shooter went plowing into his middle. Demaret stiffened, stretching to tiptoe, then his legs jackknifed and he pitched forward to lay sprawled without movement.

Without waiting to see the effect of his shot, Stony whirled toward Merker, who was down but, bracing himself on one hand, was getting back into the fight, with his gun raised toward Lullaby. Stony's Colt gun roared once as the stricken Merker pulled trigger. Lullaby, spinning around to meet this new threat, as Merker's bullet cut through the handkerchief at his neck, saw Merker sprawl forward, and just beyond Merker, the face of Abe Kincaid, rising from behind the bar, a double-barreled shotgun in his hand.

At the same moment Smoky had seen Kincaid, and he and Lullaby released their shots simultaneously. Kincaid groaned and disappeared behind the bar, the shotgun clattering loudly as it landed beside his lifeless body.

Quite abruptly the shooting ceased. Black powder smoke swirled through the room and hung in a blanket- like haze against the raftered ceiling. Someone coughed, and the noise sounded unusually loud in the sudden silence. Lullaby laughed, short and grim. "I don't see any more heads to shoot at," he said to the room at large.

Six men lay in various attitudes about the floor. Light from the suspended oil lamps shone dully on a number of ownerless weapons where they'd been dropped to the pine planking. Now and then one of the fallen men moaned. Tucson said quietly, "I guess that's all."

"It was enough." Smoky nodded. "Almost too much." There was a smear of powder grime under one eye. "Any of you get hit?"

"The crown of my Stet hat is punctured," Tucson answered.

"I had a damn close shave," Stony chuckled, gesturing toward the livid mark near the point of his jaw. "I reckon it didn't do much more than scrape off a few whiskers, though."

They became conscious now of loud voices out in the street. A man's head shoved timorously between the swinging doors. Someone at the rear gave him a shove, and then a crowd of curious men flowed into the barroom, to stop, suddenly aghast, at the scene of carnage that met its collective eye. "My Gawd," a man breathed, something of awe in his voice, "what a slaughter . . ." Others voiced similar phrases.

Tucson and his companions disregarded the crowd bunched just within the entrance, and moved around inspecting the fallen forms, huddled like discarded sacks of clothing on the barroom floor. When they had finished it was learned that Demaret, Nash, Powell, Merker, and Kincaid were dead. Bart Fielding and Lindley were unconscious, seriously wounded.

"Any one of your shots, Tucson," Smoky was saying, "was enough to finish Tulsa Nash. He was probably dying when he came in here. Only an unusually tough constitution kept him going as long as he did."

"I've examined all the guns," Lullaby put in. "There was sure plenty of lead throwing went on."

"Only we didn't waste it like the Box-V did," Stony pointed out.

"Anyway," Tucson said, "you won't have to place Demaret under arrest now, Smoky."

Smoky said tersely, "I'm satisfied, so long as he wanted that sort of settlement." He paused. "Dammit, I suppose I'll have to do something about Fielding and Lindley." He singled two men from the gaping crowd and sent one to inform the local undertaker there was business awaiting him, and the other to fetch Dr. Arden. Various men in the gathering asked questions regarding the fight, which Smoky ignored. He said to Tucson, "I never figured Kincaid had the guts to get into anything like this."

"Probably figured if he didn't, he'd lose the Box-V trade," Tucson speculated. "The whole gang of 'em seemed to lose their heads once Nash fired his final shot. It was like the starting gun in a race, with every Box-V scut trying to see who could plug one of us first—and not one of 'em with the sense to realize what it was leading to."

"Exactly the way it struck me." Smoky nodded. "Anyway, this will be the end of the Silver Spur for Vaughn and what's left of his crew—" He paused, listening. "You hear something, Tucson?"

20. Chandler Goes Down

Again came the sound. Someone was banging at the rear door of the saloon. Tucson crossed the floor in quick strides and flung back the door. Startled exclamations rose in the room as a man

248

half stumbled, half lurched into the saloon and went sprawling to the floor.

Smoky said, "What the devil!" and hurried to Tucson's side.

They lifted the man to his feet and saw that his arms and legs were tangled in a hemp lariat. A knotted bandanna that might have been employed as a gag hung loosely around his neck. His blond hair was mussed.

"Cripes!" Stony exclaimed. "It's Captain Chandler!"

Somebody else cried, "It's the Border Ranger!"

Quickly Tucson and Smoky released the ropes entangling Chandler's limbs and hoisted him to his feet. The man swayed uncertainly a moment, mumbled "Thanks," and staggered to the bar, where he poured himself a drink from one of the bottles standing there, then downed it in one swift motion. Lullaby moved swiftly to his side, steadying the man with one hand on his elbow. "You hurt?" Lullaby asked.

"Not at all." Chandler forced a wry smile. "If you except my hurt pride. I don't feel too good about this. Y'know, a man's throat can get mighty parched when he's been chewing on a gag for a while." He poured himself another stiff drink, then glanced around the room, his voice coming stronger. "Looks as though you men had had a showdown with some gun slingers."

"This is something the Box-V won't recover

from for a long spell, I'm betting." Stony nodded. "And if Luke Vaughn don't take to the idea, he knows where he can get satisfaction, I hope."

"I thought it was Box-V men I heard—at least I recognized Tulsa Nash's voice—" Rafe Chandler commenced. He stopped and started brushing dust from his clothing.

"But what happened to you?" Smoky asked.

Chandler smiled sheepishly. "I was guilty of not being as alert as I should have been—and to a Border Ranger that's akin to committing a crime, almost. You see, when I came into Torvo tonight I rode in from the south. As I was passing to the rear of this building I thought I recognized Nash's voice, so I decided to learn what I could. I took my pony around to the front, then sneaked back here to eavesdrop. Nash and the other Box-V men were plotting to raid the sheriff's office and kill you four before you could realize what was happening—"

"When did you hear this?" Tucson asked.

"Two hours or so ago. I'm not sure. I've been lying out back so long. Anyway, just as I was about to slip down to the sheriff's office to warn you, somebody on the roof dropped a lariat over my shoulders, pinning my arms fast. Then somebody hit me on the head. I can't say if there were two or three men doing the job, but they swarmed all over me, gagged me, and left me lying on the ground outside—"

"You should have yelled for help," Stony said.

"I tried, but they were too quick with the gag. I don't know how long I lay there. I was pretty groggy from the blow on the head. About the time my senses commenced to clear, I heard shots down the street. Then a short time later there was a lot of gunfire in here. That roused me to my senses and I commenced to work on my bonds. I managed to loosen them and get the gag out of my mouth. I was still pretty woozy—well, that's all there is to it. I just feel like an idiot getting caught offguard that way—say, did I hear you say that Yarrow had been murdered? I hate to hear that—"

"Not murdered. Seriously hurt, though. We'd come to arrest Demaret for attempted murder." Smoky gave brief details. "How hard was that blow you got on the head, Captain? Should it have medical attention?" He put his hand up to the back of Chandler's head. "No blood, anyway."

"It didn't even break the skin. I doubt it raised a lump. My hat cushioned the blow. It was just hard enough to stun me for a while." He looked around. "That reminds me—I had a hat."

Tucson went to the rear door and stepped outside. In a minute he returned with Chandler's black, flat-topped sombrero, which was considerably dust-smeared. Chandler thanked Tucson and placed the hat somewhat gingerly on his head.

Stony laughed and said low-voiced to Lullaby, "Score one against the Border Rangers. Matt

Yarrow and his tramp deputy may yet beat the Rangers to the final punch."

By this time still more men had crowded into the barroom and stood looking at the fallen gunmen. Smoky raised his voice: "The excitement is over, hombres. We're about to take up a collection to bury these dead. Tucson Smith will pass the hat in a minute."

There came a concerted hurrying movement toward the door, while Smoky smiled contemptuously after the retreating crowd. Tucson chuckled and said, "There's more than one way to disperse a mob of curious folks. That was masterly, Smoky."

"If I'd just told 'em to get out," Smoky said, "they'd take all the rest of the night to do it. This way . . ." He paused and shrugged his muscular shoulders, changing the subject. "Must be near time for Dr. Arden to be getting here."

The doctor entered, even as Smoky was speaking, then stopped short as his eyes flitted about the room. "Well!" he exclaimed. "It sure looks like somebody played all hell in here. What happened?"

"I'll tell it while you look over Gabe Lindley and Bart Fielding," Smoky said. "They're bad hit, but there may be a chance to pull them through."

"If I was in your shoes," Rafe Chandler offered, "I'd just as soon those scuts didn't recover."

"Someday," Smoky said quietly, "they may be

able to do some talking." He looked meaningly at Chandler.

Chandler said softly, "I see what you mean."

No one said anything for a time while Dr. Arden opened his bag and knelt at the side of Gabe Lindley. After a time he moved over to make an examination of Bart Fielding. Smoky said at length, "Before I chased that crowd out of here, I should have sent someone riding to tell Luke Vaughn we'd whittled down his outfit some. I'd make the ride myself, except I hate to leave town—"

"One of us can ride to the Box-V for you," Tucson offered.

Smoky shook his head. "No, you've done enough for one day. After what you discovered at Jackpot—" He broke off, glanced quickly toward Rafe Chandler, then, "No, I'll pick up somebody outside. There's always somebody willing to make a ride, to break bad news, among the loungers and loafers around a town—"

"Look here, Smoky," Chandler offered, smiling, "I'm not a loafer, but I'll be glad to ride to the Box-V and tell Vaughn what's happened. And I don't mind admitting I'll take a lot of joy in the telling, after the way his waddies manhandled me tonight. S'help me, I'm aiming to demand an explanation from Vaughn—"

"You're sure it was Box-V men who overpowered you?" Smoky asked.

"I'm damned if I know who else it could have

been. If Vaughn can't keep his wild bunch in check, the Border Rangers may have to take a hand in his affairs. I certainly will be pleased to ride out to the Box-V, Smoky, and tell Vaughn exactly what's happened."

"I'll appreciate it a lot," Smoky said, "if you feel able to make the ride, Captain." Chandler insisted he was all right, that he felt fine. Smoky nodded. "Do you know where the Box-V is located?"

"Good Lord, yes!" Chandler's blue eyes twinkled. "I haven't ridden the hoofs off a lot of ponies in this section without locating the various outfits."

"Well, thanks a lot," Smoky said. "And you might tell Vaughn for me, there's a showdown coming, awfully fast, and his time is running short."

"I'll do that too." Turning, Chandler hurried from the saloon. A moment later they heard the movements of his pony out at the tie rail, then the thudding of hoofs in the dusty thoroughfare.

Smoky moved over to Dr. Arden, talking while the doctor worked. Finally the medical man closed his black bag and, grunting, gained his feet. "I don't know," he said dubiously, "about those two. Right now, they're at death's door, but—"

"But you can pull 'em through, eh?" Stony snickered.

Arden looked reproachfully at Stony and turned back to Smoky. "There's not much chance for either of 'em, but I might be able to pull—er—that is—perhaps with proper attention they'd recover. Now there's two or three women I can get to take over the nursing, but where we going to keep these patients? Matt's in my spare room I always keep for such purposes—wait a minute!" He slapped his leg. "I know what. Spade Jenkins has plenty of room in his undertaking establishment, and he's got cots there. In case these hombres"—with grisly humor—"don't pull through, they'll not have so far to travel for Spade's tender ministrations."

Twenty minutes later the dead and wounded had been removed from the Silver Spur. On the sidewalks, beyond the entrance, only a few stragglers remained of the crowd that had clustered before the saloon a short time before. Smoky bolted the rear door, then located the key to the front. Tucson, Lullaby, and Stony made their way out. Smoky extinguished the oil lamps suspended above the bar, then stepped outside, locking the entrance door. Dr. Arden had accompanied the undertaker back to his establishment a short time before, and now the street was practically deserted.

Smoky, Tucson, and his pardners stood on the Silver Spur porch a moment, talking. Tucson drew a long breath. "It's been a full-testing day, men."

Lullaby said, "That hotel bed is going to look awfully good to me. And I suppose we'll have to be up bright and early to attend an inquest tomorrow morning."

Smoky shook his head. "I talked to Doc about

that. He says he'll be busy with the sheriff and those two wounded hombres tomorrow. There'll be no hurry about an inquest. We fired in self-defense, and Doc realizes that. Besides, you have to have witnesses for an inquest, and that leaves all the testifying on our shoulders. I doubt Doc will even call an inquiry."

Stony yawned. "Something was said about a hotel bed. Let's get started, before I fall asleep in the roadway."

The four men started along the sidewalk, but had progressed only about a half block when a hurrying figure approaching caught their attention.

"It's a girl," Lullaby said, noting the moving skirts.

"It's Jane!" from Smoky. He strode ahead to meet her.

Tucson heard her words, gasped out in a sort of breathless relief. "Smoky! You're all right? The man who came for Dr. Arden said there'd been a fight in the Silver Spur—and I—you—I didn't know if you had been shot—I—" The words ended in a sort of half sob as her hands clutched at Smoky's arms. "I couldn't wait any longer to find out—"

"Sure, we're all all right," Smoky said, laughing softly.

The girl suddenly became aware that Tucson and his pardners were standing directly behind Smoky now. She backed away suddenly, a certain confusion in her manner, and greeted Tucson and his pardners.

"I'm all right too," Stony chuckled.

"As if anybody cared about *you,*" Lullaby said scornfully.

"I'd have you know," Stony said indignantly, "that there's a whole lot of people worrying about my welfare—"

"Who's that?" Lullaby asked. "The directors of your life insurance company?"

"Hush up, you idiots," Tucson interposed meaningly. "Smoky has to tell Jane about the scrap, and there's no use of us hanging around to hear the story. I'm still craving that hotel bed. We'll see you tomorrow, Jane—Smoky. C'mon, pards, there's our hotel, just across the street."

They said good night, noticing just before they entered the hotel that Jane and Smoky were walking very closely together as they moved slowly along the silent, deserted street.

21. Jackpot

Tucson sat frowning in his hotel room, with the oil lamp on the dresser turned low. The partitions in the hotel were thin, and from the rooms on either side of him came the long-drawn snoring of Lullaby and Stony. They had, apparently, gone to sleep the instant they crawled between blankets. "It just don't square up, that's all," Tucson muttered softly. "Not any way I figure it. Oh well, I might as well turn in. . . ."

He had just stubbed out his cigarette in a saucer on a small table at his elbow when there came a soft knock at his door.

Tucson said, "Yes? Who is it?"

"Me, Smoky."

"Come on."

The door opened and Smoky stepped inside, closing it carefully behind him. "Cripes! You're not in bed yet. You mean to say Lullaby and Stony is making all that snoring?"

"Almost too much for just two hombres, isn't it?" Tucson chuckled. "I was just sitting here, thinking about something—how come you're still out of your blankets? Love's young dream?"

"It's not a dream any longer. It's what you might call an established fact." The happy smile vanished from Smoky's face. "But I didn't come up here to tell you about that."

"You sound like you had something on your mind."

"Plenty. Tucson, remember me telling you Jane owns that hotel in Jackpot?"

Tucson nodded. "She bought it in, dirt cheap at an auction, or something like that, figuring Jackpot would boom again someday."

"That's it. Well tonight, I don't recollect just how the subject came up—"

"Maybe I could guess," Tucson said dryly. "Young folks sometimes start talking about honeymoon trips and hotels to stay at—there you are. Hotels!"

"Something like that, I guess." A flush seeped into Smoky's tanned cheeks and he grinned.

Tucson whistled softly. "You're a fast worker, boy. You've only been here a week or a mite over—"

"When a person's certain, there's no use wasting time."

"That's true. But we were talking about hotels," Tucson hinted.

"One hotel in particular. The Jackpot Hotel. Jane happened to remember something tonight, something that was told her by the former owner of the hotel, at the time she bought the property. It didn't mean much then, but in view of what's happened—"

"Get to it, Smoky."

"Well, Jane says there's a double ceiling in the hotel lobby. The first-floor ceiling was higher than the owner liked when the hotel was first built, so he constructed another ceiling nearly two feet below the first one, the idea being that it made the lobby look cozier when the weather turned cold—"

"T'hell with the cold weather," Tucson said, eyes narrowing suddenly. "That means there's a sort of storage space between floors."

"You get the general idea."

"Yesterday when my pards and I were in that lobby," Tucson said, "we thought we heard something moving in the woodwork, but we blamed the noise on rats. And we didn't see the Cactus Man, either."

"It's my guess he heard you coming, but you'd

taken him by surprise. He must have been hidden in that storage place, but before you arrived he must have had some important business occupying him between the floors."

Tucson got to his feet and put on his hat, then slipped into his vest. He hesitated a moment. "I reckon I won't need a coat."

Smoky said, "Where you going?"

"With you."

Smoky grinned. "You guessed I wouldn't be able to resist, eh?"

Tucson nodded. "We'll have to wake the livery man and get a fresh horse. My animal had plenty travel yesterday—"

"I already got one for you, saddled and waiting, down below."

Tucson grinned. "You guessed I wouldn't be able to resist, eh?"

"We seem to read each other's minds pretty well," Smoky laughed.

"I haven't read all yours yet. There's a heap I want to know and I think you can tell me."

"Maybe I can. I've kept my mouth locked long enough. But I'll tell it on the way. I think the Glendon gang keeps men posted, on watch, at Jackpot, to see who enters. You'll remember the two that caught me between fires. I'd like to get out there before dawn and sneak into that hotel. We'll have to ride like the devil." He paused. "Do you reckon we should wake Lullaby and Stony?"

"Let 'em sleep. Besides, Torvo ought to have a couple of deputies on hand, come tomorrow, in case Luke Vaughn comes in with blood in his eye. C'mon, let's get started. We've got a ride ahead."

They closed the room door behind them and walked softly along the hall to the stairway that led down to the lobby. A sleepy-eyed night clerk looked wonderingly at them as they stepped into view.

"Damned if some people don't get a night's sleep in an awfully short time," he observed.

Tucson laughed. "We're afraid we might miss the pretty sunrise, if we sleep in."

"It's people like you that put alarm-clock companies out of business," the clerk said severely.

"That's what makes so many jobs for hotel night clerks," Smoky chuckled.

He and Tucson stepped through the door and closed it softly behind them. At the edge of the sidewalk stood two saddled horses, a rangy bay and a long-legged chestnut with wide shoulders.

"I slung your saddle on the bay," Smoky was saying. "Andy Crockett, over to the livery, assures me that while neither of these broncs will ever win a race, they'll keep going as long as you stay on their backs. He was right surprised when I woke him up—but come on, let's ride."

They vaulted into saddles and pushed swiftly out of Torvo. The moon was swinging to the west now, but the sky was clear of clouds and the horses had no difficulty flashing through the brush. The animals pounded on. At the end of an hour Tucson and Smoky drew to a halt to breathe the ponies.

"They're goers," Tucson observed. "This bay ain't really started to breathe hard yet."

Smoky glanced at the sky. "Just the same I'm afraid we won't make it before daylight."

"Didn't think we would," Tucson said. "That would be asking almost too much."

They rolled and smoked cigarettes while Smoky talked, Tucson nodding from time to time or putting in a question. Finally he tossed his cigarette on the earth and scuffed it out in the sand. "Time's a-burning," he said. "You can give me more later. It all lines up with what I've been thinking."

They got back into saddles, and the horses got under way, the ghostly forms of sagebrush, mesquite, and paloverde trees slipping swiftly to the rear in a fast-moving blur of drumming hoofbeats and wind-blown manes and tails.

All through the night they rode, stopping occasionally to rest the ponies. Glancing back, Smoky saw that the eastern sky had lightened considerably. The moon was down now, and while it was difficult to see the way, they slacked speed not a bit, leaving it to the horses to avoid any pitfalls that might lie in their path.

They came to a dry wash and stopped on the far side. Their mounts were lathered with sweat and dust now, but there'd been no abatement of speed.

Tucson stripped off his saddle and, using the saddle blanket, rubbed dry his pony's back; Smoky did likewise, then saddled up once more. A bitter exclamation from Smoky caught Tucson's attention, and he asked, "What's wrong?"

"Damn! The sun will be up before we know it." He pointed to a bright point of light touching the highest peak of the Torvo Mountains, shadowy in the distance. Here on the plain it was still dark, though it wouldn't be long now before the whole range would be bathed in the first ghostly light of dawn.

"Suppose we swing wide of Jackpot," Tucson proposed, "and come in from the other end? If there are guards out, they'll be looking for folks to approach from the direction of Torvo, mostly. We might even catch them napping this early in the morning."

"That's an idea," Smoky assented. "I'm glad we're nearly there."

Again they climbed to the horses' backs. It grew lighter; now the outlines of the creosote bush and mesquite became more clearly defined. The two riders plunged in their spurs and the ponies responded without stint as they swung slightly to the south to make a circle around Jackpot, the highest roofs of which had already been sighted from an elevation of ground. Mile after mile was kicked to the rear from beneath the flying hoofs of the tiring horses. There came a time when the animals were slowed to a walk and kept to the lower levels of earth. Finally Tucson signaled Smoky to a halt and they got down. The ponies were tethered to a branch of a mesquite tree. Tucson glanced at the foam-flecked, droop-headed, straddle-legged, panting ponies and said pityingly, "Lord, how I do hate to punish a horse this way."

"You and me both," Smoky said, "but this time it was necessary. Let's keep going."

They picked a careful way on foot between clumps of prickly pear, sagebrush, and manzanita, taking advantage of every bit of growth to conceal their advance toward Jackpot, whose buildings now stood but a scant two hundred yards distant. Wide stretches of greasewood gave a certain protection as they moved; at spots where the brush grew low they were forced to stoop and move stealthily like two Apache Indians.

The sun was up now, striking the serrated peaks of the Torvo Range with sharp splashes of golden brilliance, and with the rising of the sun the wind also lifted to blow in hot forceful gusts across the undulating plain of moving brush tips. Occasionally the wind would strike a bare spot, devoid of growth, hurling a cloud of sandy dust into the air and whirling it madly a moment before allowing the thick yellow-gray haze to settle back to earth.

Smoky, moving close to Tucson, said, "This wind and the waving clumps of brush is all to the good. If anybody's on the watch, they won't be so likely to spot our movements, with all this other movement."

Tucson nodded agreement and took advantage of a tall feathery-branched paloverde tree to advance swiftly for several yards, closely followed by Smoky. In such stealthy fashion they progressed until they had passed the first deserted shack on the southern outskirts of Jackpot. Now they could see plainly the rear doors and paneless windows of the buildings stretching along one side of Jackpot's main street. So far they'd sighted no movement in the vicinity of the town. Tucson had expected to see smoke rising above the roofs, at one point, indicating that old Joel Wyatt had his breakfast fire started, but even this was missing.

He caught Smoky's arm at sound of a sudden loud braying. "The Cactus Man's desert nightingales are there, anyhow."

"I thought I heard a horse whinny a moment ago," Smoky said, low-voiced. With a nod of his head he indicated the rear brick wall of the hotel, with its sagging back door set within a small roofed porch. "I've a hunch that anyone keeping watch will have his eye on the street side of these buildings. Are you game to make a run for it and not waste any more time sneaking along like this?"

"I was just going to suggest the same thing myself," Tucson replied. "I'm ready any time you are."

The whistling of the hot wind through the brush and old buildings drowned out any sound that might have been made by the men's running footsteps across the sandy earth. An instant later Tucson and Smoky had gained the shadow of the hotel rear wall and come to a stop at the edge of the back porch. Here they crouched, listening intently. Did they hear voices near the front of the building? Because of the noise of the wind, they couldn't be sure.

Tucson's voice just reached Smoky as he said, "Let's go."

Moving with extreme caution, testing each board as he ascended at one side of the rickety steps, Tucson gained the floor of the porch, stepped lightly over a pile of rubbish that lay there, then waited for Smoky to join him. Then, noiselessly, he shoved back the sagging back door until he'd made an opening wide enough for entrance. They found themselves in what had once been the hotel kitchen. A rust-coated cooking range was tilted on three legs; dusty utensils and broken crockery were scattered about. They crossed the kitchen and entered the former dining room, easing their feet gingerly down on boards before putting their full weight into the step. Tucson suddenly stopped, holding up one warning hand.

Beyond from the lobby they could hear voices, movements, but the words were indistinguishable. Steps sounded across the floor, moving in the direction of the entrance, and a man's voice called to someone in the street, "Hey, Waco, the boss says for you and Brose to go hitch up my wagon, and don't take all day about it, nuther." Then the sound of steps was repeated, as the speaker returned within the lobby.

"That was the Cactus Man," Tucson whispered. "Wait here." He left Smoky's side and moved stealthily through a door giving off the dining room into what had once been the hotel bar. Here a window gave on the street and, peering through its dusty broken panes, Tucson spied two riders, both unknown to him, walking their ponies in the direction of the Cactus Man's place.

So quietly, cautiously, did Tucson move that it required nearly five minutes before he rejoined Smoky in the dining room. Smoky looked questioningly at him. Tucson's lips formed the words "two riders."

The movements, voices, from the lobby continued, but Smoky and Tucson could see nothing, as yet, as they charted a cautious course across the wide dining room, with its scattered plates and cups, its overturned tables and chairs, the litter of dust and old papers about the floor and the ragged remnants of oilcloth which had once served as tablecloths. More dust swirled in through the empty window frames in one side wall. Eventually the two men had reached a point from which they could see, through the dining-room entrance from the lobby, a part of one wall and a portion of lobby floor. Beyond this entrance a man made grunting sounds, and a boot scraping on wood cut through the soughing of the wind as it blew through wide cracks and glassless openings. From above, somewhere among the bedrooms on the second floor, there came the sudden squealing of rats, and that, too, stopped as suddenly as it had commenced, even as there was an abrupt lulling of the wind for a brief moment.

Inch by slow inch Tucson and Smoky made their way to the doorway opening into the lobby. Here, side by side, they stood silently surveying the scene presented to their gaze, neither making the slightest move now, scarcely breathing in fact.

A tall man, with his back toward them, stood near the lobby desk—a tall man in dark blue corduroys, black sateen shirt with blue bandanna neckerchief, and a flat-topped sombrero slanted across his blond head. At one end of the desk was stacked a number of sardine cans, or what were meant to pass as cans of sardines. Piled on the floor, against the desk, were more of the flat tins. In the ceiling, directly above the desk where a man could easily reach it, was a dark oblong opening, where two planks had been loosened and shoved back to form an entrance to the hideout.

From somewhere beyond this opening, up above, sounded a sudden fit of dusty coughing and the cracked tones of old Joel Wyatt: "I don't know why th' hell I has ter do all th' work. I'm too old a man to have ter be scrabblin' in and out of this hole."

The tall man at the desk tilted his head upward. "Cut out your damn complaining, Joel, and get the rest of that stuff moved down here. You know we haven't any time to lose."

"Then whyn't ye come up and do it yerself?"

"Oh hell!" Tucson could see the man's black-clad back tense with angry disgust. "Come down out of there, and I'll finish the job."

There was further scraping and coughing from the opening above the desk, and then the Cactus Man's spindly legs in their faded blue denims were let down and his worn boot toes touched the desk. Panting, cursing, he came into full view and scrambled down to the floor.

"You goddam worthless old bustard," the tall man snapped. "You're no more use than—"

"Oh, my Gawd!" A sudden wail of consternation, distress, from the Cactus Man interrupted his companion's words. As he straightened up, after reaching the floor, Joel Wyatt had found himself gazing directly into the eyes of Tucson and Smoky. He tried to say more, shout a warning, but the surprise was so great that it nullified speech. He found it impossible to do more than raise one shaking finger and direct it toward the silently grim figures watching him.

"What in hell's wrong with you?" the tall man commenced. Then, suddenly, he whirled. For an instant his jaw dropped, and one hand started toward the gun at his hip. Abruptly his expression changed and a cordial smile widened his lips. "I'll be damned," he exclaimed. "The sheriff's office wasn't so far behind me after all. I was just in the act of arresting this old scoundrel. I always knew there was something queer about his cactus business. Now I've got him, dead to rights—"

Tucson said quietly, "It's no good, Chandler. Your game's up."

"Not Chandler," Smoky protested, his eyes smoldering fires of hate. "Jake Glendon's the name—he's head of the Glendon gang."

"What is this, a joke?" The tall man smiled. "Smoky, you know better than that. I'm Captain Rafe Chandler of the Border Rangers—"

"Liar!" Smoky spat. "The real Rafe Chandler is dead, and you know it—murdered by you or one of your men!"

"Now look here, Smoky Jefferson, if that's your name," Chandler—or Glendon—started sternly, "I want an explan—"

"The name's Dawson, Jeff Dawson," Smoky interrupted. "My friends call me Smoky."

"Using an alias, eh?" Glendon sneered. "Well, whatever your name, you're making a serious mistake—"

"Don't stall, Glendon," Smoky snapped. "You're finished. I stopped those telegrams you tried to send last night—telegrams signed 'J. Glenn,' if you're interested in aliases. The Atzec Sardine outfit and those two plant companies will never receive your warning. And I know you're not Captain Rafe Chandler of the Border Rangers, because the real Rafe Chandler was my closest friend—"

"You? A tramp! What can you know of the Border Rangers?" Glendon snarled.

"I happen to hold a commission as a lieutenant in the Rangers—" Smoky began.

And at that moment Glendon went for his gun! Fast as was Jake Glendon, his six-shooter jumped from holster a split second later than Smoky's weapon. Spurts of white fire crossed between the two men, the violent detonations shaking down dust from the ceiling rafters.

Tucson had jerked his Colt gun to cover old Joel Wyatt, but the Cactus Man, throwing his arms high, scrambled frantically out of the line of fire, screeching wildly, "Don't shoot! Don't shoot! I ain't takin' no hand in this game!"

Through the swirling black powder smoke Tucson saw Glendon sway back, lifting his gun as he moved. Three more spurts of flame and lead mushroomed from Smoky's six-shooter, the impact of the heavy slugs jerking Glendon from side to side and upsetting his aim, causing the man's final shot to fly wide and plow into Joel Wyatt's middle.

Tucson saw Wyatt clutch at his stomach then sit abruptly down on the floor. Again Smoky triggered his weapon. Glendon staggered back until he stumbled and fell into a lifeless heap against the hotel desk, his blue eyes wide, his long jaw slack, a wet stain spreading across his shirt front.

Tucson and Smoky paused, viewing through the drifting burned powder haze the bodies of the two fallen men. Glendon's wide-open eyes had already taken on a glassy shine. Tucson said to Smoky, "You sure pumped the life out of Glendon in fast time."

"He had it coming," Smoky said tersely as he plugged out empty shells and reloaded. "I haven't forgotten Rafe Chandler."

Tucson turned back to the Cactus Man. Wyatt was still sitting as he had fallen, a dazed, unbelieving look on his weathered features, his legs stretched out straight before him, one hand propping him up from behind. He leveled a shaking finger in the direction of the dead Glendon. "The hypercritical son of a buzzard shot me—*me*—whut was allus his friend," the old man quavered.

Tucson looked him over, seeing where Glendon's bullet had bored in. There didn't seem to be much bleeding. A wave of pity swept over Tucson. Scoundrel though he had been, still he was an old man. Tucson said, "Does it hurt much, Wyatt?"

The Cactus Man's tongue licked at dry lips. "I don't rightly know," he said slowly, as if stunned by the sudden turn of events. "No, they ain't much pain. I'm sorta numb from th' waist down, like I was parerlyzed. Can't move my laigs. Whut ye reckon's wrong? Am I bad hit?"

Tucson and Smoky exchanged glances. Tucson said to Wyatt, "Here, old-timer, you stretch out for a spell. Maybe you'll feel better later." He helped the old man to lie down, using Wyatt's crumpled hat for a pillow. Then, drawing Wyatt's gun from holster, he straightened up. Wyatt's eyes had closed; whether or not he had fainted, Tucson didn't know. He said to Smoky, "I reckon Glendon's slug got to Wyatt's spine."

Hoofbeats drummed in the street, then the sound of a man's running feet on the hotel porch. "Jake! What you and Joel shootin' at in there?" A man appeared in the doorway, drawn six-shooter in hand, then jerked back as he spied Tucson and Smoky and the two men on the floor. He gasped "Chris' A'mighty!" before Tucson thumbed a swift shot in his direction, but he had already backed out of sight, and the leaden slug whined harmlessly off through space. A second later they heard the fellow clatter down the hotel steps, his voice raised in a frantic warning to some other, unseen, individual.

Tucson leaped to the doorway and peered around the edge. A bullet splintered the edge of the door-jamb just above his head, and he jerked back out of sight. Ponies moved rapidly in the street. Tucson risked a second look and saw two riders leaving fast. He stepped out to the porch to gain a better view, and realized then the riders had only hurried to meet a second group of horsemen just entering Jackpot.

He swung swiftly back to the lobby, encountering Smoky, who was just emerging. "Get back, Smoky," Tucson snapped. "We're in for it. Here comes Luke Vaughn with a gang of his waddies. It's going to be tough!"

22. A Last-ditch Fight

The two men retreated swiftly to the lobby. Smoky said, "We could make a run for it, out the back door, but I'm afraid our broncs wouldn't hold up for long—"

"What I was thinking," Tucson said. "Vaughn and his men would overtake us on those weary broncs before we'd gone two miles." He gestured toward the stacked sardine cans, near the lifeless body of Jake Glendon. "Anyway, we don't want to leave those here. You get to the back and see what can be done about barricading that doorway. I'll take care of this front entrance. Hurry!"

Smoky turned and sped from the room. Tucson glanced quickly around, then leaped to the hotel desk. Dragging Glendon's body to one side, he swept the cans on top to the floor, then seized hold of the desk. Fortunately it wasn't nailed down. Quickly he shoved it across the floor to block the entrance, then dashed to the dining room to emerge carrying a table which he placed atop the desk. By this time he heard horses coming to a halt in the street. Knowing they'd pause to consider the situation before trying to effect an entrance, Tucson again returned to the dining room for a second table. An instant later he had added three chairs to the cluttered furniture barricading the entrance.

"They'll not come in fast, anyhow," he muttered. He could hear the Vaughn forces in the street, discussing the problem of getting inside.

Finally Vaughn raised his voice: "Smith—Jefferson! You two in there?"

"We're in here," Tucson called back, "cooking up a batch of hot lead for your arrival."

Buzzing voices, angry cursing, met this announcement, then Vaughn's voice again, "You fellers better give up; you ain't got a chance."

"What happens if we give up?" Tucson asked.

"We'll let you go. We ain't got nothin' against you two."

"What you threatening us for, then?" Tucson jeered.

Smoky came hurrying to Tucson's side. "T'hell they'd let us go," he stated. "We know too much for the safety of that crowd now." He had brought two more chairs and added them to Tucson's pile at the entrance. "The back door is blocked," he went on. "I managed to shove that big iron range against the door. The door swings in, and we'd hear anybody that tried to push that old stove back. It couldn't be done in a hurry. I took a look at the side entrance to the bar when I came through. The door there is closed. It's been nailed up for years with heavy spikes. I don't know why; but it's a break in our favor."

"What about windows in the back?"

"They're pretty high from the ground. It wouldn't be easy to get in. Of course, we'll have to go back and take a look, now and then."

"It wouldn't take much to tear that back door from its hinges."

"I thought of that. I got chairs piled atop the stove. But, like I say, we'll have to watch both entrances—"

Luke Vaughn's voice interrupted, impatient, demanding, "How about it, you two? You coming out or do you crave to die in there?"

"We like it here," Tucson called back. "Try coming in and see what a warm reception you get."

A fusillade of shots greeted Tucson's reply. Bullets crashed against the brick façade of the hotel and struck splinters from the stacked furniture at the entrance. "Cripes!" Smoky observed. "That's just a waste of good lead. I figure we could do better."

Tucson nodded and when the firing had died down they peered between the narrow openings in their barricade and glanced out to the street. Down the roadway a short distance eight horses stood at tie rails, but now no men were in sight. "Reckon they've taken cover in the buildings across the way," Tucson speculated. He glanced across the street, seeing a slight movement behind a window opening, then fired a quick shot. A yelp of pain followed the report. "Reckon I winged me a coyote!" he exclaimed.

A man darted from a doorway and made a dash between buildings. Smoky's gun jumped in his hand and the man went sprawling out of sight. "I think I'm even with you," Smoky said quietly.

They moved back from the barricade an instant before another wild volley was fired. "Let's hope we've weakened their forces some," Tucson said. He heard a slight moaning from behind. Turning, Tucson knelt at Joel Wyatt's side. The Cactus Man's eyes were open. Tucson said, "Does it hurt much, old-timer?"

"They ain't too much pain," Wyatt croaked. "I reckon I could bear thet, but I'm turrible thirsty. If I could have some water . . ."

Tucson studied the face of the old man and figured he couldn't live much longer. "Sorry, Wyatt, that's something we haven't got."

"I reckon not," Wyatt sighed. "I can't make to shift my laigs—would ye do somethin' for me? If ye can reach to my hip pocket, ye'll find a little box of pills. They're made from thet stuff whut comes in th' sardine cans. Glendon got 'em for me one time when I was poisoned from eatin' some sp'iled food. They're jest dandy for pain killin' and I allus kept 'em handy, but now I can't reach 'em."

Tucson gently rolled the old man on his side and procured the small box of pills. Opening it, he saw it contained some sizable brown pellets, two of which Wyatt crammed in his mouth, swallowing hard. Tucson settled him back to his former position. "Thankee, Smith. Ye're a white man. Th' pain will be gone right soon, I reckon. I'll jest keep them pills in my shirt pocket where I can get 'em easy, when I needs more." He sighed. "If I only had some water . . ."

Twenty minutes passed, with Tucson and Smoky taking turns watching for attacks from other directions. Now and then a shot would be fired and the bullet would ricochet through the lobby, without doing harm. Each man had made two trips to the kitchen, but all seemed quiet there.

Suddenly, from a window across the street, there commenced a steady fire, with the shots spaced at regular intervals. Tucson frowned. "I don't like this. The fellow isn't trying to hit anything. He's just shooting—wait! He's trying to hold our attention while—"

"They're figuring to come in the back way!" Smoky exclaimed.

The two men dashed for the kitchen. Someone was already banging at the door. Smoky and Tucson lifted their guns and sent shot after shot crashing through the door panel. Outside a man groaned. There were hurried steps on the porch, then a sudden splintering of boards as the ramshackle old steps gave way beneath the thudding feet. Running footsteps fled hurriedly across the sandy earth. A few vagrant shots were fired in reply. Tucson and Smoky waited a few moments, but nothing but silence greeted their ears now.

"They'll know better than to try that again," Tucson stated grimly.

"Vaughn hasn't enough men to make a real rush of it and overpower us—not so long as we're behind walls," Smoky said.

They waited an instant longer, then returned quickly to the lobby. Men were already moving up on the front porch. Smoky sent a shot screaming between the edge of the desk and the doorjamb. Someone moved away fast from the entrance, cursing as he ran. There came another ragged volley of shots from various points along the street.

"I reckon they're all around in front again," Tucson grunted.

Silence fell after a time. Now and then they'd hear voices among the besiegers, as men called to each other from building to building.

The firing settled down after a time to a few desultory shots fired at scattered intervals, the bullets crashing against the front wall of the building or striking the piled furniture at the doorway. As the sun mounted higher and higher it became hot within the lobby. Tucson and Smoky were crouched at either side of the desk, where it almost blocked the doorway, leaving at both ends a narrow crack through which they could shoot.

After a time Tucson became increasingly aware of old Wyatt's piteous pleas for water. "Dammit," Tucson said, "we've got to do something about this." He raised his voice: "Vaughn! Luke Vaughn!"

After a moment came the reply from a hidden point across the street. "What you want, Smith? Ready to give up?"

"Not on your life. But how about a five minutes' truce until I can go out and get some water? Old Wyatt's in a pretty bad way——"

A jeering laugh cut short the request. "We're not that easy, Smith," Vaughn yelled back. "So you're getting thirsty, are you? And you thought I'd fall for that kind of a dodge?"

Another man called out, "T'hell with Wyatt and you too!"

"Heartless bunch of bustards," Smoky muttered.

The firing from across the street died down now. "They think they can wait us out," Tucson growled. "They're figuring when we get thirsty enough we'll give up."

It became hotter in the room. Wyatt's moaning increased. He half raised himself on one elbow and then sank back with a groan. "I heerd whut them useless coyotes said." He spoke faintly. "Wouldn't even let a pal have water when . . ." The voice died off, then came stronger. "Anyway, ye tried, Smith.

My thanks to ye. . . ." After a time the old man's feeble complaints were renewed.

Tucson stood it as long as he could. "Dammit, I'm going to get him some water—"

"Don't be a fool, Tucson. They'd mow you down the minute you stepped out on the street," Smoky protested.

"I don't intend to step out on the street. Wait a minute." Tucson rose from his crouching position and hurried out to the kitchen. Moving as quietly as possible, he drew back the stove, then opened the door a trifle and peered out. Some distance away, one man stood on guard, seated on an old beer case. Directly at Tucson's feet, crumpled on the sagging rear porch, was the body of a dead man. Tucson closed the door and hurried back to Smoky.

"All quiet at this end," Smoky answered Tucson's inquiry.

"We got one scut when they rushed the rear door," Tucson said. "There's one fellow on guard, out back; that hombre named Port Osborn. Remember him, he testified at the coroner's inquest a few days back."

Smoky nodded. "Dumb as dishwater, that so-and-so."

"Listen," Tucson said, "that watering trough is about half a block down the street. Vaughn and his men are all watching the front of this building. I figure I can slip out the back way, run along the rear of the buildings, and then cut through to the water trough—"

"But, Tucson—"

"You'd like a drink, too, wouldn't you? Here's what you do. Take Glendon's gun and Wyatt's, have 'em loaded full, with yours. Give me a few moments to reach the back, then you start throwing lead as fast as you can. Keep the firing going steady, as though there were two of us here. That's bound to keep the Box-V's concentration centered on this building, while I do my job down the street. But keep those guns rolling. The Vaughn men are bound to reply. They'll think we're getting ready to make a dash for it. But you stay back where you won't get hit. Move around so they can't shoot at your flashes."

He waited until Smoky had procured the other guns and fully loaded the weapons, then started for the rear door. As he entered the kitchen he seized one of several old galvanized buckets standing there, then slowly opened the door. At almost the same instant he heard the explosions of Smoky's guns. Immediately the Vaughn men replied to the fire.

The roofed porch was in deep shadow when Tucson stepped over the dead man and made his way across the sagging porch floor. The short flight of steps that led to the ground were now but tumbled boards with rusty nails sticking from their ends, and as Tucson jumped to the earth the movement attracted the eye of the guard, Port Osborn.

Osborn started up from the beer case on which he'd been sitting, opened his mouth to yell, then reached for his gun. Before it was half out of holster a shot from Tucson's six-shooter had sent the man sprawling in the sand, the report of the gun being drowned in the steady firing that was taking place at the front of the building.

Tucson gave Osborn one brief glance, saw the man hadn't moved since he'd fallen, then started a swift dash for the water trough, running with wide steps along the rear walls of the buildings. A minute after he'd fired his shot he was making his way quickly toward the street, passing between the walls of the old livery and a rock and adobe structure. Another instant saw him crouched low, with the watering trough just ahead. Supposing the trough was empty! No, it couldn't be. Horses had undoubtedly been watered that morning. . . .

Tucson cast a swift glance along the street in the direction of the hotel as he passed from the deep shadow between buildings into the brilliant sunlight of the sidewalk. He could hear the staccato explosions of the guns and see the drifting smoke hovering above the roadway in the vicinity of the besieged building, though none of the Box-V men was in sight. Only a number of horses, tethered to hitch rails some distance beyond, gave any indication of movement in the sun-baked dusty thoroughfare. Expecting every moment to feel the wind of a bullet passing near, or even the shock of pain as a slug ripped into his body, Tucson crouched low and hurried out to the trough.

A feeling of exultation coursed through him as he saw that the big wooden trough was half full. Swiftly he dipped the bucket into the lukewarm depths and brought it up brimming. Then, whirling, he disappeared once more between buildings, a long low breath of relief whistling from his parted lips.

The guns were still pounding as he hurriedly retraced his steps along the rear of the buildings, this time, however, unable to cover the distance at a run for fear of spilling too much of the precious fluid he'd risked his life to secure. He swore, begrudgingly, each time a few drops splashed over the rim of the bucket. It seemed ages passed before he once more reached the shelter of the hotel rear porch. Here he paused but an instant to flash a single glance in the direction of the fallen Port Osborn. The man lay as he had dropped, beside the beer case, and apparently hadn't moved since Tucson shot him down.

"Anyway," Tucson panted, "the Box-V hasn't discovered yet that their rear guard is out of the fight."

He pushed on into the kitchen, closed the door, and again shoved the heavy iron stove against it, and set some chairs on top of the stove in such position that the slightest movement would dislodge them. Then he hurried on into the lobby, picking up a cup on his way.

Smoky whirled to meet him, at the sound of Tucson's steps, then a vast look of relief crossed his powder-grimed features. "Damned if you didn't do it"—glancing at the bucket. "Take over and throw some lead, while I reload. Did you have any trouble?"

"I handed out some." Tucson triggered a shot toward a movement behind a window on the other side, but was rewarded with only the sound of crashing glass. He went on, "I dropped that guard out back."

"T'hell you say." Tucson gave brief details. Empty shells clattered to the floor as Smoky plugged out cylinders and shoved in fresh cartridges. Again he took his place at the barricade. A moment later Tucson was supporting old Wyatt's head and holding a cup of water to his lips.

The old man swallowed greedily, gratitude glistening in his eyes. "Gawd, thet was good," he breathed at last. "Makes me feel like a new man, could I only move my laigs. I won't forgit this, Smith. Ain't many hombres would risk their life for an enemy."

Tucson said, "Forget it," and moved back to Smoky's side with the water. They both drank and decided they'd never tasted anything sweeter. "I realize now how Wyatt feels," Tucson said, adding low-voiced to Smoky, "That old coot certainly hangs onto life."

The firing fell off to a few scattered shots. From somewhere without Luke Vaughn's voice reached into the lobby: "Hey, Smith!"

"Spill it," Tucson yelled back.

"If you don't surrender, we'll set fire to the building."

Tucson's eyes met Smoky's, then Smoky shook his head. "The brick walls wouldn't burn. Anyway, I don't think they'd do it. They wouldn't risk losing the opium in those cans. They're too greedy for that." He lifted his voice, "Go ahead, Vaughn. Start burning!"

A savage curse greeted the reply, followed by several shots that flew high across the lobby and thudded into the back wall.

Tucson said, "With that guard dead at the back, we might make a getaway. Only thing, I don't think our horses would be much good without a drink, and"—he smiled grimly—"I don't think we could risk bringing them to the trough."

"We could set fire to the building, ourselves, and destroy the opium," Smoky said reluctantly, "and, maybe, make a clean getaway, but I sort of hate—"

"You hate to burn Jane's building and you hate to run from such scuts," Tucson finished.

"That's about it. I'd like to play out this string for a spell and see what happens. We've killed two that we know of, and maybe wounded two or three more. At best, that only leaves six against us. If our horses can rest until night fall, and Vaughn and his men don't rush us, we might get away by the rear. Still, I hate to leave this opium."

"We'll stay," Tucson announced. "If it's a last-ditch fight, so be it. I figure, maybe—" He turned at a query from old Wyatt, then carried the water bucket to the Cactus Man's side and gave him another drink. As he was about to rejoin Smoky, Wyatt plucked at his arm. "What's on your mind?" Tucson asked.

"Look here, Smith," the old scoundrel said, "ye been right good to me. I'd like to lend ye a hand in this fight. Them bustards outside wouldn't give me no drink, but you risked yore life to bring me water. I been an old sinner, I know, but I repented. Ain't no better way to salvation I know of than to take a shot at them Box-V varmints, if ye'll trust me with my gun."

"Don't you realize you're seriously wounded, Wyatt?" Tucson asked.

"I know it better nor you, Smith. I can feel the blood tricklin' slow-like inside my guts, but there ain't no real bad pain there. I reckon Glendon's slug must've went clean through to my backbone. But if ye'd jest drag me to thet doorway and give me my hawg laig, please. I can't last much longer. I know I'm dyin', but it'd be a heap satisfactual if ye'd give me thet last chance t'prove I ain't all wicked."

Tucson glanced inquiringly at Smoky. Smoky considered, then nodded. Tucson shrugged. "All right, if you want to try, Wyatt."

"Thankee, boys. But ye'll have to drag me to thet doorway, Smith. My hull lower body is par'lyzed, and I can't make no move on my own."

Tucson moved him to the entrance where he could peer out between one end of the desk and doorjamb. "Prop me agin th' side of th' doorway, Smith. Nope, there ain't much pain. I can jest feel th' lifeblood oozin' away inside. Now hand me thet gun."

It seemed a foolish risk to take, yet Tucson and Smoky were convinced that the Cactus Man sincerely regretted his past deeds and would do all possible, according to his lights, to redeem himself. Tucson handed him the six-shooter. Wyatt said, "Thankee," then strained his voice to call to the besiegers: "I'm in this fight, too, ye lousy, two-bit, gall-sored, spring-halted sons uv bustards! Keep yer heads down, or I'll blast th' livin' hell outten ye! I'm ridin' to glory on th' low-life soul of any dirty stinkin' catamount thet lines hisself in my sights!"

His taunt brought on a burst of gunfire that quickly subsided, but not before several slugs had shattered the woodwork near Wyatt's head. The old man seemed to bear a charmed life. Coolly he held his fire until the right moment came. Suddenly he tilted the gun and pulled trigger. From across the street came a sudden cry of agony.

"I winged me a varmint, boys!" Wyatt exulted. "Sounded like Brose Gerard's caterwaulin'. He was allus a stinker an' crybaby."

Smoky and Tucson exchanged thin smiles. Smoky said, "Good work, Wyatt," then to Tucson, "Keep watch while I strip the cartridge belt from Glendon's body. We mustn't run short of ammunition."

23. Conclusion

Morning passed and noon arrived. There'd been a definite falling off in the firing and Tucson became uneasy. Probably Vaughn and his crew were cooking up some fresh deviltry. Various trips to the kitchen had proved that the Box-V men hadn't yet discovered the death of their rear guard; otherwise there'd likely been another man there to replace the dead Osborn. Tucson, Smoky, and old Wyatt had all been sparing in their use of ammunition. The Cactus Man was a marvel of endurance, considering his wound. He'd have short lapses of unconsciousness, then would revive apparently as strong as ever, despite his ashen-gray pallor.

Tucson felt Wyatt couldn't hold out much longer—and yet he did. "I been a wicked sinner," he'd mutter every now and then, "but this is my redemption." And his eyes would brighten momentarily and he'd peer through the crack in hope of seeing a mark to shoot at. After a time he said, "If only I'd never met Jake Glendon and told him about thet double ceilin' there. I rec'lected it from th' old days. Thet was my downfall; and then they started bringin' th' dope across th' border into Lamedero, down on th' salt flats. From there the Box-V crew brought it here for hidin', until I could send it out in my cactuses."

"Wyatt," Smoky asked, "who was it killed Rafe Chandler?"

"He was the fourth one killed over here," Wyatt replied. "We was allus afeared somebody would uncover our hidin' place. First it was Jane Yarrow's dad whut come snoopin' 'round, then two of Matt Yarrow's deputies. They was bushwhacked by various guards Vaughn and Glendon kept here on watch. Me, I never killed nobody. Them two thet tried to kill you, Smoky; it was done like thet. Only you turned th' table on Jerky Trumble and Whittaker. Whittaker had just joined up with Vaughn and nobody knowed much about him." Smoky interrupted to ask again about Chandler. "Oh, ye mean th' Border Ranger whut come here? Three Box-V men jumped him one night and took him prisoner. Knocked him cold. Then Glendon changed clothes with him, picked up a shotgun, and blowed his features all t'hell. Then they fixed things to make it look like suicide."

Smoky asked grimly, "What was the idea of Glendon posing as a Border Ranger?"

"Matt Yarrow was makin' him uneasy. He

wanted Yarrow to think he was dead. A suicide note was left with the corpse of the Ranger, but the boys got careless and took his horse away, but left a six-shooter. Glendon was sore as hell. But he posed as a Ranger so's he could talk to Yarrow and find out whut th' law was doin'."

Smoky said to Tucson, "I knew it was Rafe Chandler you'd found dead, as soon as Matt mentioned the dead man had a streak of gray hair across the back of his head. That was the result of an old railroad accident. Rafe had told me about it more than once. I could have convinced Matt at once the supposed suicide wasn't Jake Glendon, but I wanted to see how far Glendon would go. Besides, if I'd arrested him at once, the rest of the gang might have got away. I should have told you sooner, but you get damn secretive in this business."

"I'd more or less guessed he was a fake," Tucson said. "Border Rangers don't generally spend so much time killing horses. They'll ride when they have to, but I figure Chandler was tearing around lining up shipments of dope and keeping in touch with Vaughn. How'd you get into this?"

"I'd been on another case, bank robbery job, when Rafe Chandler was sent to this section to look into the dope running. Rangers are supposed to keep headquarters informed of their activities, and when nothing was heard from Rafe after a reasonable period we knew something had gone wrong. I was available by that time, so they sent me to investigate. I decided to arrive disguised as a tramp, and planned to get myself kicked off at Torvo. It was just accident that Matt grabbed me for his deputy—" He broke off to send a shot winging from his Colt gun toward a window across the street, then said, "Dammit, I think I missed."

Three shots fired at ragged intervals flattened against the front wall or sped harmlessly across the lobby. Smoky continued, "I had to send a code message by Jane to headquarters, so she knew I had some connection with the Rangers, but she kept it secret."

"I rec'lect th' fust day ye come here," Wyatt put in, in a tired voice, "that day you met Glendon and he borrowed some 'baccy off'n ye. He was supposed to meet Vaughn in Jackpot thet day, but he swung wide and circled back to stop Vaughn. Th' two of 'em watched from a high ridge, expectin' thet Whittaker an' Trumble would finish ye off, but it turned out different—'specially after Smith and his pards arrived. Then when Vaughn and Glendon saw ye fellers takin' th' bodies to town, Vaughn rode fast to get ahead, and he give Nash orders to kill Jerky Trumble. They was afeared Jerky would recover and talk. I hear ye nigh pinned thet murder to Nash, Smith, 'cause he dropped his plug of 'baccy . . ." Wyatt's voice grew faint and he closed his eyes.

Tucson said to Smoky, "I still wonder why

Glendon stopped Nash from shooting me that night in Sundown Saloon. There was something awfully queer about that."

A feeble snort issued from Wyatt. "Thet was an act he put on. He was right leery of ye, Smith. Thet act was all fixed up between him and Tulsa. Glendon hoped it would put him in your good graces and ye'd get friendly and spill whutever ye might know. Heh-heh"—it was but a feeble cackle that parted the old man's pallid lips. "Yesterday, Smith, ye nigh cotched me bringin' some cans from thet hole up there. I just pulled th' boards closed in time, and I nigh baked, waitin' for you fellers to leave. Then when I found the dollar ye left for two cans, I knowed the fat was in the fire, 'cause only one can held fish, as ye know by this time, I reckon. I spied ye when ye left Jackpot, headin' west, and I figgered ye was leavin' this section fer good, when ye didn't start toward Torvo. . . . Could I have some water agin?"

Tucson gave him a drink. The water was low in the bucket now. He looked closely at Wyatt and saw the fingers of death were closing in fast. Tucson said, "Joel, do you happen to know what was Glendon's idea in saying he'd been over-powered back of the Silver Spur last night?"

A wan smile crossed the bearded face. "He told me about thet. Figgered he'd fooled ye, he did. It was his plan that Nash and them others should wipe you fellers out, but the plan went wrong. That put Glendon in a spot. He knowed he'd been seen around town, and somebody might wonder why he didn't come to your aid when the shootin' started in the Silver Spur. So he wropped some rope around his carcass and pertended like he'd been hit on th' head and gagged. It didn't work, did it?"

"Not for a minute," Tucson replied. "He claimed he'd heard Tulsa and the others plotting to kill us, some two hours before the fight in the Silver Spur, and we hadn't returned but about an hour before, so Tulsa didn't even know we were due to arrive in Torvo that night. And when a man's unconscious, he doesn't know how much time has elapsed when he becomes conscious again. That was a bad break Glendon made."

"He made another mistake about the same time," Smoky put in. "He said he'd heard me mention Matt had been shot. He couldn't have heard that, if he'd been unconscious as he claimed. Oh, there's plenty of proof against Glendon if he were alive to be tried. Last night, Tucson, after I left to take Jane home, I got to thinking it might be a good idea to send a telegram to have somebody check into the sheriff of Bandinera County, to see if he's been doing his job—"

"He ain't." Wyatt's voice was weaker now. "Th' shurf of Bandinera was in Glendon's pay, and as big a crook as ye'll find."

"I'm glad I sent that wire then," Smoky said. "Anyway, while we were at the depot the night

294

operator mentioned to Jane that the Border Ranger had been in and wrote some telegrams. That was right after Glendon had left the Silver Spur, saying he would ride to the Box-V for me. The night man, having been eating his midnight snack, hadn't got around to sending the wires yet. Jane explained a few things, and we stopped the messages from going out. They were signed J. Glenn and addressed to the sardine company and the two plant outfits, advising them to watch their step, or words to that effect."

"It was that hint you dropped to Glendon," Tucson said, "about us discovering something at Jackpot that got Glendon stirred up——" He paused to send a quick shot whining into the street where a man had appeared momentarily, but had only the satisfaction of seeing his bullet rip into a plank in the opposite sidewalk. "Dammit, I can't talk and watch at the same time," he growled. "That's another slug wasted."

"We're doing all right," Smoky commented. "But I'd like to know what Vaughn is doing. Him and his men are too quiet to suit me." He returned to the conversation: "I had an idea that hint might scare Glendon into action. I noted he was only too glad to make the ride to the Box-V."

"He rode to the Box-V, all right," Wyatt said feebly. "Killed a hawss gettin' there. He roused out Vaughn and told him to bring his men as quick as possible, so's we could all move the stuff to the

Box-V. He wanted the hands for a bodyguard in case any trouble showed up. I reckon Vaughn was so shocked about th' death of Tulsa and them others, he didn't git started as soon as he should . . ." A painful sigh welled up from the old man's chest and he fumbled for his box of pills.

Tucson said, "It looks like the Glendon gang has really caught it in the neck this time." He paused. "Smoky, nobody's thrown a shot this way for a long spell. Something's up. I reckon I'll drift back to the rear and see if everything's all right there."

He was but halfway to the kitchen when he heard Smoky's cry of alarm. "Tucson! Quick! Here they come!"

Tucson whirled and ran back to the lobby, gun in hand. "What's up?"

Smoky's eye was glued to the crack between desk and doorjamb. He spoke without turning his head. "They've got a big timber they're going to use as a battering ram. They're figuring to rush us—smash down this barricade."

"Let 'em come!" Tucson exclaimed. He glanced quickly at Joel Wyatt, eyes closed, sagging against the doorjamb. "I'll get the old man out of there."

The Cactus Man's eyes opened. "Don't you tech me, Smith. I can't live anyway. This is my chance to—"

What the old man was about to say was lost in the rush of feet pounding up the hotel steps. They heard Wyatt's gun explode once. Tucson yelled, "Smoky, hold your fire until they start in—"

The battering ram had touched the desk and piled chairs and commenced to shove them to one side, when it was suddenly dropped on the porch with a resounding thud in the midst of confused cries and stampeding feet.

There came a sudden rush of hoofbeats along the street and a loud voice that carried from end to end of Jackpot: "Charge 'em Rangers! Don't let a man escape!"

"Give 'em hell!" roared a second voice.

And then the first again: "You're surrounded! Throw down your guns if you don't want to be killed!"

There was a burst of gunfire, then sudden cries for mercy.

Smoky looked inquiringly at Tucson. Tucson exclaimed, "Those were Lullaby's and Stony's voices. Where in hell did they gather the Rangers?"

The two men pulled the furniture aside and rushed out, leaping over the battering ram in their progress. A scene of confusion met their eyes. A number of saddled but riderless horses were trotting aimlessly about the street, and there was a great deal of yelling and whooping from Lullaby and Stony, who sat their mounts, guns in hands, in the midst of the bedlam.

"Shoot at the first move, Rangers!" Lullaby was bawling. "We've got 'em surrounded!" Tucson surmised the Rangers were hidden among buildings.

At the edge of the road stood what remained of the Box-V forces: three men, their arms flung high in the air. Two men lay dead in the dusty roadway. One of the prisoners was Luke Vaughn, his face ashen.

"I surrender!" Vaughn cried shrilly. "I ain't making no fight."

Tucson yelled, "Stony—Lullaby!"

"You all right, pard?" Stony yelled, relief in his voice.

"You will run off without us, eh?" Lullaby jeered. "Let this be a lesson to you and Smoky. Take the guns off these scuts. There's ropes on those ponies wandering loose. Tie up the prisoners and let's *habla* a mite." He and Stony climbed down from their ponies.

Smoky and Tucson secured ropes. A few minutes later Vaughn, and his two men who still lived, were trussed up like fowls and seated at the edge of the sidewalk. Tucson asked Lullaby, "Why don't you tell the Rangers they can come out now?"

"Rangers!" Lullaby burst into uproarious laughter. "Even you're fooled, eh? Stony, we're better than we thought we were."

"One of us is, anyway," Stony chuckled.

Lullaby explained. "There ain't any Rangers. That was all bluff, and Vaughn and his coyotes fell for it." He paused to laugh at Vaughn's scowling face. "There's just me'n Stony. The wind was in the right direction and we could hear shots while we was still some distance off, so we sneaked in here, figuring they must have you and Smoky holed up someplace. Then we spied on Vaughn and his sidewinders fixing a battering ram, out back of one of the buildings. We hid until they was ready to start and had their backs to us. Their horses was tied down the street a piece, so we released 'em and when the right time come we hit 'em a few slashes with our ropes and started 'em stampedin' down the street. We come ridin' after, yelling to beat hell and throwing lead. The surprise come so sudden that Vaughn and his lousy rattlers failed to recognize their own horses and thought an army had descended on 'em. But it looks like you had the gang whittled down. What happened?"

"You damned idiots," Tucson said fondly. Then to Smoky, "You tell 'em about it. I'll be right back."

Turning, he dashed up the hotel steps and into the lobby. There he stopped short. Joel Wyatt still sat propped against the edge of the doorjamb, but the gun had fallen from his lifeless fingers, his eyes were wide, and his mouth hung open. Tucson said softly, "You didn't do so bad, at that, old-timer," then swung away and returned to the street. He said to Smoky when he had rejoined his friends, "The Cactus Man is finished."

"I still don't know how he held on so long—"

"Tucson," Lullaby interrupted excitedly, "Smoky

tells us that he's a Ranger and that that other Ranger was really Jake Glendon. Dammit, I always smelled something fishy about him."

"Sardines, maybe," Stony chuckled.

Lullaby brightened, then said with a martyred air, "Sure, I'm hungry, but I can stand the pangs a mite longer, until I've heard what happened here—"

"What I want to know," Tucson cut in, "is what brought you to Jackpot in such timely fashion?"

"It was Jane's doings," Stony explained. "Seems she said something to Smoky last night about there being a double ceiling in the hotel, or something like that. Anyway, after she went to bed she got to worrying for fear he'd go investigating. She couldn't get to sleep. So she dressed and went to the sheriff's office. Not finding Smoky there, she headed direct for the hotel. The next thing we knew, she came knocking at my hotel door, with the hotel clerk shocked and trying to tell her it wasn't ladylike to come to gentlemen's rooms in the middle of the night. So then Lullaby and I went to get Tucson, and he was already missing, so we knew the two of you had headed for Jackpot. And Jane was worried nigh sick for fear there'd be something rash done. Them's her exact words, ain't they, Lullaby?"

Lullaby nodded. "So there wa'n't nothing for us to do except saddle up and ride to beat hell for Jackpot. And here we are." His face clouded. "Dang you, Tucson, running out on us this way!"

"Smoky and I thought we didn't need your help on a little job like this." Tucson smiled. He glanced at the dead men in the road and then at the prisoners. "There's two more bodies out back of the hotel, and two in the lobby."

Luke Vaughn raised his voice from the sidewalk. His ankles had a rope around them and his hands were tied behind his back. "There's another corpse in that building yonderly, Mr. Smith. I don't know which of you fellers shot him."

Smoky said tersely, "You seem mighty willing to talk, all of a sudden, Vaughn."

Vaughn shrugged his shoulders. "I know when I'm licked. With Glendon dead, I can tell you a lot of things about the dope ring, if you'll promise to see my sentence is made lighter."

"Promise hell," Smoky said grimly. "If you get anything less than hanging, you'll be lucky." He turned back to Tucson. "Do you suppose we could get finished up here? I want to send a telegram off to my headquarters as soon as possible—"

"And you know a girl who sends the best telegrams," Lullaby grinned, "so—"

"Look here," Tucson proposed to Smoky, "I figure my pards and I can clean things up here. Why don't you catch up a horse and hurry back to Torvo? There's no use Jane being worried any longer than necessary. You get on along. We'll bring in the prisoners, horses, and sardine cans. You can get the news to Matt too."

"I'd sure like to," Smoky said eagerly, "if you don't think—"

"Dammit," Stony said, "get going, Smoky. How long do you intend to keep that girl waiting?"

Five minutes later Smoky was mounted and thundering down Jackpot's dusty street, a yellow cloud boiling up at his rear. The Three Mesquiteers looked after him until he had disappeared from view, then glanced back at their prisoners. "Well," Stony said, "I suppose we can get on with our job now."

"That can wait a few minutes," Lullaby protested. "There's a limit to my patience, and I'm still in the dark as to all that did happen here. Tell it, Tucson."

"Yes, Papa," Stony snickered, "tell us a story."

A hot wind blew down the street, ruffling the manes of the waiting horses. The sunlight was bright on the three pardners standing close together. Tucson smiled. "Once upon a time," he commenced, "there were three footloose saddle tramps, and they came riding into a town called Torvo . . ."

(Allan) William Colt MacDonald was born in Detroit, Michigan in 1891. His formal education concluded after his first three months of high school when he went to work as a lathe operator for Dodge Brothers' Motor Company. His first commercial writing consisted of advertising copy and articles for trade publications. While working in the advertising industry, MacDonald began contributing stories of varying lengths to pulp magazines and his first novel, a Western story, was published by Clayton House in *Ace-high Magazine* in 1925. MacDonald later commented that when this first novel appeared in book form as *Restless Guns* in 1929, 'I quit my job cold.' From the time of that decision on, MacDonald's career became a long string of successes in pulp magazines, hardcover books, films, and eventually original and reprint paperback editions. The Three Mesquiteers, MacDonald's most famous characters, were introduced in 1933 in *Law of the Forty-fives*. His other most famous character creation was Gregory Quist, a railroad detective. Some of MacDonald's finest work occurs outside his series, especially the well researched *Stir Up the Dust* which was published first in a British edition in 1950 and *The Mad Marshal* in 1958. MacDonald's only son, Wallace, recalled how much fun his father had writing Western fiction. It is an apt observation since countless readers have enjoyed his stories now for nearly three quarters of a century.

Center Point Publishing
600 Brooks Road • PO Box 1
Thorndike ME 04986-0001 USA

(207) 568-3717

**US & Canada:
1 800 929-9108**
www.centerpointlargeprint.com